Happiest in Denial

Cassandra Cordini

Published by OMNE Publishing in 2022

A catalogue record for this book is available from the National Library of Australia

This book is available in print and eBook formats.

Author's Note

This story, and all the names, characters, and incidents portrayed in this book are fictitious. No identification with actual persons (living or deceased), places, buildings and products are intended or should be inferred.

This story contains strong adult themes and may trigger stressful episodes, if the reader has experienced domestic violence or sexual abuse. If this story triggers anything for you, please ring Lifeline on 13 11 14.

Contents

Why her?...1995
Chapter 1

Marriage can be a tricky thing. Couples never really know what they are signing up for. They all think their spouses are "the one". But are they really? Life also has a hidden agenda, throwing roadblocks in our paths of happiness as it eagerly watches with anticipation, to see what we do next. Will we plough through them, go over them, around them or avoid them by making a complete detour? People's choices are also impossible to predict. Mia was at a stage in her life when she was slowly becoming aware of these things.

Mia and Wolfie had been married for seven years and were celebrating the arrival of their second child. Chloe was the perfect baby. During her first three weeks, she did nothing but feed and sleep, and was more settled than her brother, Alex, at the same age.

I have my pigeon pair, my little darlings. A nice home, a loving husband. I'm so happy.

Late one morning, Mia sat in her mother Natalia's kitchen drinking the warm brew she had prepared, the lightly caramelized and almost nutty scent of her percolated coffee hanging in the air. Mia was exhausted from the nightmares that plagued her and kept her awake. With her mouth dry, her brow furrowed and wringing her hands, she hesitantly whispered to her mother, "Mamma, sometimes when I'm breast-feeding Chloe and I'm gently stroking her, she makes this kind of annoyed sound. I feel like she's telling me off!"

Natalia placed her hands palm-to-palm, in the prayer position, as she looked up to the heavens and replied, "Please, don't be ridiculous, Mia! You don't want a baby with problems. I'm sure you are imagining things." As much as she could, Mia tried to push these worrying thoughts from her mind.

When Chloe was four weeks old, she became more alert and aware of her surroundings, and this was when Mia started noticing other things. Chloe liked to sleep in the most convoluted, awkward positions and disliked being swaddled. Also, her pupils never stayed in the centre of her eye when she was awake, like normal pupils do; both eyes were always off to the upper left side, as if she was continually peering at something around the corner. Mia sensed something ominous and had not yet voiced her concerns to her husband.

She took Chloe to the baby health sister for her check-up by a round-faced brunette called Narelle.

"Why do you think my baby is always looking to the left like that? I mean, look at her. Why does she seem to be comfortable when she is all twisted and contorted?"

Narelle replied, smiling broadly and with a relaxed voice, "It's just because she was crooked in the womb. Don't worry, she'll grow out of it." However, the feeling of dread that gathered in her gut could not be ignored.

Since Chloe was due for her vaccination, Mia took her to see Dr Knight, their family doctor. She placed her daughter on her lap, as he prepared his syringe, and Chloe instinctively wiggled into her favoured twisted position. Her head on Mia's left thigh, torso over to the right and her legs back over to the left.

Mia said, "You know she always wants to be crooked like this. It's weird but that's what she likes."

Dr Knight, seemingly unworried, chuckled as he injected Chloe in the thigh, and responded, "All babies are different, aren't they?" Chloe who was already half asleep did not have any reaction.

Finally, when she was nine weeks old, Mia decided to make an appointment with the hospital, wanting a definitive answer once and for all. In the consultation room, the paediatrician listened to Mia's summary of her daughter's life to date. Dr Tucker performed some simple tests to check her reflexes. Her knees jerked as something resembling a small hammer struck her semi-flexed knees. He then held her elbow between his thumb and fingers, tapped his thumb at first on her bicep, and then used the tiny hammer so that her elbow jerked in response. He then shone a light into her eyes, and watched her pupils dilate and constrict. He held her in his outstretched arms as he deliberately spun 360 degrees a couple of times in his swivel chair. Chloe's eyes did their familiar dance quickly to the right and then settled to the left again.

Dr Tucker was a man in his fifties with gold-rimmed glasses that sat at the end of his nose. He made eye contact with Mia, reaching for his doctor's pad, his bushy eyebrows having shifted slightly upwards and his forehead tightening. "I agree that there's something wrong. Let's get an ultrasound done. She can sit on your lap while you hold her. The test can be done through the top of her head, through the fontanelle. It won't hurt, and it might give us an answer."

They were ushered to another part of the hospital and into a dark room. She held Chloe on her lap as a sharped-faced sonographer squeezed slimy gel onto the tip of her probe and placed this atop Chloe's head.

Mia watched the monitor; a fan of grainy white, a blob of black appeared.

"What's that?"

"I don't know. The doctor will need to look at the film and make his findings. He will then discuss these with you," she said, her voice having risen an octave as she stretched over pushing buttons so the machine clicked and beeped. Her maternal intuition told her immediately there was something wrong. The sonographer made no eye contact with her but kept her eyes fixated on the screen, her face looking troubled.

She called her husband from the hospital. He said he would meet her there. Mia and Chloe were once again ushered into another waiting room. She waited there anxiously for more than half an hour, sensing that something was off kilter. Finally, the nurse called them in to see Dr Tucker again. Mia entered the small office carrying Chloe, who had not made a sound, and found him sitting there studying a printed report that he held in his hand. He looked apprehensive.

"I've had a look at Chloe's ultrasound and there is something there. There's a mass that's approximately one third of the left side of her brain in size. I've made a call to Professor Fourrier at the Children's Hospital; he's a neurologist and top in his field. He will see you today, and I've organised an ambulance to take you both there immediately."

"What is it?" asked Mia. "What's the mass?"

"In layman's terms, she's had a stroke. It would have happened just before, during, or straight after birth, but Professor Fourrier will be able to tell you more." Mia's shoulders drooped as the tears streamed down her cheeks. He paused as he took her hand and gave it a squeeze; this act of kindness caressed her aching soul.

Mia stepped out of his office to find Wolfie waiting. Concerned, she updated him on Dr Tucker's findings. He wanted to find out more before drawing any conclusions. The ambulance arrived, and Mia and Chloe were escorted into the back of the waiting vehicle. Wolfie followed in his new company car. It was a forty-minute ride in the ambulance. Mia sat rigidly on a seat; the colour having drained from her face with her hands clenched tightly in her lap. Chloe slept on the bed, looking tiny and helpless.

At the Children's Hospital, they were expedited through the Emergency Department to another room where Wolfie met them. Professor Fourrier sauntered in. He was a tall, wiry looking man with a head of white hair and a wrinkled face. He wore an oversized lab coat and as he approached them the ID badge that hung from his lapel swung from side to side.

He advised, "The next step will be to perform an MRI. This will give us a clearer image of what's going on inside. Since she is so small, we can probably get away with giving her a small dose of Phenergan, which should be enough to make her drowsy and lie still for the test." Wolfie and Mia gave their consent.

From behind a glass window, they watched a listless Chloe slowly slide into a tunnel. Various images appeared on the screen now with that familiar black mass. As soon as the procedure was completed, they were taken to a large sterile ward with rows of empty beds. In green vinyl armchairs at the end of Chloe's bed, under the harsh fluorescent lights, they waited for Professor Fourrier. Two cumbersome looking bandages held an intravenous line in place, from her delicate arm to a drip, whilst another machine monitored her vital signs, periodically beeping softly.

"I'm worried that something's really wrong with her," Mia confided to Wolfie.

"Let's just wait and see what the doctor says. I'm sure it's nothing major," he replied calmly. She had an uneasy feeling in the pit of her stomach that was getting stronger by the minute.

Professor Fourrier entered the room and pulled up a chair to face them. He spoke to them in a matter-of-fact tone. "I've just been looking at your daughter's films, and from what I can see, she has had what we call an infarct, or as Dr Tucker has explained, she's had a stroke. A blood vessel in her brain has burst causing extensive damage, and that's what the black mass is. It's basically dead tissue. This large mass of scar tissue covers a third of the whole left side of her brain."

Once again, the tears flowed freely down Mia's face. He continued, "This most likely happened at the time of birth ... She'll most likely never walk, never talk … She'll be in a vegetative state and will probably have cerebral palsy ..."

The room spun and Mia suddenly felt lightheaded and was trembling all over. Wolfie, who had not uttered a word, squared his already squared shoulders, but then stood up and stormed out of the ward. She was trying to focus on the doctor's moving lips but could not make sense of anything he was saying. She could no longer absorb any more of the dreadful, grim future he was painting for Chloe. She sat there, shedding tears, her shoulders shaking uncontrollably from her sobbing. He remained unmoved and continued with his unpleasant prognosis.

When he had finished, Mia asked, "So what happens next? What do we do now?"

He replied, "Just live your life normally. The damage is done."

"Will it get worse?"

"No, the damage has been done."

She felt a surge of warm love rise as she looked across to Chloe, lying still in her oversized bed, and it spread throughout her like a fountain as the neurologist's words echoed in her head.

No, not my daughter! That can't be right. I'm sure you already have more movement than that. Never! I'll make sure that you're the best version of yourself! I love you so, so much. I didn't think I could love you more than I do, but I do! We'll get through this together. I promise I'll do everything to help you.

She made Chloe a secret promise, a secret pact, right then and there, not asked for but given freely and with love. Mia emerged from the building wondering where Wolfie was, having no idea where he had parked. She found him sitting on a wooden bench in the nearby carpark, shoulders now slumped and a scowl on his face, looking down at the hands that lay limp in his lap. They walked to the car in silence, both absorbed in their tortured thoughts.

She strapped Chloe into the car capsule and got in. Mia's face was streaked black from her running mascara, and it was smeared around her eyes, making her look like a panda bear. Her eyeballs were glazed, her hair a mess and her characteristically impeccably applied red lipstick was smudged. Wolfie concentrated on driving.

"Why has this happened to her? How could this happen to her? Where is God? Why did he let this happen?" she asked, distraught.

Wolfie wanted to know if the doctor had said anything else. They did not discuss his abrupt departure. That was the last thing on Mia's mind. They were driving back to her parents' house to collect Alex. As they pulled up in their driveway, Natalia came out to greet them.

She asked in her thick Italian accent and all smiles, "Well? It was nothing? You were worrying for no reason?"

"She's had a stroke," replied Mia curtly.

"NO! NO!", screamed Natalia as she ran to the baby capsule that Mia held, "Oh my God! No!"

Gino came out to see what the commotion was. Natalia was crying, completely devastated. When they explained, he was also visibly upset, though he shed no tears. Mia had only ever seen her father cry once, when his mother had died.

Mia studied the scene with her eyes wide and her shoulders hunched. There was a palpable sense of despair in the air and in her body. She glanced over at Wolfie, her pillar of strength. He watched all of this unfold without showing any emotion. Her idyllic life seemed to be in danger, and no one around her seemed capable of handling these looming events. It was then that she heard it, a friendly voice in her head, that gave her strength and the resolve to help her daughter. It was loud, and it was clear, *"YOU'VE GOT THIS! YOU CAN DO IT!"*

Eleven Years Earlier

Chance Encounter ...1984
Chapter 2

It was the morning peak hour, students and businesspeople crowded the platform. As the train rolled in, Mia Fidelio stepped aboard, and took the stairs to the upper deck. Commuters sat facing the direction the train was taking with vacuous expressions on their faces, revealing the boredom of their repetitive lives.

Oh great, it looks like standing room only! Hang on a minute; it must be my lucky day!

She found the only empty seat, which meant looking out at everyone in the carriage, and travelling against the direction of the train's movement.

Well, I guess it beats standing for fifty minutes!

It was a tight space for someone with a small behind, and she just fit. She pinched her legs together and twisted them slightly to the right so as not to knock knees with the mature business executive opposite her wearing a peeved look.

Mia was 18 years old with hazel eyes, high cheek bones and shoulder-length chestnut blonde, sun-streaked hair. She was on her way to university, where she was in the second semester of her first year of an accounting degree. She noticed a young girl sitting on her mother's knee, shyly playing with a doll. She smiled at Mia who smiled back at her. She looked about four years old which was the age that Mia had emigrated from Italy with her mother Natalia, her father Gino, and her older brother, Nino, who at the time was five and a half. During her childhood, Mia also remembered sitting on her mother's knee or at her feet while she knitted and listening to her mother's stories about her as a baby while she was still in Italy and after they had moved to Australia. Natalia had said jokingly, "Your first word was NO! I should have known what a difficult child you would be."

"Why? I think it shows strength of character. I knew what I wanted from six months or maybe it showed that you never let me do anything, and that you were overprotective," laughed Mia, who was often able to see both sides of an argument.

A part of her remembered fondly the stories her mother had told her, about when they were newcomers to Australia, did not speak the language, did not know anyone, and how they had struggled at first. Unable to find work in their chosen fields, her father worked night shift in a local factory whilst her mother stayed home and looked after the children. One afternoon, Natalia picked Mia up from kindergarten. Natalia pulled the collar up on her coat as they walked home; Mia skipped alongside her mother as the dry orange leaves crunched beneath her feet. When they got home, Mia bounded up the stairs in a hurry to watch her favourite cartoon. She turned on their second-hand black and white TV but only a grainy image appeared and there was no sound.

Mia frustratingly fidgeted with the knob as she said, "Fuck TV! Fuck TV!"

"Oh, look, Mia is speaking English very well," said Natalia proudly to Gino.

"Do you know what she's saying?" and he enlightened her.

"Is that what they learn at school!" exclaimed Natalia horrified, having been raised by Catholic nuns in an orphanage.

Her mother also told her stories of how she had met Gino at a youth centre over a game of table tennis, and how they had quickly become inseparable from then on. Going dancing and standing ankle deep in the snow, in her stilettos and thin coat, kissing for hours. It all sounded so romantic. When her parents married, Natalia was only 20 and Gino was only 19. It was Mia's hope that she would also find and marry the man of her dreams.

Natalia was blue-eyed, with a fair complexion and a full head of tight, blonde curls and permanently had a crisp white apron tied around her waist.

Gino was a stockily built man with charcoal hair, and Mia had inherited his magnanimous personality. They went to English school and her father eventually retrained as an IT manager and found work in the city. Now, when he left in the morning, he reeked of Aramis, his favourite fragrance. He suffocated Mia when he walked past. It was as if he had climbed into the bottle of cologne and back out again.

Mia remembered being about seven, when she found her parents in their room one weekend lying on the bed animatedly laughing and chatting with the window curtains fully drawn back and the sun streaming in on them. She hovered in the doorway.

"Hello, little Mia, what are you doing standing there, come in. What do you know?" said Gino merrily.

Mia climbed onto the end of their bed and sat on her heels, as she excitedly said with a smile and shiny eyes, "I heard a joke at school. Do you want to hear it?" Gino laughed, "Alright."

"Tarzan and Jane were lying naked, when Tarzan pointed to her boobies and said, 'What are those?' 'Those are my headlights,' said Jane. Then she pointed to his rude bit and said, 'What's that?' 'That's my tail,' said Tarzan. He then pointed to her private parts and said, 'What's that?' 'That's my pussy cat,' replied Jane. They were hugging when Tarzan yelled, 'JANE! JANE! Turn on your headlights! Your pussy cat's swallowing my tail!' "

Her father roared with laughter and her mother chuckled. Though Mia did not understand the whole concept of the joke, she loved to make her parents laugh.

Natalia turned to Gino and asked, "Would you have ever told your mother a joke like that?"

"Never! She would have washed my mouth out with soap!"

Natalia was shaking her head as she said, "I can't believe what she is learning at school."

Whenever Mia heard a joke, any joke, she would eagerly come home to tell her parents, especially her father.

When her parents or their neighbours would ask her, "What do you want to be when you grow up?"

She would reply proudly, "Someone who makes people laugh."

As she grew and her parents asked her this same question she would reply, "I want to be a comedian and a scientist who helps people by finding cures for diseases and I want to be married and have six children!"

Natalia would laugh and say, "We'll talk about it then."

As the rest of the family was still back in Italy, they were loving and close-knit. Mia was baffled when at show and tell the other children would stand up and talk about visiting their cousins or grandparents, as she had no concept of these extended family relationships. She would come home and ask her mother about them and loved sitting at the table enjoying *la merendina* after school, sometimes a warm bowl of milk with biscotti for dipping or a scoop of fresh ricotta with sugar sprinkled over the top, and today, a slice of fresh bread, spread thickly with sweetened condensed milk, while her mother fussed in the kitchen, telling her the names and ages of her cousins and any family stories she could think of.

Even though Mia had her older brother, Nino, she could not relate to some of the games he enjoyed, such as playing with his two favourite cars, the Ferrari and Lamborghini that he would collide with his trucks or building towers out of his wooden blocks that he would destroy with planes crashing into them. She often wondered what it would be like to have a sister who could play with her and her dolls for whom her mother had knitted an assortment of outfits. As the four of them lived in a one-bedroomed unit, she never had any friends come to visit, nor did she go on any play dates. Mia found herself yearning for a pet and was forever rescuing injured animals that she found in the neighbourhood, such as a bird with a wounded wing which she nursed back to health or when a black and white kitten had followed her home. As her mother poured some cream in a saucer and fed the kitten some ham, she explained, "We are not allowed to have pets in our unit."

Eventually, they were able to move to a house when Mia was 15 and she was able to establish a close relationship with her Nonna who had come to Australia to live with them when Nonno died. Nonna was always dressed in black from head to toe and being set in her ways refused to learn English; as a result, Mia became fluent in Italian. Now that she was 18, as well as Nonna, there were also two younger siblings; Vincent was 10 years old, and Sophie was four. Mia often helped out with her sister and enjoyed taking her to a playgroup when she had time off from university. She was popular with their neighbours as well, and frequently babysat for them for some pocket money, and had even posted an ad in their local newspaper for babysitting jobs.

As Mia stirred from her thoughts, she realised the train had not moved and was still at the platform. Overhead, the musical chimes sounded, signalling the announcement about to be made by the wry train driver. "Ladies and gentlemen, can I have your attention please, we apologise for the delay but we're waiting for the green light to go ahead. If you'd like to, please shake your fists angrily at the train passing us to your right, as they are the reason for our delay." Passengers snickered, including the man opposite in pinstripes, and she did too. He continued, "We thank you for your patience and will be departing shortly."

Mia was feeling fabulous. Her hair was braided, and she loved the outfit she had chosen, denim jeans with a long-sleeved denim blouse with a lace frilled bodice and brown patent leather slip-ons with big bows. Good clothes always lifted her mood and gave her a feeling of empowerment. She was very aware of fashion trends but followed her own instincts. Although almost anything she tried looked great on her, her style was quintessentially classy and polished. She never ventured outside with unwashed hair or an outfit that did not match, and she enjoyed the theatricality of dressing.

Mia sat on the train, single and contented. She had been kissed by two boys but that's as far as it had gone, having vowed to never have sex before marriage, a legacy of her Catholic upbringing. The train pulled into Town Hall station and she noticed a young man stand to exit. He caught her eye because he was tall and handsome, with brown hair and eyes and a slim build. He had a confident, determined look on his bronzed face, and there was a rugged quality about him. It was unusual to be so tanned at the start of spring. He looked like a typical student with faded jeans, white sneakers, a navy-blue Lacoste polo shirt, a beige jacket and a giant khaki coloured bag flung over his left shoulder. She wondered if he attended the same university.

She did not give him another thought as the doors opened and she hopped off the train. The hot air seemed to sit on the underground platform like a panting dog and it leapt up to greet her. It was stifling. She caught a glimpse of him as he disappeared into the sea of people that engulfed him on the platform. It was so crowded that she seemed to glide with the crush of the crowd. She made her way through the masses of feverish bodies to get to campus. Today, she only had two subjects. After attending her Business Statistics tutorial, she walked the short distance to her Microeconomics lecture where the students were already gathering outside the lecture hall. Who should be standing there but the boy she had seen on the train with a girl whom she naturally assumed was his girlfriend. They were deep in conversation and laughing at something he had said. She walked towards them as they loitered near the entrance door. He spoke to her, "Hi! You're in my Business Stats class."

"I don't think so."

"Didn't you just finish your class? That room over there." He indicated to the room she had just exited.

"Yes."

"Then that's the same class."

"Well, I didn't realise you were in my class. I usually come in just as it's starting and sit up the back, so I don't pay any attention to who is in the room. It's such a monotonous subject, and that lecturer!" She rolled her eyes.

"I'm Wolfie. This is Bae-Sook."

"Hi. I'm Mia. I'm sorry. What was your name again?" she asked, turning to take in the small Asian girl to his right. She was shorter than Mia with black wavy hair and seemed quiet and reserved.

"Bae-Sook," she answered timidly.

"Bae-Sook?" Mia repeated inquisitively. "I think it's the first time I've ever met anyone with that name."

He quickly added loudly, "It's easy to remember! Just think of "Hey Sook"! Like you're calling over a gigantic sook. That's what I do." He was grinning as he spoke. Mia was looking at Bae-Sook, who was chuckling.

Why are you laughing? Is he your boyfriend? Is he joking?

Turning to him, Mia asked, "I'm sorry. Did you say your name was Wolfie? That's unusual."

He replied proudly, "It's my nickname. It's easier than my full German name which is Wolfgang."

They entered the lecture hall and sat together. Wolfie plonked himself firmly between them. He continued quietly talking to Mia. He was articulate with a clever sense of humour. She quickly realised that Bae-Sook, though not his girlfriend, would like to be, giggling at everything he said.

They eventually exchanged numbers, with him adding, "If it's a nice day Friday, why don't you come over for a hit of tennis?"

"Okay," she answered casually.

Swept Off Her Feet
Chapter 3

On Thursday, Mia sat next to her friend, Julie, in her Principles of Marketing class while their lecturer stood at the front of the room talking about the different groups of shoppers, from laggards to innovators. Mia whispered to Julie, "Do you think it's going to be a nice day tomorrow? It looks like rain." Gazing out the window, "I've met this guy. He said we should have a hit of tennis if it's a nice day. Do you think I should go?"

Julie tucked the hair of the shoulder-length bob that framed her sweet, heart-shaped face behind her ear, as she turned to Mia, her blue eyes filled with excitement, "Yes. Go, definitely."

"But I can't even play tennis. I mean it's been years since I've picked up a racquet, let alone stepped onto a tennis court. Besides, I'm over boys. Stupid creatures! It's only been a month since I broke up with Simon."

"I still think you should go. What have you got to lose?"

Mia shrugged and looked away into the distance.

Friday arrived, and both Mia and Wolfie had the day off to study. Most students quickly learned how to plan and organise their subjects into the first four days of the week to leave Friday free. She called Wolfie and organised their tennis match. He offered to pick her up and arrived in his father's bright green micro car.

Mia lived in a typical Australian weatherboard home that was a mess inside. Halfway through renovations, the builder had broken his jaw playing football and stopped working. The walls in the lounge room were half done, partly sanded and painted. On top of that, Mia's father, who had always suffered back pain, had just come out of hospital after having had traction treatment, and he was still recuperating. To be included in family gatherings, he lay on a door set up as a bed in the middle of the lounge room.

Wolfie walked in and was greeted by Mia's parents and this dreadful disarray of furniture and half-completed workmanship. He looked handsome and athletic in his tennis whites. Mia wore a T-shirt and matching navy-blue Bermuda shorts with giant white hibiscus flowers all over them. Wearing the shorts that she had made, made her feel confident.

Wolfie who had been talking to Gino, walked over to the TV to find a better channel for him; the knob, however, came off in his hand. He stood there looking a little dumbfounded.

"Don't worry about it. It was already like that," Mia said as she ushered him out of the house.

In the car, they talked, and it was easy. So easy she forgot to be nervous. He concentrated on the road as he asked her lots of questions. Just a hint of a curl fell across his forehead, a golden tanned face with carved features, the cheek bones, the thickly lashed eyelids, the full lips. The smile that curved his mouth and when it reached his eyes, crinkled the corners. It made her stomach feel jittery.

They arrived at his parents' house. It was an enormous home in a leafy North Shore suburb, sprawled across a huge one-acre block at the end of a very long, pebbled battle-axe drive. As they drove down the driveway and turned the bend, Mia saw a grass tennis court, a pool, an outdoor spa and a large pond covered in enormous lily pads. He parked under the double carport in front of the double garage. From there, she saw unused horse stables and a large cabana, where his father conducted his consultancy practice.

"When you said, 'Let's have a hit', I thought you meant at some local council courts. I didn't realise that you had a tennis court."

They entered his house through the oversized wooden antique door, and she gazed around at this spacious home, with its colourful Gabbeh rugs contrasting with the white shaggy carpet. Every wall she could see was covered in modern surrealistic artwork, and every room was filled with antiques.

Oh, my goodness! This is so embarrassing! He lives in a mansion and my house is falling down around my ears. What must he think? He never said anything! I had no idea! Well, at least it shows he's humble, not bragging about it; besides I guess it's not his house; it's his parents.

As they stepped out of the foyer, which was flanked by two five-foot-tall turquoise urns, he introduced her to his father.

"Sam this is Mia. Mia this is Sam."

Fancy calling your parents by their first name! That's different. I guess different household, different rules.

Sam was from Berlin. He was an older gentleman with white curly hair and blue beady twinkling eyes. He was short and stout, with an enormous belly and roared loudly with laughter at every opportunity.

"Hello, Mia. Have you just returned from Hawaii?" he asked in a thick German accent.

"Hawaii? No. Why do you ask?"

"Those flowery shorts!" he added with a majestic cackle.

They made their way down to the tennis court and started off with some warm-up shots and then had their game. Wolfie was a better tennis player than Mia, and when she managed to hit the ball back to him, she could tell that he had been holding back, for he would sometimes display his talent by launching a ball across the court at such a fast pace that she had no time to react. Since it was a warm day, they then walked back to the house for a drink. As she sat in the kitchen, and he poured her a glass of pulp free freshly squeezed orange juice, he continued bombarding her with questions. It made her giggle. She felt like he was a reporter for a news channel and wondered if he was nervous.

"What's your favourite food?"

"I love Italian food, and especially pasta!"

"What movies do you like to watch?"

"I love James Bond movies and I've read all the books written by Ian Fleming. I adore Roger Moore."

"I don't think there are any 007 movies currently screening," he said flicking through the newspaper, "but there is a movie playing tonight starring Roger Moore. It's a thriller and he's playing a psychiatrist. Do you want to go see it?"

"Sure."

After this first date, their paths crossed frequently at university. They hung out in the cafeteria, eating custard tarts that he had introduced her to, or grabbing a drink at the university bar. They had been seeing each other for three weeks, but she could not ignore the vague sense of disquiet she felt about him. Though uncertain of her reasoning, she decided to give him another chance to prove her wrong.

On Saturday night, they saw a movie in the city and then popped into a café. Mia ordered a Coke, which was something she rarely did, but tonight she was feeling particularly thirsty after the big bucket of popcorn he had insisted on buying. He ordered a cup cake with thick cream and a cherry on top as well as a strawberry milkshake. She momentarily looked away at something Wolfie had pointed to, before turning back to her drink.

"My Coke looks weird, kind of creamy. Can Coke go off?" Mia asked as she stirred the contents of her red plastic cup with her straw. He sniggered.

"I'm not drinking that. I think there's something wrong with it," she said as she pushed it away.

He almost roared with laughter, "I dropped my cherry in your Coke. That's some of the cream." He thought his prank was hilarious. "It was a joke."

Him and his puerile prank! That's it. He's so childish and immature. I won't be seeing him again!

The following day, who should pull up to her house in his bright green vehicle? Wolfie. He had arrived unannounced and uninvited. Mia went outside to meet him. He presented her with a bunch of pink flowers, a heart shaped red box of chocolates and a greeting card. The card had a picture of a smiling monkey on the front, holding a bunch of bananas in one hand and a single peeled banana in the other. It read, "Sure had a great time!" Inside the card, on a bright orange background, there was a picture of a bunch of bananas, "THANKS A BUNCH!"

Wolfie had written:

Dear Mia,

Just a quick word if I may,
For such a lovely day.
No more being a rat,
My apologies,
You certainly don't deserve that.

I hope you will like this card,
With the chocolates,
From this clever little bard.

Ohhhh, he's so sweet. What a nice, thoughtful gesture.

She liked the way he had apologised when he had been in the wrong. She believed the first to apologise was the bravest, the first to forgive the strongest and the first to forget the happiest.

Wolfie spoiled Mia by taking her to see the ballet, classical concerts at the Opera House, plays, various other concerts, and tennis tournaments. This was a whole new world to Mia, who had never gone anywhere with her parents, only ever going out on school excursions and never having eaten out. Tonight, he was taking her out to a fancy French restaurant. She wore an off-the-shoulder burgundy chiffon dress that stopped above her knee and accentuated her perky, high bust. In order to match his height, she also wore her five-inch stilettos.

"WOW! You look amazing! That dress is absolutely gorgeous," he exclaimed in appreciation.

"Thank you. I love this dress and I love the colour," she replied with a smile.

"You really have a flare for fashion and a fabulous sense of dress, don't you? You always look great."

"I like to look my best. I think it says a lot about who you are. I think clothes are powerful. I know if I get up in the morning feeling a little drab, when I put on a bright colour, I instantly feel better. Don't you?"

"No, not really. I tend to dress to be comfortable."

Two complete strangers walking by complimented her on her dress, and Mia was sure she saw Wolfie's chest swell each time with pride that she was on his arm.

Their meal was delicious and again, even though she offered to pay half, he refused. Eventually, he accepted since he did not have a part-time job like she did, and she also was proud and wanted to pay her own way. He lived off the savings from his job in a gap year when he had worked in the share registry of a large multinational, and his father also gave him a small weekly allowance. Mia worked at the cash register at a large discount grocery chain on Thursday night and Saturday. She earned enough to pay her way through university and for incidentals such as clothing, outings and textbooks and never asked her parents for a cent.

He would also meet her at the train station in the morning, so they could travel to university together. He would hop off the train and find her at the designated point of halfway along the platform. Most mornings, he would arrive with a hot chocolate and a chocolate croissant for them both. If she shivered because it was cold, he would take off his jumper and say, "Here put this on, you look cold." He was kind and caring.

He finally plucked up the courage to kiss her on a date at the beach. Wolfie put his arms around her and as he planted a soft kiss on her lips, she felt an eruption of butterflies break free inside her. She relaxed into his body and did not want to pull away as the thrill still fluttered inside her. She could not think of anywhere she wanted to be more than in Wolfie's gentle, protective embrace.

They had now been dating for three months and it had been going well. His generous and romantic nature also ensured that there was a steady stream of flowers and cards with thoughtful messages. He gave her a card that read, "You're the kind who makes me want to kiss your feet…", on the front was an animation of a girl standing and kneeling next to her a man kissing her feet. Inside the card read "….and work my way up!!" He had penned a poem:

To the girl of my dreams,
I'm so elated when I'm with you,
I hope you feel the same way too.

These last three months have been my best,
They easily beat all the rest.

You know there is no competition,
The others are left behind in attrition.

Curvy curves, heavenly hair and lips like roses,
Revealed by those wiggly hip poses,

But if you have it, flaunt it, why not,
Go, give it your best shot.
Don't ever tell me to take a hike,
Cause you're the only one I'll ever like.

Could anyone doubt his infatuation, even if his writing style would not win him poet of the year? She felt that his words echoed the euphoria they both felt for each other. It was not only his beautiful words, but he was chivalrous too. When he came to pick her up, he always opened the car door for her and waited until she was securely stowed, long legs and skirts tucked in before he would secure the door. He would often hold her coat open for her so she could slide her arms into the sleeves. One morning on the way to university, under the umbrella he held, they huddled together as the rain pelted down. His other arm was protectively wrapped around her waist. There were puddles everywhere and as they crossed the road in front of a construction site, Wolfie stepped into a puddle which sent a glob of mud onto Mia's boot.

"Oh yuck!" she exclaimed as she giggled. When they were out of the rain and safely at university, he reached for the handkerchief in his pocket and bent over as he wiped the mud off her shoe. Everything inside her went to mush.

He was studying for a Marketing degree, but they shared many core subjects. As the curriculum had not changed, Wolfie gave Mia his notes and assignments from a subject he had received a credit in. She had been moved by his thoughtfulness and kindness. He repeatedly told her that meeting her was the best thing that had ever happened to him, and she felt the same way, and his actions demonstrated his regard for her.

She was savouring the romantic liaisons with her man. His kisses were now hot and steamy. It was common practice for them to spend hours kissing in the university library, Mia sitting on his knee. His tongue gently pushing into her mouth, his breath shuddering with desire, both caught in the passion. They spent hours rolling around on the grass in a secluded park, kissing and cuddling, sensuously lost in the moment. His hands moved teasingly over her body as he easily turned her on. When they were alone, his mouth would gently make its way to her nipples, which he circled with his tongue, licked and sucked. He loved massaging her firm breasts with both hands, and as he pushed her panties to one side, she instinctively spread her legs as he pushed two fingers inside her, in, out, in sweet rhythm; feeling her wetness, dipping inside her, she groaned in pleasure as he continued driving her wild with desire, her spine rising in an arc. She was delirious, bosom heaving, flooded with hot, liquid sensations that burned in her loins, filled with lustful wanting. Wolfie always tried to coax her into taking things a little further in their relationship. While she could not get enough of him, she was still hesitant to cross that line.

Wolfie got into the habit of picking her up after work on a Saturday and they would then spend the evening together. Having strict Catholic parents and being the firstborn daughter, meant she had to pave the way for her little sister. Mia had to be home by 10pm on a weeknight and by midnight on a Saturday night. She could only go out once at night during the week and only once on the weekend. She had to be home on Sundays. Wolfie found her parents' strictness frustrating as he could not get enough of her. He had never met anyone like Mia before, unpretentious, and breathtaking, as well as kind and sweet. She was positive, with an irreverent sense of humour and gifted at always being able to see the funny side of everything. He was impressed by her ability to recall and retell jokes when he could not remember any.

"Can you make a sentence using the words defence, defeat and detail?" asked Mia.

"No", replied Wolfie, waiting for the punch line.

Putting on her thickest Italian accent and with fingers pursed and talking with her hands, she said, "De cow, jumped over de fence, and de feet came first and de tail last." And burst out laughing. She always laughed at her own jokes. He chuckled, adoring her playfulness and zest for life. They were falling in love.

They shared similarities; like her he was European. Both his parents were German, and he had emigrated with them when he was five. He was the oldest and only had a brother. Wolfgang Andre Schmidt was called Wolfie by his family. Mia liked his nickname because it made him sound like a friendly, cuddly pet dog. Sometimes they even referred to him as "The Wolf." He was proud of his German heritage and thought his name sounded unique and strong. He maintained close bonds with Germany and spoke of his frequent visits to his grandparents who still resided there. He kept in regular contact with them through letters and phone calls. It showed a softer side to him; he loved his family, was caring and family oriented.

They had been dating for about six months and he was beginning to open up to her, as they lay on the carpet in the study playing backgammon, in front of the floor to ceiling window with the sun streaming in on them, he said, “I can’t wait to be a grandfather. I want to be as close to my grandchildren as my grandparents are to me.” He paused as he continued, “Family is very important. My grandparents have always been there for me. Family and respect are the most important things in life and should be shown at all times.”

Mia, who was getting hot in the sun, sat up, swept the hair off the back of her neck and tied it on top of her head in a high ponytail. The long, tanned nape of her neck was beautiful, just like the skin of a peach. She replied, “I agree with you 100 percent. Family is important and we should show respect at all times, not just to family, but to everyone.”

“Communication is also important. You should have seen the way my folks carried on during their divorce. It got ugly.”

“I don’t know anyone who’s divorced. How old were you?” she asked, hugging her knees to her chest.

“Seventeen.” He cried as he said, “I could never put my children through something as traumatic as that. That’s why communication is so important.” He sounded sincere, as he wiped tears from his eyes. “Now my father has remarried Tammy, and she’s moved in with her three daughters. A blended family also never works.”

“Why did they get divorced? What happened?”

He packed away the backgammon checkers into the side racks of the board as he said, “My mother, Sabine, approached me and told me she was going to leave Sam. She said she couldn’t live with him a minute longer. I said, ‘That’s fine but do it quickly. Don’t let it drag on and on.’ But she didn’t, and the fights, screaming matches and drama were relentless. They hadn’t been getting on for years and later I found out that my mom had been having an affair. I think a lot of women do. She didn’t do it quickly like she’d promised!”

“Oh wow, that’s tough, but hang on a minute, I think a lot of men have affairs too. It’s not one sided. I think if partners have affairs, it’s usually because they are unhappy with something in their marriage. Something’s missing and they are looking for love elsewhere, or they're bored; something is making them unhappy."

"She should never have cheated on my father! She should have just left if she was unhappy! I haven't spoken to her since!"

"What? But she's still your mum! You don't know what really went on between them. That was three years ago; don't you miss her? Why did it drag on if they both wanted it to end?"

"I'll eventually speak to her again and I think it dragged on because Sam had to pay her out her share, but he didn't have the funds, so she couldn't go anywhere. They even argued over their vinyl record collection. In the end, they had to flip a coin to see who would go first. They then took turns from there, one record at a time."

"That sounds fair and probably the best way to split it, if they were no longer getting along. It sounds like things became vindictive and nasty. I think most divorces end up like that."

"It was pathetic. I could never get divorced. I've seen what it can do, and how it destroys families." He shed tears as he said, "And if I ever did, I would never behave the way my folks did. It would be amicable. I could never be so spiteful and vindictive. When Sabine finally did leave, I suffered a break-down. I had a massive depression, during which time I stayed locked in my room for six months, and hardly ventured out! I was also prescribed anti-depressants, that helped me, but I'm fine now and don't take or need these anymore."

She listened to his tale but could not relate, having never met anyone who had suffered from depression. He seemed fine to her. Everything about him seemed well adjusted. He gave such a strong impression of having learnt a lot from his ordeal. He spoke so eloquently about what he wanted from life. He was 20, and Mia was his first girlfriend.

"I've never had the confidence to ask girls out before, even when they had shown interest. I was just so shy. You're lucky you came along when you did, because I was just about to ask Bae-Sook out."

"I haven't seen her at university in a while. Have you?"

"No, I think she's gone back to Malaysia. She was only out here as part of a student exchange program."

Mia reflected on their conversation and appreciated his honesty in sharing the most challenging time of his life which she thought was admirable. The vulnerability that he displayed disarmed her, and she longed to be near to him both physically and emotionally, and to help take away his pain.

Deflowered
Chapter 4

The passion was bubbling between them and Wolfie was continually putting pressure on her to have sex. Mia, still reluctant, was feeling pushed into a corner. One day, when her mother was doing the laundry, she decided that it would be a good time to seek some guidance but knowing full well that the subject was still taboo. As her Mum stood there sorting the whites from the colours, she dived right in, "Mamma, what do you think about sex before marriage?"

Her Mother snapped, "Mia, if you can't wait until you're married, don't come home pregnant! Go on the pill and don't come and tell me how good it was." Mia walked back to her room dejected, still confused and indecisive.

There are times when I can't wait to move out! Have my freedom, do what I want and not worry about getting judged by you!

The feelings she had for Wolfie were unlike anything she had ever felt before. Mia was at her happiest when with him, and when she saw him, her soul danced. When she uttered the words, "I love you", he chuckled and hugged her close, wrapping his arms around her. It took three weeks for him to tell her that he loved her too. She finally gave in to him, and agreed to have sex, even though she was not ready for it, but because they loved each other, and it seemed like the logical next step. Wolfie took Mia to a romantic French restaurant, *Le Petit Escargot*, by the water with a gorgeous view of Sydney Harbour and then back to his place. His parents were open to their children bringing home their partners and letting them stay the night. However, Mia's parents would never consider this, not even allowing her to have a boy in her bedroom with the door open! The furniture in his bedroom was adorned with gold leaf and boasted a wooden bed, a wardrobe and a desk. He switched on a standing floor lamp which instantly illuminated the room as if it were broad daylight. He draped a multi-coloured silk scarf over the lamp to soften the harsh light and this had the effect of casting colours of the rainbow across the room, which made it feel romantic and relaxing.

"You smell and taste so good," he purred as he leaned in to kiss her. He could smell her, a delicate blend of strawberries and cream that he always loved. Taking her face in his hands, and looking deeply into her eyes, he kissed her more softly, as if every taste was like drinking ambrosia, the drink of the gods. He moved away, still looking deep into her eyes, holding her face in his hands, then pulled her in to kiss her again. She felt her body yielding and then a strong pang of affection for him. They both got undressed and huddled under the sheets. Here he kissed and caressed her. The tip of his tongue circled her nipple, delicately at first as it hardened to the soft flicks of his tongue; he pounced hungrily on it with his mouth, sucking and gently nibbling its ripeness. He repeated this on the other side, then softly kissed the length of her body making his way to her hips. He gently parted her legs and hovered admiringly over her clitoris before continuing to lick, kiss and suck, his tongue discovering pleasure spots she had never even known existed.

After a while, Wolfie whispered, "Do you want to try a 69?"

Mia replied, "Okay," but had no idea what this was.

She sat up next to him in bed. He was now lying on his back. He tapped her derriere as he said, "Come up here," indicating to his head. She got into all fours over him with his guidance. Mia found herself face to face with his genitalia and was horrified. She had no idea what to do, and had never seen a penis up close before, let alone an erect one.

What an ugly thing! So veiny.

In time, she would come to love an erect penis, and look forward to it, but not tonight. She suddenly felt his tongue dart deep between her inner thighs and realised what he was expecting. She could not and did not reciprocate.

He changed position, so he was now on top. Mia lay there motionless. She did not make a sound. She felt tense. Her beliefs, instilled from birth, held her in an iron grip at that moment. He tried entering her, but her body was unyielding. He also found it disturbing that she lay there unmoving. He could not penetrate her and eventually gave up. He rolled over, so he was lying next to her, still pressed against her. She felt relief.

Just then, there was an eruption of flames. The scarf had caught alight. Wolfie sprang out of bed, grabbed it and tried shaking it to put the fire out, but this only made the flames grow. This instantly illuminated the room again, revealing him standing there stark naked. He looked like a stick figure. He threw the flaming scarf to the floor, folding it over as he stomped and extinguished the fire. They laughed with each other and Mia realised that the deep knot of tension inside her was no longer there.

After their evening, she noticed a change in his behaviour. Though they still spent every minute of every day together whenever or wherever they could, Wolfie no longer kissed and caressed her as he had done before. It was driving her crazy. She longed for his magic touch, tender embraces and passionate kisses. His Christmas card to her read, "You can pinch and squeeze your Christmas present from me all you want!", and on the inside, "but remember I bruise easily!"

Dear Mia,

Have a Merry Christmas and a prosperous New Year; I certainly had a lovely year because of you. Thank you.

Love Wolfie xxxx

What's going on? Why so formal? Where's my poem? He sounds like a business acquaintance rather than a would-be hot-blooded lover.

Eventually, it was Mia who wanted to try again and this time he was the reluctant one. It took about a month for them to become amorous once more. His whole family had gone out for the evening and they had the house to themselves. His bedroom was softly lit from the many candles Wolfie had scattered throughout. The flames danced softly casting shadows on the walls that looked like a cheering crowd. As their lips touched, softly at first and then harder, his hand slipped behind her neck, pulling her in for a warm, deep kiss that seemed to stop time. Heart and hormones stuttered inside her. He slowly unbuttoned her shirt, unclipped her bra, and as her breasts sprang free, she groaned pushing them towards him. She wanted him, wanted his touch, wanted it hard and fast. He entered her, but only about halfway before he lost his erection and gave up. When Wolfie next saw her, he said, "I've been thinking that it might be a good idea that we go and see a sex therapist, and I've made an appointment."

Mia was shocked, "Why?"

"Things in the bedroom appear more difficult than they need to be. I've found a sex therapist who specialises in female sexual dysfunction."

"What …? I don't think there's anything wrong with me. Apart from being a virgin and not wanting to have sex until I was married. Don't you think you're overreacting?"

"No, and I think she could really help. There's no harm in hearing what she has to say, and it will probably be beneficial for us both. I'm going and it would be great if you could join me." Mia laughed nervously.

The sex therapist's office was in the city, close to campus. Marnie was in her thirties, of medium build with shoulder-length dark curly hair and saucer-eyed. Scattered across her office were many colourful pamphlets and paraphernalia on anything to do with sex, and on her desk, she had 3D models of both the male and female reproductive systems.

Wolfie explained their first encounter. "She just lay there. Motionless. I kept trying but she was too tight and eventually I had to give up. It was a disaster!"

"I told him from the beginning that I wanted to wait until I was married but gave in to him because he was relentless with his requests for sex, even though deep down I did not feel ready. I really didn't want to," protested Mia.

Marnie turned to Wolfie, as she crossed the legs of her elegant cream trousers and said, "Had you continued, you would have been a rapist."

Taken aback he replied, "I'm not a rapist."

"Yes, if you had continued and forced yourself on her, then that would have been rape. She didn't want to. You were forcing her. That's rape." Wolfie didn't know how to take this. He was now the surprised and shocked one.

Mia felt like a bit of justice had been thrown her way. She almost wanted to give herself a high five. He had made her feel guilty for not wanting to give up her virginity when he had decided it was time for her to do so. Listening to Marnie explain it, he seemed to understand.

Marnie's eagerness to talk about anything sexual so openly made Mia uncomfortable. She sat there squirming in her chair. Marnie talked about the smells and the odour of the vagina when aroused, and how primitive woman was hairy at the back of her thighs, trapping these odours to attract males. She spoke about sex with such enthusiasm and gusto that Mia found it impossible to sit still. Listening to her sprout on the joys of love making, all kinds of love making, including oral sex, was almost unbearable for Mia who sat there red-faced and giggling nervously. She talked freely about masturbation, and was all for it, and was perfectly happy that her three-year-old son was now starting to play with himself.

"I've told him it's perfectly natural, but we don't do that in front of other people. You have to do that in your room."

Marnie said, "Dolphins are the only other animals on the planet that have sex for pleasure."

Now I have to worry about horny dolphins. Great! Like that time, I went to Sea World when I was about ten years old, and we stood next to a dolphin pen, the smell of the sea, the deep hues of green and blue, the ripple of the water as a gentle breeze caressed its surface. A dolphin swam up to us and threw a piece of seaweed that landed at my feet. I remember thinking, "Why did you do that?" Mum said, "Look! He wants to play with you! Throw it back! Throw it back!" I picked up the green mass and threw it; he promptly caught it and tossed it right back at my feet again.

We all laughed. There was a long whistle in the distance and the dolphin swam away to his handler. I wonder if that dolphin was a horn-bag too, like Marnie seems to be.

She was quickly snapped back from her childhood memory and into the present with Marnie, who had picked up one of her models of the vagina and was talking about the clitoris and the G spot. Mia was tittering and trying not to laugh out loud, which only made it worse. She was nervous, shy, tense, and self-conscious all at the same time, and came close to wetting her pants from embarrassment. Wolfie calmly sat there listening, asking lots of questions like he always did. Occasionally, he would turn to Mia and say, "Can you stop laughing?" Which only made her erupt into fits of hysterical laughter.

Each time he said this to her, Marnie would say, "It's okay. I would rather have Mia laugh than cry." Which of course would send Mia into a further spasm of giggles.

After their session, they walked to a local restaurant for some lunch, his arm around her waist.

"So, what did you think of that? You couldn't stop laughing!"

"Oh, my goodness! I've never been so embarrassed and uncomfortable in my life. She's so comfortable talking about sex and what about her little boy masturbating?"

"She was pretty good though. I thought it was worthwhile. Mind you, I didn't like being called a rapist."

"She's right though, if you had continued, it would have been rape. I wasn't ready to go all the way the first time; that's what you wanted, not me, even though I had agreed and that's why I just lay there. I wasn't into it. I'm glad you stopped when you did. It made me feel closer to you." She took his arm and gave it a little squeeze as she said this, convinced that he would understand.

They saw Marnie a couple more times and on their third attempt in the bedroom they had success. When he was finished, he held her in his arms. She lay there timidly looking up at him, her head tucked into his chest with half-closed lids. She was feeling vulnerable but safe in his warm, strong arms. When he lifted his head, and looked into her eyes, she was in the greatest love story ever told. While she had no comparison, she felt absolutely certain she had just experienced the true meaning of every love song and poem ever written. Sex with him marked the crossing of a threshold to trust and intimacy. In her eyes, he could do no wrong.

I absolutely adore you! You're my knight in shining armour. My lover. My Prince Charming. I'm so lucky to have found you.

"Look at you. Looking up at me like a shy schoolgirl. You are so beautiful, and so sweet, Mia." He held her close.

She had lost her virginity at 19. Wolfie was 21. They had been dating for about seven months. After their first success, there was no stopping them. Their lips would meet tenderly for a kiss and in no time her lips would be fully parted for his, which he would eagerly lock onto hers. She kissed him with a wild fervour that he matched, their tongues wrestling with each other. She passionately ran her hands the length of his back as she hugged him close, over his shoulders and entwined her fingers in his thick hair. He held her close so that she could feel his hard body against hers, engrossed in their own private paradise. He continued kissing her and then moved to her neck, caressing her with his lips, stopping at the pulse point before capturing her earlobe and sucking it. She gasped breathlessly. His lips crushed hers, his tongue seeking and searching, punishing and soothing all at once. He was driving her wild with desire.

His hands stroked the length of her body as they made their way to her breasts which he freed from her tight-fitting bodice. She wriggled out of her undies and skirt. He continued licking and sucking her nipples, each one in turn. His hand made its way to her thighs as he paused before her hot humid valley. He teased her by gently caressing her inner thigh, drawing a circle that got closer and closer to its target. His hand found her throbbing womanhood which he caressed and rubbed causing delicious friction as she moved into his hand. She felt a flutter of excitement; as he slipped two fingers inside her and began thrusting, she cried out into his mouth as he deepened his kiss. He was driving her crazy.

She turned to him as she undid his belt and dropped his trousers to the floor, and then his shirt and she helped to quickly remove his briefs. She kissed him hungrily as her hands found his throbbing manhood which she began rubbing, holding and squeezing, hardening with her touch. Both enjoyed exploring each other's bodies as they climbed into bed, and he mounted her. He slid inside her and began thrusting. When he was on the brink, he changed positions and took her from behind. He shuddered and collapsed on her as he climaxed deep inside her.

They had sex weekly if not more often, and at least twice on every occasion. After a short rest, he was always more than willing to have another round with her. She was enjoying sex with him, getting to know the way his body and her body responded to each other's. Trying new positions in this loving, safe environment.

One evening Wolfie surprised her with a black lace suspender belt and matching stockings and asked her to wear them. He helped her put them on as he murmured, "You look so, so sexy." For once in her life, she felt it, because of how her skin felt at his melting touch. The raw energy pumping from him enthralled her and from the hardness of his cock, she could tell he wanted her too. He stood behind her as he slid his hands over her naked breasts, rubbing the nipples with his palms. She tipped her head back and moaned. Waves of white-hot desire rippled through her. She wanted him inside her and she wanted him now. When it was over, she relaxed into the curve of his body, enjoying the stickiness of their bodies from sweat and the scent of sex, feeling completely satiated and loved.

As she removed her lingerie, he said, "Take them home. They're for you."

"Are you crazy! What if my mother finds them? She's a snoop and regularly goes through my stuff. No way!"

"Okay. I'll keep them here. You can wear them when you come over."

Often, after they had made love and lay together, Wolfie would marvel at her perfect figure. He admired her naked body, saying, "You're so beautiful, Mia. Look at your curves." His words were filled with lust and his face full of admiration, as he stroked the length of her body, following the rise of her breasts to the fall of her waist and then to the rise of her buttocks; he gazed at her in awe. He was a man obsessed.

Chemistry or Compatibility Chapter 5

Wolfie arrived at university on Valentine's Day, carrying a big bouquet of flowers which he presented to Mia, red carnations, her favourite. Everything inside her turned to mush as he walked up to her, wrapped an arm around her, pulled her close and kissed her like a man who seriously meant it. He also gave her a large purple card, embossed in bold yellow writing. It read, "Your Body Is Like Church", and on the inside, "The best part is the organ. Happy Valentine's Day."

Dearest Mia,

I can't stop thinking of you,
Each and every day,

It must be those rosy, red lips,
Hazel eyes and dazzling smile.
Not to mention other admirable features,
Such as a deep, humid, wooded valley,

With two tall pink crested mountain tops,
Nearly – all within easy reach.

Or is it your understanding, caring,
Honesty, and kind-hearted nature?

May our happiness continue forever.
Thanking my Valentine from the bottom of my heart.

Reading his heated words made her heart quiver and released a thrill that made her tingle all over. Seeing a sex therapist had also helped her understand the taboo surrounding her sexuality and how little she knew about it. She felt so close to him now, closer than ever. She thought about him constantly. It was as if her life had been put on hold until he had arrived and now, she suddenly knew the reason why she had been placed on this earth.

That evening they lay together on his bed cuddling, he said, "I wish I'd met you when I was 16." Mia was flattered. There was a real connection between them.

Then he said, "I really could have used you then."

"Used me!!! Why is that?"

"I really needed a girlfriend at 16. My hormones were racing."

"You do realise that I would have been 14 years old, and there is no way that I would have had sex with you or anyone else at 14!" He laughed awkwardly quickly changing the subject.

***

Mia could hear her mother in the kitchen, banging wooden cupboards, shuffling and sorting a collection of metal pots. She could smell the sauce she was making from homegrown tomatoes, the distinctive woody fragrance of nutmeg hanging in the air, the richness of the sautéed garlic and onions wafting to her room, making her salivate. Their home always smelling like a cosy Italian restaurant. Her mother had begun cooking some of her favourites early today as part of Mia's birthday dinner preparation.

This winter seemed colder and more miserable than ever, she thought, as she wrapped a scarf tightly around her neck. She wore multiple layers, a beanie and a blanket over her knees. She sat at the small desk in the room she shared with her sister, working on the essay due Friday, realising that she had probably not given herself enough time to prepare. Growing up she had always been encouraged to excel academically. In primary school when she was dux of the school, her father had taken her to the local bookstore to buy any book she desired as a reward. Mia had chosen an encyclopedia on animals. Later her father had wrapped her expensive book in plastic to keep it in its pristine condition. She remembered coming home proudly in high school having scored 95% in her algebra test. She had clashed with her father when he had said something unexpected, "Why couldn't you work a little harder and get 100%. You were only five points off a perfect score." His lack of pride in her accomplishment had infuriated her. She'd yelled at him, "Why can't you be happy with 95%? I came first in class! The next mark was 68%." His nostrils flared, and his eyes turned black. He looked like a snorting toro about to charge, and he suddenly seemed taller and more ferocious. She realised she was the matador in a red cape. He sent her to her room for disrespecting him. She happily obliged. Having only ever attended public schools, Mia had still done exceptionally well, coming in the top 10% of the state for most of her subjects.

"Wolfie is here, Mia!" called out her mother, and snapped her back to reality. The news caught her off guard, as she had not been expecting him until later that evening. She jumped up and hurriedly ripped off her leg warmers, beanie, scarf and two additional layers of tops that she tossed onto the chair before straightening her hair and quietly walking into the lounge room.

Wolfie delivered a box with a big red ribbon. As they sat together on the sofa, she wildly tugged at the ribbon and the wrapping and lifted the lid. As she parted the chiffon paper, it revealed a folded white, cotton nightie, elegantly trimmed with lace and bows. It was worn off the shoulders and fell to her ankles. There was an envelope. It read, "To My Lovely Linguine!" On the back, Wolfie had written, "Now that you're not a "teen". We know where you've been", and a smiley face. She opened the card with anticipation.

"A birthday memo: You are hereby instructed to enjoy life, smile, be happy, relax and be good to yourself." Wolfie had added, "Signed Mr Know it all!!!".

There was a ridiculous looking, brightly animated character with a flower in his hat. Inside the card read, "…effective immediately! Happy Birthday!"

To my gorgeous, smiling, beautiful girl,

You're so dear, kind and sweet,
Putting up with me is no mean feat,

I love holding you in a tight embrace,
With you wearing nothing except silk and lace,
Always tell me what's on your mind,
Please let me help you relax and unwind,
I love to see you bright and happy,
and rue the day that you would ever be unhappy,

I wish to be with you come what may,
You'll have to fight to keep me at bay,

Your gown is soft and white,
For you to wear every night,
And fondly remember your love at first sight.

Love forever Wolfie xxxx

"Let me take you out for a quick hot chocolate and then maybe we could get some lunch?" enthused Wolfie.

"But I'm working on my 3,000-word essay which is due Friday!" moaned Mia, starting to feel anxious as she realised she might need to pull some all-nighters to meet her deadline.

"You've still got plenty of time. Come on, Mia, it's your birthday! Live a little."

Mia called out to her mother in the kitchen as she walked over, "Mamma, is it OK if I go out with Wolfie for lunch, since it's my birthday. I promise to dust and vacuum clean on the weekend."

"Do what you want!" snapped her mother who seemed suddenly annoyed.

Mia turned to Wolfie, "Just let me grab my coat and change my shoes."

In the car Mia said, "I don't know what my mother's problem is. Last time she yelled at me saying that I treat the house like a hotel, that all I did was eat and sleep there. I don't know what she's on about! I am certainly home a lot more than I'm out."

"Maybe she's jealous that you're starting to live your own life."

"I don't know what it is. Sometimes I feel that she doesn't like the fact that I have a boyfriend. I also have to do my chores when she wants, birthday or not, because otherwise, she is furious with me. I'll buy her a tea bun when we're at the shops; that always seems to calm her down."

"I don't have to do any chores, apart from help out my father in the garden sometimes. We have a lady, Mrs Lambrinos, who comes in once a week to clean the house, change the bed linen and anything else Tammy wants."
"You're lucky. We've never had a cleaning lady and I don't think we ever will."

***

Wolfie showered Mia with gifts and tokens of his appreciation. It was not uncommon for him to bring her treats of delicious little cakes from his local patisserie, or brightly wrapped handmade truffle chocolates. He would often buy her a coffee or some lunch when they were at university. Mia reciprocated and had spent hours knitting him a jumper. Moreover, after he had complained that Mrs. Lambrinos failed to return his handkerchiefs after doing the laundry, she had bought him a dozen and embroidered his first initial on each of them. They also never argued, got on well and enjoyed each other's company. Her heart and eyes were awestruck by him. He was not only her boyfriend, but her lover, confidante and best friend.

On their second Christmas together, Wolfie arrived for lunch at Mia's place. His family always celebrated on Christmas Eve, which meant he was free on Christmas day. After pulling on some cracker bonbons, laughing at the dad jokes inside and adorning themselves with colourful paper crowns, Wolfie gave Mia her gift. A small green velvet box that contained a gold ring, engraved with the words, "Love always Wolfie". She felt a flutter of excitement in her stomach and wondered if this was a sign of things to come. Would he one day soon, give her an engagement ring? Deep down, though, she felt a tinge of doubt about a future with him but could not explain why. Was the voice inside her head an enemy trying to sabotage the wonderful future that lay ahead, or was it her intuition, a warm friend warning her to proceed with caution?

In his card he had written: Thank you for another lovely year. I believe we have become closer which is so important to me. It's been great to have your love and support when I needed it the most. You are a lovely and kind person. I'm a very lucky bloke and know it. I'm curious to see what the next few years hold for us, and I hope that one day shortly you will be my wife. That would be fantastic!

Congratulations on your great results!

Love always Wolfie xxxx

She believed him to be the one for her.

Later, when he had gone and she sat alone in her room admiring the ring on her finger, she picked at the bit of cuticle sticking up on the side of her finger. She ripped at it and felt the stinging pain and clenched her jaw as it started to bleed. A thick red drop oozed and pooled in her nail bed. She placed it in her mouth, sucking the blood away.

***

Their relationship continued in this blissful state, with his never-ending beautiful cards giving her so much pleasure. Her following birthday, he gave her a card which had an animation of a cranky looking fat cat on the front wearing a party hat. Emblazed in giant red letters were the words "BIRTHDAY GREETINGS" and inside "from Old Sourpuss."

Wolfie wrote: You're the light at the end of my tunnel. I always love to see your radiant smile. I'm happy when you're happy. Your caring and loving manner is particularly special. I owe you so much and I thank you from the bottom of my heart. Without you, there would only be mere existence. There would be no love, no tenderness or understanding.

My love for you increases daily as does my affection. It grows for you with the dawning of each new day. I can never love you enough.

Love to eternity and beyond Wolfie xxxx

Mia laughed as she put down the card and turning to Wolfie said, "The light at the end of the tunnel isn't always a guiding light. Sometimes it's the light of an oncoming train! You'd better watch out, Wolfie!" She laughed again.

"Mia, you are my guiding light. Without you, I would just be surviving, but with you I feel I am truly living. I love you so, so much."

"I love you too, Wolfie, and I was kidding. I love your warm words and when you write me poetry." Nobody had ever written her poetry before. She loved his cards and even though she knew deep down that he would never be a Keats or a Shakespeare, his sweet words showed that he loved her too. He was far from perfect, but then who was?

"I'm glad you appreciate them because they take me hours to write!"

"I love them, Wolfie, and I love you!" she said as she straddled him and covered his face with a thousand kisses.

Living in Sin
Chapter 6

Wolfie graduated from university and was eager to start a new chapter in his life. He began working for a large IT company in their marketing department, rented a one-bedroom apartment on the first floor of a secure block in the city, and moved in with his meagre possessions, his bed and the clothes on his back. Despite his family's wealth, he would not see any of it unless there was an inheritance. When he was settled in, he called Mia and said, "Hey babe, I've settled in and I'm looking forward to you joining me, so when are you moving in?"

"Hello darling, I want to move in and be with you, but my parents are never going to go for it. They're very traditional and will want me to stay at home until I'm married. They will never approve of what is, in their eyes, their daughter living in sin," she replied, feeling torn.

"Come on Mia, I love you and want to start our life together. You said you'd move in, and I hate living on my own. I want you by my side. Don't you want to be with me?"

"Of course, I do. I love you, but I worry about my parents' reaction. I'll move in with you if we get engaged and have the wedding date set, then I think my parents might be more accepting of this arrangement." She felt pressured and wanted to keep everyone around her happy as well as herself.

He agreed to get engaged and they shopped together for an engagement ring. As he did not have any savings, they settled on a small nine-carat gold ring with a crumb for a diamond that was on sale. He proposed in his lounge room one afternoon on bended knee, as she sat in an armchair watching television. Mia ecstatically said "YES!" and even shed tears of joy as she knelt down to face him, looking into his eyes and threading her arms around his neck. She loved him and could not wait to begin their life as husband and wife.

Knowing her parents would be upset that she wanted to leave, let alone live with a man, she was unsure how to broach the subject with them. Finally, one evening Wolfie dropped in at her house so they could announce their engagement. Her father was grinning as he opened a bottle of champagne, and poured generous measures into each flute, the bubbles fizzing over the top. He then proposed a toast, "Let's have a toast to your future. May you both have a happy life together." They all clinked glasses, raised them and she downed the gently fizzing liquid in one go.

They chatted for a while. She smiled, feeling a flutter of courage as the champagne bubbles went to her head. Then Mia announced, "Wolfie has found an apartment in the city and now that we've set a date in September for our wedding, I've decided to move in with him." Her parents were visibly disappointed, particularly her father. Gino's mood shifted from being elated by the news of their engagement to lukewarm enthusiasm for them living together. Her mother was no longer smiling; her face looked strained, and she was not making eye contact with Mia or Wolfie. Her father now wore a scowl as he said, "Why did you share the news that you were moving in with him like that? We raised you better than that Mia. Your mother and I don't like the idea of you moving in with him before you're married, and what about your degree? If you get married, you'll never finish it!"

"Papa, I'm determined to finish my degree no matter what, but I also want to be with the man I love and the man that I'm going to marry."

Her father continued, "We've raised you with integrity and the strongest moral fibre, and HE should be respecting your background and traditions more than he is." The evening continued with moments of awkward silence and stilted conversation, and when Wolfie left, Mia went straight to bed as the situation was still very fraught.

***

The news was well received by their friends who had expected it. They were such a "loved up couple". That was how everyone felt, everyone except his brother, Thomas. "You're not seriously going to marry your first girlfriend? The only girl you've ever been with."

Wolfie stood by his decision, "I love her, and she loves me and that's all that matters. I've never felt like this about anyone before. She's the one for me."

This did not endear Thomas to Mia. She had heard stories of his many female conquests. Women seemed to throw themselves at his feet, and he bedded every single one of them. Once conquered, he moved on to the next. Thomas was far more polished than Wolfie, taller, blonde, blue-eyed, had a muscular build and left a trail of broken hearts behind him. He was a real Lothario, so this did not surprise her, but it felt like sabotage none the less. She had caught the better brother, the decent one.

A couple of weeks later, Mia moved in with Wolfie; it was the end of January. Thankfully it was when her whole family were out for the day. Her parents would be upset with her leaving in such a way, so Mia hid a long letter for her mother in her bathroom vanity behind her make-up bag. In it, she explained to her mum that although she loved her and her family, Wolfie was her future, and she wanted to spend her life with him. She explained that they were in love and that her mum did not know his true character, which was one of understanding and appreciation of her. She promised to get in touch, after she had settled in with him. Wolfie came by with his father's station wagon, and they loaded up the bookcase she had bought along with her books and clothes. Not happy with her plans to move out, her parents had forbidden her from taking her bed or any of the other furnishings in her room. Wolfie and Mia were starting out with very little, but they had each other.

She landed herself a full-time job in a chartered accountancy firm, which left her with no choice but to finish her degree as a part-time student, meaning an additional six months of study. Mia had a term deposit of $2,000 which she broke for them to use. Together, they shopped for pots, pans, broom, cutlery, glasses, vacuum cleaner, mop, cleaning supplies and a small two-seater sofa. During the week, they would head off to work, walking through Hyde Park together. At night, while he watched TV, Mia would squeeze in some study, sitting in the same room as him. It was new, it was fun, it was exciting, and it was freedom! Since neither one of them could cook and were surrounded by affordable restaurants, it meant they often ate out.

The weekends were great! They were keen to seize the day and would take long, leisurely walks together in the sun. They strolled around the Sydney Botanical Gardens, along the harbour foreshore, and ventured into the red-light district out of curiosity, his arm always lovingly around her. At home, whenever he walked past her, he would grab her, squeeze and kiss her. He would come up behind her and cup her breasts in his hands, tenderly kissing her neck. It gave her goose bumps all over. He could not keep his hands off her, and she loved the attention. At night, Wolfie would say, "Why don't you have your shower and slip into something comfortable?" He would then shower and join her in bed. Their love making sessions were always hot and steamy. Reaching over he began kissing her neck, gentle touches at first growing deeper, his fingers burrowing through her hair. His mouth pressed against hers and his tongue hungrily pushing into hers, his breath quavering with wanton yearning, and they were both caught in a moment of desire. She moved her hands over his chest, circling his nipples, gently tugging at them and then over his shoulders. His hands moved across her body, the curve of her rib cage and over her lacey bra, then pulling it down to expose her left nipple which he circled and flicked with his tongue, making her gasp. He pounced on it with his mouth, gently sucking and biting at her hardening nipple. He said, "I think the other one is jealous. We can't have that," as he repeated the same ritual with her right nipple. With each lick and touch, she felt an electric current pulse through her body, from her breast to between her thighs, her wetness growing rapidly. He moved his hands to her back where he unclipped her bra. He massaged her breasts as he pushed them together and inserted both nipples into his mouth at the same time and sucked. She moaned in exquisite delight. His lips brushed her neck, and he licked the length of her body, his tongue in flicks and swirls, working down her body as his fingers peeled off her panties. She was now in a garter belt and stockings. Spreading her legs, he blew lightly on her swollen clitoris, then stroked it with his cock as she groaned in almost unbearable pleasure. Finally, he dipped into her, and as they rocked together, his eyes shut tight, his hands clenching and rucking the sheets, he exploded inside her, his spent body buckling and collapsing on her. She lay on the mattress, trying to catch her breath. He placed a towel underneath her thighs to catch the damp patch that felt ice-cold against her skin, the passion subsiding and reality rushing back in, as she felt her skin pulling on the surface of her inner thighs as his cum dried. He held her in his arms for a while, stroking the length of her body, before they would fall asleep.

***

Mia decided to call her parents. She dialled their number with trepidation. She started to leave a message when her father answered. "Hello."

"Hello, Papa. It's Mia. How are you?"

"I've been better," he said in a curt aggressive tone.

"Is Mamma there?"

She could hear her mother in the background, "No! No! I'm not talking to her!"

"Your mother is upset with the way you left, we both are, and doesn't want to talk to you."

"Papa, I love you and I love Mamma, but I love Wolfie and want to spend the rest of my life with him. I left Mamma a letter explaining this to her behind her make-up bag. He's the one for me. I'm going to marry him, we are only living together for a short while, but we are definitely getting married! Can't you please accept this and be happy for me?" she begged tearily.

"Mia, we're not happy with the way you left," but she heard his voice softening as he added, "Just give her time. I'll talk to her. She just needs time to calm down." Mia hung up the phone, her eyes were full of tears.

"Are you alright Mia? What did they say?" asked Wolfie with genuine concern.

"Papa said he would talk to her but she wouldn't come to the phone. I heard her in the background; she was furious and sounded really hurt. I feel terrible with the mess things are in. It's all my fault. I should have handled it better, but I love my parents and I love you. I hope they don't stop talking to me because of all of this. I couldn't bear it."

"I love you too. Come here and let me give you a hug." He wrapped his strong arms around her. She instantly felt better. "Don't worry, things will calm down. It's probably just the shock of having their first child move out."

"Your parents didn't react in such an adverse way," she replied.

"No, my parents are a bit more open minded and not as old fashioned as yours, plus they're used to us being away from home. Both Thomas and I often went to visit our grandparents by ourselves from the age of 12. It'll work out, you'll see. It's going to be alright. Don't worry, I love you, Mia." He continued hugging her. Even though she worried about her parents' opinion of her, she felt comfortable knowing that she had Wolfie and his love by her side.

***

Having grown up with a stay-at-home Mum, Mia instinctively gravitated towards the kitchen and being the homemaker, even though she was working full-time and studying. They were still figuring things out as they went along. One evening she decided to give cooking a go. There was not much in the refrigerator, two good quality steaks and some potatoes in the drawer. She fried the steak, peeled the potatoes and thought she would boil them up and serve them with butter. She had set the table in anticipation of Wolfie's arrival. When he came home, he was pleased to find her cooking, "Barefoot, not pregnant but in the kitchen. I'm hungry and it smells good. What are you cooking?"

"Steak and potatoes."

"Is it nearly done?"

The potatoes were still boiling. Wolfie sat at their new dining table. He waited to be served, while Mia fussed in the kitchen.

"How much longer is it going to be? I'm starving." Since he was growing restless, she decided to serve him. She drained the potatoes and brought everything to the table. She placed a steak on his plate and tried picking up a potato with a fork but could not pierce it. She laughed, "Oops, I think the potatoes are slightly undercooked."

Wolfie tried to cut into a spud but it was rock hard, and he flew into a rage. "What the hell is this? I come home after a hard day's work and you serve me this rubbish?" he bellowed.

Mia was stunned. He continued yelling and pushed his plate aside with such force that it almost flew off the other end of the table. He refused to even eat the steak, though there was nothing wrong with it.

"You know I don't know how to cook." This only infuriated him.

"I'll do better next time," she said as she cleared the table. He had never spoken so harshly to her before and it frightened her. He stormed off to the bedroom and slammed the door shut behind him. Mia wondered what had just happened.

She did not see him for the rest of the evening, and later when she went to bed, he was sound asleep. Mia tried to get to sleep but too much was going around in her head. Instead, she lay there, listening to his calm, regular breathing. She must have dozed off, because she awoke early in the morning, feeling her hot breath on the pillow. He was acting as though nothing had happened, and was back to his jovial self. She was confused, as she thought they had both agreed, "to never let the sun set on anger."

When she broached the subject, he admitted, "Look, I overreacted. I'm under a lot of pressure at work and I hate that place." Mia forgave him.

Since Mia's parents were still strongly opposed to their daughter living in sin during her engagement, Wolfie agreed to move the wedding date forward to April. He was more than happy to do anything to help ease the tension between Mia and her parents. Consequently, this had the effect of releasing the strain on the relationship between the four of them. That afternoon Mia's parents were dropping in for a coffee. Since their unit was very small, Wolfie suggested that they all go out to a café downstairs and around the corner from their apartment block. The four of them walked into the "Wise Monkey" café, nestled among many residential buildings opposite Hyde Park. As they all sat down, Wolfie announced, "I'll get the coffee." Mia's parents protested, but he insisted; finally, they relented. Turning to Mia's parents, Wolfie asked, "What can I get you?"

"I'll have a skinny cappuccino please," replied Natalia.

"A short black for me, thanks mate," replied Gino.

Wolfie walked over to the counter and ordered. He then came back and sat down next to Natalia and opposite Mia.

"I've ordered the coffee." He looked at Mia, "I forgot what coffee you wanted, so you'll have to go up and order your own." Mia, somewhat miffed and surprised got up and ordered herself a latte. She would have to talk to him later about his unusual behaviour, but not now in front of her parents.

When Mia's parents were driving home. Natalia said, "Did you see the way he spoke to her? The way he made her go and pay for her own coffee. He wasn't very nice."

"I've told you before, I don't like him. He always acts superior, and there's something about him that's not quite right. I can't put my finger on it. He always acts so smug and arrogant. I don't know what Mia sees in him."

"It's because she's in love, but what can we do? Maybe that's what young people do these days, have separate finances. I guess if she loves him and wants to be with him; we can't say anything. It's her life."

"I know, I know, but I don't have to like the guy and I don't. She probably wouldn't listen to us. She can be so stubborn, but I think she's making a big mistake. I mean look at him, the way he talks and acts. He thinks he is so good because he comes from a rich family. It's not him who's rich. It's his father."

"I didn't tell you what she told me; last time they went to the Discount Mart to buy some things for the house, he waited outside and refused to go in."

"Why?"

"He told her he couldn't shop there in case someone saw him."

"That's ridiculous! He's such a snob, but Mia just doesn't see it."

"Well, if he's good to her and treats her right and she's happy, we can't ask for more, but I'm worried for her. We can't tell her not to marry him. It's her choice." They sat in silence the rest of the way home.

Once back home, Mia and Wolfie had another fight. This time it was over him buying coffee for everyone except her. He was still angry with her over the dinner incident.

You can be so frustratingly immature at times! But I'm sure with good communication, we'll be able to sort it out.

***

Wolfie came home one afternoon with exciting news. Oma had wired them $10,000 as a wedding gift. Mia read the card from Oma, written in perfect English, her words kind and sincere.

"WOW! That is so generous of her!"

They were both very excited about the money. This would give them a significant boost financially. This small windfall from Oma would help with a deposit on a unit of their own, which is what they decided to do with the money.

A couple of days later, Wolfie approached her, "I think we should get a prenup."

Mia laughed, "A prenup? For what? We don't have any assets."

"For the money."

"What money?" Mia asked confused.

"You know, the money we got from Oma."

"The wedding present."

"But it's from my grandmother, and we'll eventually have other savings and a home … I was thinking the prenup could go something like this, if we stay married for one year, you would be entitled to 10% of the money, two years 20% and so on, and at five years you get 50%"

"Are you kidding? That's the lamest thing I've ever heard." He was, however, quite serious.

"It's a gift from my family," he wailed. "Your family haven't given us anything."

"My family are paying a third of the wedding costs and the only reason you've received that money is because you're marrying me. The money is not solely yours. It's a gift to both of us because we're getting married, together, you and me."

How can he not understand this?!!! A wedding present is for two people starting their life together. How can he not see this?

Eventually, she gave him an ultimatum, "If you want me to sign a prenup there won't be a wedding and you can send the money back to Oma!" He acceded. Mia was confused by Wolfie's behaviour, but later he admitted, "You never know if a marriage will work. They say one in three ends in divorce. I mean, look at my parents."

"Yes. But look at my parents; they're still very much in love and happily married. It's like you said, you have to work at your relationship, have good communication and never take the other party for granted. It's simple really."

"I guess. I know that I do really love you, Mia, and really want this to work."

"Don't worry, it will. What could possibly go wrong? Besides, together we can conquer anything right?" She lifted her hand for a high five. He laughed as he high-fived her, "OK. If you say so." She passionately looked to a future with him as his wife.

That afternoon, Mia heard a joke. Now that she knew what a blow job was, and the fact that she had never given him one in the whole two and a half years that they had been dating, seemed apt.

"Why is a bride smiling when she's walking down the aisle?"

Wolfie laughed a little, as he anticipated the punch line, "Why?"

"Because she knows she's just given her last blow job!" Mia erupted in laughter.

"Very good," laughed Wolfie, "very good."

He would still occasionally ask her delicately, but she could never bring herself to even try, saying, "But that's disgusting. You pee out of that thing and you want me to put it in my mouth? Gross!" He did not persist. He respected her and her decision. He loved her and understood and accepted the protected upbringing she had had.

On the weekend, they held hands, fingers intertwined as they happily laughed and chatted together, the sun warming their faces and the warm wind whipping through their hair. As they walked around the local park, he fell suddenly quiet, deep in thought, when he asked, "What are we going to do with our bank accounts when we're married?"

"What do you mean?"

"Well, I was thinking, maybe we should keep our finances separate. I can transfer a monthly payment into your account so that we have about the same amount of money each." Mia had not quite finished her degree and was earning slightly less than Wolfie.

"That makes absolutely no sense! We will have a joint account. Both of our pays will go into this account and from there we will pay our joint expenses."

"Really? You want to do that?" asked Wolfie rhetorically. "I thought it would be easier if I transferred $100 into your account monthly."

"Why on earth would I want that? When you think I've been 'bad' you won't pay me anything? I've seen the way your father uses money as a weapon against Tammy."

If Sam and Tammy had an argument, or she had done something that had displeased him, then she would go without grocery money for the week. She was a homemaker and did not work, so there were times when she could not buy food or petrol. It appeared the Schmidt men had all mistreated their wives at some stage, in one way or another, but Mia was sure that Wolfie was different. They had good communication and he was always willing to discuss things.

Mia continued adamantly, "We will be Mr & Mrs Schmidt, and we will have a joint bank account. You know, what's yours is mine and mine is yours?"

"Okay, if that's the way you want to do it." He seemed to be willing to learn and try things Mia's way.

The next day, Mia called her mother to update her on recent events. Nonna answered the phone and she divulged to her, details of the wedding gift, and their finances.

Nonna interjected, "He is the man of the house."

"Nonna, that doesn't give him the right to have everything his way. Times have changed and I'm working too. A marriage is a partnership. I'm not his chattel to do with as he pleases."

Her mum picked up the other line and quickly caught up on events. "He has very funny ideas," said Natalia.

"I know, but I think it's because his parents got divorced. I think it's scarred him, but at least he's open to discussing things and trying new ways."

The following weekend, as they spent time together and were walking along Hyde Park they came upon a sign, "Tarot Readings Done Here".

He asked, "Have you ever had your fortune read?"

"No, never. I don't believe in it," she replied nonchalantly.

"Why not give it a go? Just for fun," he enthused.

They entered the small shop and went down a circular staircase that took them to a large space below street level. The tarot reader, who was a nondescript young man, proceeded to masterly shuffle a deck of tarot cards. He then handed Mia the deck for her to cut. She sat there with a deadpan face, trying not to give any readable body language to this obvious charlatan. Wolfie watched.

He placed some cards on the table between them in a sequence. He then turned over a card revealing eight wands, "I see swift travel for you overseas in the foreseeable future to either Bali or Thailand."

Well, duh! Considering we live on an island and most people our age travel to those destinations!

The next card from the deck was the Six of Wands, "I see you making money from a creative outlet. You won't make a lot but enough. Some sort of side business, I don't know why, but I'm being shown you moving furniture."

Mia amusedly replied, "I'm sorry, but I have no idea what you're talking about. I don't move furniture and nor do I ever see myself doing that in the future."

He continued, "You will never have any big windfall, such as an inheritance or lotto."

Mia again tickled, said sarcastically, "You're full of good news, aren't you?"

There were now lots of cards face up on the table. He smiled wryly as he said calmly, "I can see you marrying soon."

Well, duh! Considering I'm wearing an engagement ring!

The room seemed to darken, or had she imagined this, as he continued almost in a trance, "But he is not the one for you, and it will not last. You will marry again, later in life and you will be happy because this man will be your one true love."

Mia thanked him for his reading, and they merrily went on their way. When they were back on street level, Wolfie asked, a little peeved, "So who's the guy?"

"Who?" asked Mia.

"The guy? Who is he?" he demanded.

"What guy?" asked a confused Mia.

"The guy he was talking about?"

Mia laughed at Wolfie. "You believe that!" she declared and laughed some more. "How should I know who he is? According to him it's some guy in the future. I don't know. I haven't met him yet." She laughed harder. "Don't tell me you believed that nonsense! It was all so vague." Wolfie was ominously quiet.

***

Wolfie had finally had enough of his job and just quit, but luckily, he had been able to find a better one that offered a higher salary and included a company car. One Wednesday evening, he drove to the university to pick

Mia up since her lecture finished at 9pm. She was beginning to realise that Wolfie had a very short temper. She had not witnessed this when they had been dating, but now living with him, things were different. He could snap at the smallest thing and then he would take it out on her. Wolfie greeted her outside her class. As they walked to the car, he said, "I notice my white tennis socks have a pink tinge to them now."

"Sorry about that, they wound up in the coloured wash. By the time I noticed it was too late. It's only slight, eventually they'll go white again."

"I can't wear them. They look gay, only poofters wear pink!" he said contemptuously.

"Don't be so childish! Anyone can wear pink!" she snorted in derision.

He stormed off ahead adding, "You can make your own way home!" and disappeared.

She walked to the bus stop but the next one was in half an hour. It was just as quick to walk the half hour home instead. She commenced her trek in her high heels, keeping her eyes open for a taxi, but none passed. The streets were dark and completely isolated. Mia felt vulnerable and unsafe. This was not a situation that she would have put herself in.

How can you just leave me like this and drive off? Why put me at risk? FUCK YOU!

Pomp
Chapter 7

The cost of the wedding would be split three ways between Mia's family, Wolfie's family, and themselves. It would not be outrageous as both had decided to be sensible and add any savings to Oma's gift to put towards a deposit instead. Though Mia would have preferred a church wedding, Wolfie, having been brought up in a more secular family, was strongly opposed to it. Hence, they wed in the backyard of his parents' house. Sam had ensured that the magnificent gardens were immaculately manicured. The hedges had been shaped into animals, a reclining cat, and a family of bears standing in a row. The grass tennis court had been resurfaced and the swimming pool glistened clean in the sun. The long meandering driveway meant total privacy for their special day.

Mia had wanted something simple yet elegant. Her gown was made of raw silk and her veil was attached to a head band made of pearls that rested over her forehead like a crown. There were silver diamante butterflies scattered throughout her bejewelled tiara. She had decided not to approach her groom with the veil pulled over her face. She did not want him unveiling her. The whole concept made her feel like his chattel, which was not how she saw herself. Julie was her maid of honour, as the two had become close, and Mia had jokingly said, "It's your fault I'm getting married, because you encouraged me to go on that first date with him!" The pink bridesmaids' dresses contrasted beautifully with Mia's dress. Julie and Wolfie's three stepsisters resembled springtime nymphs in their rented lace dresses and matching flower crowns. Her little sister, Sophie, was excited to be the flower girl. She wore a white dress, a sparkling tiara and held a basket of rose petals, looking like a miniature bride herself.

Every detail filled Mia with joy, from selecting their matching gold wedding bands, through to ordering the Italian wedding cake with the cake topper being a couple leaning in for a kiss. It felt like she was organising a big party for the first day of the rest of their lives. Mia had decided that, be it superstitious or not, it was bad luck for the groom to see his bride before the wedding. She had not wanted them to get off to a cursed start and had slept at her parents' house.

Their wedding day arrived. Thomas arrived in Sam's Mercedes, to drive Julie, Sophie and herself to the venue. They pulled up at Wolfie's parents' house and Wolfie's stepsisters met them in the study at the front of the house where they all hid, whilst the wedding guests waited in the garden at the rear of the house. Rhonda, a school friend and budding photographer, had agreed to take their wedding photos as a wedding gift. She busily snapped away as their guests happily stood chatting amongst themselves on the green lawn or on the sun-drenched terrace, speckled with giant earthenware pots featuring frangipanis, which were Sam's favourite flower. The pergola offered shade with the intertwined branches of a thickly growing grape vine. Sabine looked elegant wearing a sinamay hat with stylish rakishness, in her blush sundress, with auburn hair framing her face. After listening to Mia, Wolfie had reached out to his mother and mended their fractured relationship. He was pleased that she would witness their nuptials. He liked the better version of himself he became around Mia.

Overhead, the sun was shining in a cobalt blue, cloudless sky. It was unusually warm for this time of the year. Birds sang sweetly in the huge trees that lined the property. Another friend from university, Jay, had agreed to be their DJ for free. Mendelssohn's Bridal Waltz began. One by one, the flower girl and then the bridesmaids walked down the grass aisle between the parted sea of wedding guests, which consisted mainly of their university friends.

Mia stood there alone waiting for her father. Suddenly she was gripped by fear. Instantly, she felt a knot in the pit of her stomach and heard a voice in her head, chanting a whispered refrain, *for the rest of your life, for the rest of your life.*

I don't think I can do this! Why have I decided to marry him now? Is it too soon? I could have waited. Is it because I've had sex before marriage? Is it because we're lovers? Am I marrying him because I feel obligated?

She snapped herself out of it when her father entered the room and offered her his arm. It was a good thing she was in flats as her father, clearly nervous, was walking hurriedly, and it was as if they were on the verge of breaking into a hundred-metre sprint. She heard gasps of admiration from her guests as she walked past. Mia was captivating and revelling in it. As they approached the marriage celebrant, and she saw Wolfie, she felt herself calming down. Her father gently guided her towards him, as if he were entrusting her to him. Wolfie looked handsome as he stood in front of the other groomsmen, Mia's brothers, his brother, Thomas, and Stephen, his best man and his friend since primary school. They all looked dashing in their black suits with red roses in their lapels.

Nerves. That's all it was. Just a case of cold feet. Everybody gets them.

They recited the vows they had written themselves, after having considered what the traditional marriage vows were. They had sat together one afternoon and, with her eyebrows furrowed, Mia said, "I like these bits, to have and to hold, from this day forward, for richer, for poorer, in sickness and in health, and forsaking all others, but I'm not keen on this next bit, for better and worse. Why on earth would it get worse and why would anyone wish for that?"

"I don't know. It does sound strange, and I don't agree with it either. So far, it's been better and better, and I don't see why it would change. Let's change it to better and better," he said as the smile reached his eyes.

"My sentiments exactly." She threw an arm around him as she pulled him in to her and gave him a soft kiss on the cheek, "I'm not too keen on this next bit either, where I promise to obey you. Why would I obey you? That sounds so archaic; you're my husband not my father. That's out as well." She scribbled a line through it. "What do you think of this next bit, to love and to cherish, until death us do part?"

"Well again, I don't see why it has to end there? I believe our love is stronger than that. Let's change it to, 'to love and to cherish, to eternity and beyond.' " Mia smiled as she happily jotted down their changes. Mia was 21 and Wolfie 23. They promised to love each other, through "sickness and in health", and to "eternity and beyond". They vowed to love each other for "better and better", not for "better and worse." They were both young and idealistic.

Their marriage celebrant, Lloyd, read an Apache wedding poem:

"Now you will feel no rain, for each of you will shelter the other. Now each of you will not feel the cold, for each of you will be warmth to the other. Now you are two people, but there is one life before you. Go now to your dwelling, to enter the days of your togetherness, and may your days be good and long upon the earth."

She believed his words and felt it would always be so for them.

"I now pronounce you husband and wife. You may kiss the bride," he continued with a smile.

They had discussed the kiss and planned a long, lingering one rather than the small peck couples usually give each other. Mia was feeling apprehensive. As he leaned in, she whispered, "Just a little one, just a little one." However, he enveloped her in his arms and tipped her back as he kissed her, long and passionately. Their guests clapped and cheered. He continued kissing her for a minute or more. When they both finally came up for air, Mia was smiling and laughing. She did truly love him. They both felt their love was invincible.

Felicità Coniugale ... 1987
Chapter 8

Stephen drove them to a secret northern beach location for the weekend. He had surprised them with a honeymoon, which was a generous wedding gift, as they had not budgeted for one. It was their first weekend as Mr & Mrs Schmidt.

Mia dazzled Wolfie with a lacy white corset, knickers, suspender belt and stockings. In the low light, with the white curtains fluttering behind her, she looked like an angel. He reached for the bottle of wine. There was the squeaky sound of the corkscrew twisting into the cork, and then the "Pop!" as it was removed from the neck of the bottle. As he poured her a glass of wine, the velvety red liquid made its familiar sound – glub, glub, glub. She gazed out of the window of their accommodation, high on a hill; there was nothing but a peaceful expanse of blue ocean in sight. He walked up behind her and wrapped one arm around her waist. His other hand raised the glass to her lips. She sipped the wine they shared from the same glass, and she sighed and settled back into his warmth. He began nibbling her ear and whispering soft words; she felt a flutter of excitement deep within her belly as goosebumps ran wildly across the length of her skin. She slowly pressed herself back against him. What started with a small spark, quickly turned into a blaze. She wanted him as much as he wanted her.

The following morning, they were having breakfast on the terrace overlooking the ocean with the sun shining brightly overhead. As they feasted on croissants and freshly brewed coffee, Wolfie admired Mia's face with a mellow and tender expression.

"You're beautiful, Mia," he said with adoration in his eyes. She smiled her megawatt smile, feeling overwhelmed by love and flattery. No hairbrush, make-up, wet hair, and he still found her attractive. She knew she had made the right choice. He was definitely the one for her. They spent most of their short honeymoon in bed making love. Wolfie reached a new peak, eight times during their two-day stay. She relished being in his manly embrace, smelling him, having skin to skin contact, feeling connected and secure.

Their wedding had only cost $6,000 in total. Mia was pleased with her frugality. The savings, along with Oma's wedding gift, had enabled them to put a deposit down on their new apartment, close to the CBD. They bought a one-bedroom unit in an older style block that had been refurbished and moved in. A lot of windows lined the north side which provided plenty of natural light and a constant source of sunlight streamed in. At night, they could clearly see all the lights from the city skyline. In retrospect, it was small and pokey but to them it felt like a palace and they were rapturous!

When they had moved the last box into the apartment, Wolfie had suggested that they fumigate it after experiencing the many cockroaches in their rental unit. He had purchased a cockroach bomb from the local supermarket.

"Alright, I just have to put this in the centre of the room and press this button. We can then go for a walk and come back in a couple of hours and there should be no more vermin around." He detonated it. The contents from the aerosol can sprayed into their loungeroom, like a genie spurting from a bottle.

"Run!" cried Wolfie, "Quick! Let's get out of here!" They both bolted for the front door, and as they exited, it slammed shut behind them and deadlocked.

"Have you got keys on you?" he asked.

"No. I thought you did!"

"No. I don't have any," he replied with genuine bewilderment.

Mia erupted into laughter, "Oh no! We're locked out!"

Wolfie joined in. "Oh well, let's go get a bite to eat. We can worry about it later." Luckily, he still had his wallet on him.

They continued laughing together. These were the moments that she cherished. The new happy memories that they were weaving together, as each other's life companion. One Saturday morning, the phone rang and Mia answered it.

"Hey, Mia. It's Julie. How are you?"

"Oh, my goodness, Julie, it's so great to hear from you! I haven't seen you since the wedding. How are you? It's weird the last couple of days I haven't been able to stop thinking about you. I was going to give you a call. You must be psychic!" They both laughed. The girls exchanged pleasantries and caught up on what had been happening in their lives.

"I've got something to tell you. I have some news," Julie said.

"Okay. What is it?"

"I'm pregnant."

"What! Pregnant! What happened? Well, I know what happened, but what? What are you going to do? Can I help? Is there anything you need?"

Julie was laughing, more at her friend's hysteria than anything else. "No, no. It's not like that. I'm keeping the baby. It's Toby's. We're just seeing what happens. It's still a new relationship and I'm not rushing into anything."

"Good idea." They talked some more before agreeing to catch up soon.

"Who was that?" asked Wolfie, noticing that she looked distracted.

"Julie, and you're never going to believe this. She's pregnant! The baby's due any day now."

"What? Pregnant? Has she got a boyfriend? Is she getting married?" He sounded puzzled.

"Well, it wasn't an act of God. There wasn't any immaculate conception. It does take two. I can demonstrate if you'd like," Mia said with a wink and a laugh.

"Smart arse." His voice was sharper than she was used to, as he continued more calmly, "You know what I mean."

Mia rolled her eyes as she replied, "She's been seeing this guy, Toby. He's an engineering student but it's new. They're just playing it by ear."

"I'm surprised she found someone. I mean don't get me wrong, she's nice but she's so tall and flat as a pancake."

"Can you not be so shallow?"

"It's true, she's even taller than me. If you had been taller than me, I never would have asked you out."

"Are you serious?"

"Yes. I wouldn't have liked that. I'm glad it's not us, and that we're not the ones in that situation," he said, sounding relieved.

"Yeah, it's a bit early. Imagine if that happened to us, especially now with a big fat mortgage."

"I don't think we can even think about having kids till we have at least $10,000 saved up," he added matter-of-factly.

"What …? $10,000? Where did you get that magical number from?"

"You'll need to take time off work to look after the baby or go part-time, and we'll still have the same bills."

"A baby budget?" She was amused. "I bet you there are a lot of people, probably the majority, who just fall pregnant with no plan B. My parents never had any savings when they had children and somehow managed. I think you just adapt."

"No. When we decide to have children, we'll need to have saved at least $10,000."

Mia was surprised at how deadly serious he was being. She had never known anyone to think this way, especially someone who came from such an affluent, privileged background. This was the first time she had ever heard of his baby budget.

"Then we're never going to have any, because I don't ever see us being able to do that, now that we have a mortgage," she replied.

***

They settled into married life. Wolfie had decided to change jobs and had landed a job in sales. Mia thought that he had not given his last job a real chance. The company had been willing to give him a stint in all their divisions in their undergraduate program to see which one he preferred. He had decided that this job was not for him in less than three months. He had just come home one day to announce that he had quit. Luckily, he had easily secured a job with another large multinational, in an area of interest to him. However, this now meant that he would be away travelling, Monday through to Friday, every week. She had come from a bustling, noisy family, then moved in with him. Mia had never been alone in her life and hated it. At night, she felt scared, even though the building was secure. As their only time together was on the weekends, Wolfie would want to spend it solely with her. He would stay with her as long as he could, before leaving for the week.

One weekend, her girlfriend Jessica dropped in for a visit unannounced. Mia was happy to see her, "Let's get a coffee downstairs. Are you coming Wolfie?"

"You two go. I'm happy to read my paper." Mia spent a couple of hours with her friend before returning home.

"Hey, Wolfie, I'm back. Do you want to go and do something? Jessica said to say 'bye too.' "

"Does she have to come see you when I'm home? I only get to see you on the weekend."

"You could have joined us."

"She's as boring as bat shit and I don't know what you see in her and why you're even friends."

"She's a really nice person, and we've been friends since primary school, and I like her," Mia replied, a little disappointed.

On another occasion, Felicity rang Mia to ask her to join the girls for a night of clubbing. Wolfie said, "She only wants you there because she's so ugly and is looking for a boyfriend. I don't know why you're friends with her; you're both at different stages of life now and she's just using you."

"She's not ugly! Don't be so horrible!" He did not like any of the friends she had made prior to knowing him and would often criticise them. She slowly noticed how she was losing contact with them. It was a gradual process, but it seemed inexorable.

To keep busy in his absence Mia got into the habit of doing the housework in their little unit. It was a very tight space, so it did not take long. During the week, she would go out with her work colleagues and sometimes have a girlfriend stay the night. She occasionally hosted a dinner party. Anything to avoid being alone all the time. Sometimes she was content in her own company, but she preferred to have her friends and family around her.

When he was home, they usually spent most of their days outdoors, taking long walks and soaking up the sun. There was always a physical connection between them, either his arm was around her waist, or he held her hand, his fingers entwined with hers. There was lots of conversation between them too. They talked about their jobs. Mia always had gossip about her girlfriends and their relationships and Wolfie loved to hear about their dating dramas.

"You won't believe this, but you know that girl, Kim, in the office, that I can't stand? The one no one likes. We bumped into her once at the shops."

"Oh yeah, I remember," he replied.

"She confided in me that her husband has left her. He's found himself a girlfriend."

"What? Really?" he said in disbelief.

"He's blaming her because she once said something sarcastically to him like, 'You'd be lucky to find someone else who'd put up with your shit, but if you do go for it.' He's now saying he didn't have any trouble finding someone better."

"How old is he?"

"I think they're both in their fifties and have been married for more than 20 years with three kids. He's a smoker, short, fat and balding. She was telling me that he constantly puts her down but wants sex six times a day."

"Six times. You'd like that," he said, proud of his quip.

"Not when he sounds like such a dickhead! And then I'd never get anything else done!" Wolfie laughed and Mia continued, "She said she's never in the mood because he's always so nasty to her! I can't stand her, but when she was telling me her story, I felt sorry for her; I had tears in my eyes. I know she's a bitch, but she doesn't deserve this."

"He sounds like such a loser. He's destroying his family. I would never do that." An elderly couple walked past holding hands, both with their heads full of grey, their shoulders hunched. He said, "That'll be us one day." Mia believed this would be true.

Wolfie would have Mia in stitches with his dry sense of humour, his sarcasm and wit but when it would take a turn for the worse, she found it distasteful. A lady hurriedly passed them wearing a flowing black skirt and a large T-Shirt that covered her abundant frame. She was clearly not wearing a bra and her ample breasts were held up in place by her large round stomach. She wore thongs, which he disapproved of, saying, "Only Westies and bogans wear thongs," and forbade Mia from ever owning a pair. Her black hair was gathered on top of her head in a ponytail that fell in half, like rabbit ears on either side of her head, and the tips were a faded blonde.

"Oh, look at her. Now she's fugly!" which meant fucking ugly. He let out a majestic cackle that sounded like Sam's. "What a stunner!" When he turned his sarcasm onto other people, he never really laughed; it was more of an evil chuckle.

Living close to the hub of Sydney's gay community, they often saw gays, lesbians and queers. A gay couple walked past them holding hands.

"I wonder which one of them is the pillow biter?" whispered Wolfie.

"Why don't you run up and ask them? You might find out in more ways than one," she replied, laughing teasingly.

"Hey! I'm no poof …" He was cut off mid-sentence by a motorcyclist displaying his showmanship on his back wheel as he revved loudly past them. Wolfie looked disgusted and judgemental. "What an idiot!" and he called out after him, "We'll see you wrapped around the next telegraph pole, you bloody wanker!"

When she had had enough of the constant barrage of distasteful criticism, she would remark sarcastically, "Aren't I lucky to have met your high standards?"

He would laugh, "That's right. See how lucky you are." She would roll her eyes.

One Sunday morning, Mia opened her eyes and stretched. The room was bright from the sunlight streaming into their bedroom. She was ready to seize the day. She looked over at Wolfie who was sound asleep. Knowing he could easily sleep in till noon, she snuggled closer to him and wrapped her body around his. He moaned moving away from her. She blew on his ear and tried to nibble it but he threw the sheet over his head. Finally, she straddled him, "Wake up! Wake up!" She shook him playfully. "Come on! It's a beautiful day, let's go get some rays." Laughing, he rolled over on top of her, but she was squirming so much that they slipped off the bed with a thump. There was a moment's delay, then they both burst out laughing. He then started tickling her, until she was laughing uncontrollably, legs kicking wildly and she was screaming and begging for him to stop.

Once, they were dressed and ready, they left their apartment and stepped onto the street, it was like a different world. There was already traffic buzzing everywhere, people walking about, and a bus roared loudly as it passed them. He paused, waiting for the noise to subside. "What would you like to do today, Mia?"

"Let's go for a walk around the Botanical Gardens," she replied, full of bubbling energy.

"No, I don't feel like doing that. Let's go to Darling Harbour instead." Mia was slowly becoming aware that he never wanted to do anything she suggested. It did not make sense to her why he bothered to ask. He always decided what they did and where they should eat, but she chose to ignore it as the weekends were so precious.

They were adjusting to cohabitation and Mia refused to let the little irritations common to any relationship upset her. She never objected to the toilet seat being left up or down. She never complained when he flossed and left flakes of plague decorating the mirror. She did not care if the toothpaste was initially squeezed out from the middle, rather than from the end. It was his idea that they have separate tubes of toothpaste.

Mia sometimes invited her parents over for dinner on Saturday nights. She would shop, prepare all the food, and clean their apartment, while he rested and recuperated from the amount of driving he had done throughout the week. She got into the habit of doing both of their laundry, as he would not be there to collect it from the shared laundry on the rooftop.

For her birthday that year he gave her some exquisite lingerie wrapped perfectly in small cardboard boxes with silk ribbons, and an enormous stuffed brown bear wearing a large red velvet bow. He thought the bear resembled him as it had a potbelly and a friendly face, and therefore would keep her company in their bed in his absence.

One morning, he stood holding a mug of tea as he stared out of the kitchen window. She quietly placed her warm hands over his eyes and planted a damp kiss on the back of his neck. He barely bothered to turn around and look at her. She noticed that since moving into their apartment, Wolfie was cuddling her less. He no longer sneaked up behind her to give her a big bear hug or grab and feel her up like he used too, and she missed his random displays of affection. When she quizzed him about this change in behaviour, he answered, "Well things are different now. We have a mortgage."

"But don't you still love me? Whether we have a mortgage or not?"

"Yes, but I'm just saying that things are different now," he said, dismissively. Mia did not understand what he meant and why he would not elucidate. He had voiced some discomfort at having a mortgage and she thought that he was maybe feeling a bit of financial pressure. Though they had to be sensible, they were still a long way from poverty, and still had enough money to eat out and buy clothes. This had been something she had enjoyed, initially only owning one business suit and two pairs of office shoes. Mia, with her eye for fashion and a bargain, had quickly amassed a wardrobe any businesswoman would have envied, but had still been frugal and very strategic with her shopping.

Wolfie approved of her choices, though he forbade her from wearing leg warmers, which were still the rage, and from buying cardigans, because he said "only old women wear them". Track suits and track pants, he also frowned upon as he thought they looked "too daggy", as did Sloppy Joe's, sneakers and twin sets. Mia liked knitted twin sets, thinking they could look quite stylish teamed with the right accessories, but never bought any of the items that he did not approve of. There were even certain colours that he forbade her from wearing, such as brown, and dark green. That was fine with her, as she did not like these shades either.

When it came to personal grooming, Wolfie seemed to throw on the first thing he pulled out of his wardrobe. The most treasured garment that he wore constantly was a pair of beige corduroy trousers. Even though she believed this colour and fabric to be unsophisticated, she never prevented him from doing or wearing what he wanted. When he wore these, she would gently suggest, "I think a pair of jeans might go better with that shirt." He would respond, "I don't care how I look, I'm not trying to impress anyone. I'm comfortable and that's what matters." She took him shopping for his birthday and bought him some stylish new clothes. When he wore them, she showered him with compliments. That was her style, ignoring the behaviour that she did not approve of, and praising the good. It was the same with his office attire; his suits and ties were conservative and neutral colours; his business shirts were white or light shades of blue.

Now that they lived together, Mia was becoming aware of the differences between them. For one, her libido was higher than his, and she now resorted to keeping a calendar of the number of times they had sex, marking the day she got lucky with a red cross and hung it on the back of their bedroom door. She had felt obliged to do this because whenever she dropped a hungry hint, he always responded with, "What!? Again! You just got it recently." She could now show him unequivocally that this was false. They then agreed to have sex once a week on the weekend. Mia was often the initiator. Though he complained about having to "perform" and that all she had to do "was lie there", she found it softened him towards her, and he was always nicer to her for a while afterwards. She noticed that if they had sex, they would also fight a lot less.

One night, Wolfie was taking a shower and Mia was bored. She decided to sneak up on him. She tiptoed into the bathroom, which was full of steam, the water running at full speed. She quietly approached the shower curtain, and ripped it open with a "RAHHH!". She was shocked to find him sitting in the bathtub, with a huge erection.

"What are you doing?" asked a bemused Mia.

"Nothing," he replied calmly. Her expectation had been that he would be angry at being scared by her, but there had been no response, which to her meant he was guilty of something. He continued, "Sometimes, it's relaxing to just sit here and have the water run. Haven't you ever tried it?" he asked as the water pounded the top of his head, and he continued rubbing the water from his torso never looking up at her.

"No," Mia responded, as she closed the door and walked away.

Why did you lie? It's clear you were masturbating. Why didn't you ask me for sex? I'm always up for it and always want it. I was only in the next room, all alone. Now you won't want sex but what about me?

It was never mentioned again. Mia felt like she had intruded on his private moment and did not understand his need to masturbate. She was confused and a little hurt, as she was always ready for action, but his libido seemed to have dwindled. The saying, "Treat them mean, keep them keen", floated around in the back of her mind. She sometimes felt that he manipulated her to keep her hungry and interested.

Regardless of these shortcomings, she loved him. She had chosen him, and it would work. Life was good. After all, sex was only a small part of married life; it was not the be all and end all of a loving relationship. Their first Christmas as husband and wife came and it was a joyous time for them both. She bought him a gold fob watch and had it engraved. "Once upon a time, I met you."

"It's perfect. It reminds me of my grandfather's watch," he said warmly.

"I know. That's why I got it for you."

"I love the inscription and I love you, Mia." He gave her a kiss and a squeeze.

He had bought her something practical, a leather satchel that she could use for work as well as a sexy red negligee.

The front of his card had a picture of a wife in a Christmas apron standing in front of a boiling pot on the stove, unimpressed with hands on hips, and in the doorway her husband in a brown business suit, looking at his gold watch, obviously late again: "To my wife at Christmas. I know at times I've made you roast, and at times I've made you stew ... but any time and all the time my favourite dish is you." When she opened the card, there was a three-dimensional pop-up of a husband kissing his smiling wife in front of a Christmas tree, "MERRY CHRISTMAS WITH LOVE".

Dear Mia,

I wish you a wonderful Xmas and a Happy New Year. Let this next year be even better for us.

Love Wolfie xxxx

Mia said, "Hey! Where's my poem? Don't tell me now that we're married, I'm not going to get any ever again?"

He chuckled, "I've been busy with work and they take me hours to write. I just didn't have time; I promise you'll get one next time."

***

When they were dating, she never noticed his nasty temperament. He had always been calm and rational, but now she saw that there was a nasty side to him as well. There were more and more explosions. This was all new to her. When he was in a rage, he would take it out on her, blaming her for whatever he believed was wrong. She thought he easily lived up to his nickname "the wolf". She noticed that he began coming home from work, tired and in a deplorable mood. He would then deliberately aggravate her. If she was doing some sewing, a crossword puzzle or even reading a book, he would make silly comments and nit-pick, to interrupt and bother her.

The smell of tobacco wafted through the open window. Downstairs, in the street, a group of friends chatted while they smoked, having just left one of the many restaurants. Mia closed the window in anticipation of Wolfie's arrival.

He yelled out a greeting as he walked in and started sniffing the air wildly like a crazed dog, "Is that cigarette smoke? It's disgusting!"

"I've just closed the window. There's a group outside smoking."

"Arseholes!"

She was sitting at the dining table doing her accounting homework, wearing a cardigan her mother had knitted her. He sniggered as he asked, "Has Grandma come to visit?" She ignored him.

"You're not cold, are you?" he prodded.

She wrapped her cardigan tightly around her, "Yes, it's cold sitting here, reading and not moving."

He sneered, "Grandma's studying? Where's your rocking chair, Grandma?" This was said slyly to annoy her. It was as though he was thrashing a dormant wasp nest with a big stick. Mia knew what he was doing, provoking her until she snapped, but she found that she could only ignore his behaviour for so long.

"Can you shut up and leave me alone!" she shrieked. Once she was in full fury, he seemed pleased with himself. Once again, she had behaved like his fighting fish.

He always waited till she was calm, before he would ask, "Are you happy, Mia?" This meant that he was in a good mood, and she could finally have a rational conversation with him. Eventually, he reduced his provocative behaviour, but it was always hard work. She had not seen this before and she had never seen her parents interacting in this way.

She also noticed that he no longer apologised. If she bumped him as she walked past, or interjected when he was speaking, she would instinctively say, "I'm sorry" or "I beg your pardon". He had stopped altogether even when it was his fault and it often was.

"You don't say sorry anymore like you used to? Why is that?"

He brushed her off with his snarly reply, "I've had enough." Mia was quiet.

What have you had enough of exactly and why are you taking it out on me?

One evening Wolfie's faced had dropped and he looked close to tears. He sat on the sofa rubbing his hands together over and over again.

"Are you alright, Babe?" she asked, concerned.

He stumbled as he answered, "I have to … I have to tell you something," he said, clenching his jaw.

She sat down next to him as she took his hand, "What is it?"

"I've started taking anti-depressants. I feel like I'm not coping with things, working and having a mortgage. I'm tired all the time because I'm not sleeping well. I have a heaviness in my chest and feel dizzy all the time."

Mia was relieved as she said, "Oh, that explains a lot. I thought something was really wrong with the mood swings and temper tantrums you were having." She gave him a hug as she said, "It's OK, Babe, if you need to take them, it's fine. I'd rather you take the medication if you need it, than live with an unhappy monster. Let me know what I can do to help. OK?"

"I love you, Mia." He looked at her meaningfully and Mia felt a shiver of pleasure. He grabbed her face and kissed her again and again.

She giggled as she replied, "I love you too, Wolfie, and I'll always be here for you." She loved him when she married him and loved him still. She had picked him as her husband. She understood that this was proper grown-up love, complete with responsibilities and difficulties. She knew in her heart that if she needed to be strong for them both, then she would do that.

The Affair? Chapter 9

Mia had also decided to change jobs for more money, but also hoping that wider experience would take her career in a new direction. She had started as a Junior Auditor in a Chartered firm but quickly got tired of the role. She visited customers' premises keen to find any kind of fraud in their books. However, many green ticks later, there was still nothing. It was repetitive, tedious work and she got bored quickly. Now she'd found a role in a small firm of five, walking distance from their apartment in the city. This new role offered her the preparation of accounts to balance sheet and tax returns, and she looked forward to developing her skills.

Mia liked her new manager, Norman, whom she found friendly and charming. He was ten years older than her and exuded confidence and a natural elegance. Every day, he wore cuff linked shirts and an array of flamboyant neckties. His business shirts provided a splash of colour that broke up the monotony of the bland office. Mia found him fascinating. He spoke lovingly of Jason, his three-year-old son. The photo frames of his smiling young face covered his desk; the boy with curly black hair and the big cheeky grin he'd obviously inherited from his father. Norman was her mentor and immediately took her under his wing. They quickly grew close. He was slightly taller than her in her heels with a muscular build. He was single and spoke warmly of the mother of his son.

"Jason's mum is an incredible mother, and I can't remember why we broke up. We still get along and talk every day. She's currently in a relationship, and when she's in one then usually I'm not, and vice versa. I hope that one day the timing will be right, and we can get back together and be a family."

Mia had never met anyone like Norman before. Although there were two partners, he practically ran the firm, being knowledgeable in finance matters, even in editing accounting software. He looked suave with his smouldering brown eyes and dark curly hair and his Mediterranean charm was hard to resist, and he was fun to be around. She found him dashing and debonair. When they drove out to visit clients, Norman would pick her up in his sports car. It was low to the ground and hugged the corners tightly. He would keep the conversation flowing, talking about music, food and the clients they were about to meet.

One evening, Mia rang her parents, she talked enthusiastically about her new job and gushed Norman's praises.

Gino said, "Be careful."

Be careful of what? Norman's such a nice man! He's always smiling and positive. There is nothing to be careful or concerned about. Dad's just being Dad. Overprotective.

On Monday as they drove to a client and were stuck in traffic Norman asked, "Have you seen that new shampoo ad on TV?"

"Which one?"

"I think it's for Detangle. It's in a green bottle. It shows all those girls in the shower washing their hair, all lathered up and stroking shampoo bottles while they're singing."

"Oh yeah, I know the one you mean. That's a very lame ad."

"Yeah, I know … but we all know what they are thinking about when they are stroking those shampoo bottles close to their mouth. Don't we?" He laughed almost with a wink.

"Oh yeah." Mia laughed too. The ad was obviously very suggestive, at least to Norman.

Mia had not been offended by it. Though it was cringeworthy, she had not given it another thought, other than it was so obvious what the advertisers were trying to do. Everyone had heard the adage that sex sells. She did not give Norman's comments another thought. They had become close and now talked about everything. He was like a big brother to her, and she trusted and admired him, hoping to be as successful as he was one day soon.

They began attending the gym together after work because it was more motivating than going alone. Otherwise, she would work out until she broke into a sweat, usually after ten minutes and then leave. Going to the gym with someone meant that Mia tried a little harder. Wolfie had said, "I don't do gyms," and was always away with work. She would only see him on the weekend. Since she disliked going home to their empty apartment, she jumped at the chance to go to the gym with Norman.

One evening after their workout Norman said, "Let's meet up in the sauna."

Mia had never been in one before and did not know what to wear.

I'll take off my tights and just keep my leotard on.

She was sitting in the dark, perspiring and feeling hot. Norman came in wearing a towel and sat behind her. They were alone and casually chatting about the client they had visited earlier in the day. Norman started giving her a neck and shoulder massage.

"WOW, I can feel some big knots."

"Always. I think that's where all of my tension gets stored."

He was kneading the skin along her neck. Mia was feeling goose bumps.

"Ouch! Not so rough there, it hurts. That's better. Gosh, that feels so good."

I like this. It feels great. I love being massaged. Who doesn't?

His hands slid along her collarbones and seemed to be making their way to her breasts. He reached them and began massaging them as he said, "I like the firm breasts of a 23-year-old."

Mia froze.

Oh, shit! What should I do now? Is this crossing a line? It's just a massage… I think I like this.

Suddenly, the door sprang open, Norman ripped his hands away from her guiltily, as another man joined them.

Norman said, "I've got an early start tomorrow. I'd better go. I'll see you tomorrow." And with that, he left.

That was odd. Why did he jump as if he had something to hide? That was weird and kind of sexy.

When they saw each other in the office, it was as if nothing had happened, and it was never mentioned.

Phew! Nothing to worry about, everything is fine.

They still occasionally had lunch together, especially if they were visiting a client. Sometimes on a Friday evening after work, they would go out for drinks; Mia was not used to drinking and would feel giddy after two glasses of wine.

The following Friday evening, they were having a drink at a local bar and were once again talking about relationships. Something that Norman always liked to discuss.

"Where did you meet your husband?"

"At university."

"Was he your first?"

"Yes."

His hand gently bumped hers as he answered, "I like that."

What was that? Did he deliberately caress my hand or was that an accidental bump? I don't feel so good. That wine's gone straight to my head.

"I'll get you another glass of white."

"No. No, I can't. Two is plenty. I'm feeling a little sick and light-headed. I think it's time for me to go home." With that, she stood up to leave.

"I'll walk you out." He escorted her.

Outside, they said their goodbyes and Norman leaned in to give her a kiss and kissed her on the lips. It was just a peck. Mia had not expected this. She puckered up and gave him a peck back. He then said, "Come here for a minute," as he led her by the hand and walked through a door on his left that led to a car park.

Once in this stairwell, he became an octopus. He was trying to kiss her whilst lifting her skirt and fumbling with his pants.

Mia was trying to push his hands away from her, trying to pull her skirt back down again. "No, no, no." He responded with, "Yes, yes, yes."

What are you doing? Let go. Get off of me! Stop it! Stop! No! No! NO!

The next thing he had picked her up and was holding her against the wall. He was inside her. It all happened so quickly. Mia did not have time to react. Her head was spinning. A couple of thrusts and he was done. He held Mia in his lap, as he sat down on the step. Her eyes filled with tears. She said, "I feel like crying."

"Don't cry," came his curt reply, but there was no tenderness from him, nothing. She understood; he had only been interested in satisfying himself. She stood up, straightened her garments and left. He gave her a perfunctory kiss. She was confused. She made her way to the bus stop. As she sat there, tears filled her eyes and thoughts swirled through her head.

How did this happen? I didn't want this. I trusted him. He knows I'm married. How could he? Why did he do that? How could I let this happen? What do I do now? Do I tell Wolfie? Did I lead him on? I was nice to him. Polite with him. Laughed at his jokes. I admired him. I thought he was terrific. Was this all my fault? Did I deserve this? I must have asked for it. Maybe I sent mixed messages. I am a terrible person and a terrible wife. I should never have let this happen.

She went home crying and confused. Blaming and feeling disappointed with herself.

Mia returned to work on Monday and Norman treated her the same way as he had prior to their Friday night rendezvous. She felt uneasy around him and was trying to have as little interaction with him as possible. She thought that he was regretting what had happened, like she was.

In the weekly Monday morning staff meeting, as they sat in the partners' office, Norman said, "I'm just reminding you all that I'm on leave next week, for the week. I'm taking my son to Byron Bay. I think it would be a good idea if Mia and I come in on Saturday morning so that I can hand over to her what needs to be done as a priority in my absence."

The partners agreed, and Mia had no choice but to agree too. The week leading up to Saturday was uneventful. Norman made no reference to what had happened the Friday earlier and neither did she. Mia believed that things between them were back to normal.

By Saturday morning, Wolfie had not returned home as there had been flooding and the roads were blocked. Mia arrived at work punctually at nine. She wore a pair of khaki trousers with a long-sleeved crew knit, that went all the way up to her neck and a pair of comfortable flats. She looked presentable in her conservative, casual attire and had deliberately chosen not to wear anything revealing or eye-catching.

Mia thought they would just talk about work and that their meeting would be over quickly. They sat in Norman's office. She was taking notes as he discussed the needs of various clients; for one she would have to go through all their real estate agent's statements summarising income and expenses for the numerous rental properties they owned. He handed her all the documentation that he had as well as a shoe box full of receipts and invoices. Mia did not say anything but could see it was going to be a laborious process. He showed her a giant manual ledger that belonged to another client, which they used for paying staff, and he was showing her how she would have to summarise all the columns to prepare the payments summaries for their employees. They were old school and had not digitalised their payroll system. Mia was taking extensive notes, and everything was going well.

He printed out a document that he wanted to go through with her. Mia volunteered to retrieve it from the printer. As she was walking back to his office, he came out, and stood there. She held the piece of paper in her hand, and as she walked toward him, he put his arm around her and pulled her close. She stopped dead in her tracks. He kissed her on the lips as she tried to pull away, but he had her in a firm grip. He now had both his hands around her, and she stepped backwards, trying to escape his embrace. She shook her head as she pushed on his chest. She said, "No", he replied, "Yes".

She was walking backwards trying to move away from him, but he would not let go of her. Again, she said, "No," again he replied, "Yes, yes," in whispered tones like it was a game. Mia was scared. He was bigger and stronger than her, and she was alone in a completely desolate office block with him. How could she escape? He had previously been able to pick her up in one swift move. She did not want things to turn violent, and she feared for her safety. She tried to unsuccessfully push him away again and again, and continued trying to move away, but he was unrelenting. Since this had already happened once, she felt she had no choice. In the end, she lay on the couch and let him do what he wanted. She did not participate in any way. She made no sound and was completely motionless.

He was on top of her thrusting. Mia did not want to be there. About halfway through his thrusts, he stopped to look at her and asked, "Are you all right?"

"I love it," she lied. She wanted him off her and wanted it to be over. She did not want this! He finished quickly and for that she was thankful. He climbed off, and she pulled up her underpants and trousers. He had not undressed her or himself, and she knew she was just another notch on his belt. He continued their meeting. Although she was looking and listening to him, she heard nothing. As she was leaving the office, Norman said, "Don't tell your husband."

Mia decided then and there that she would tell Wolfie. She did not want this to continue and did not know how to stop it and did not understand how it had even begun. Nothing in her previous life had prepared her to recognise a sexual predator, especially one who was so good at recognising someone vulnerable. She was still blaming herself and when Wolfie arrived home she could not bring herself to tell him though she tried. The following week, Norman would be out of the office, so she would be safe.

How do I tell Wolfie that I have cheated on him?

He was the man she had fallen in love with. The man she had chosen to build her life with. The man with whom she had made a home. She yearned for the smile he would have for her, happy to see her after his weeklong absence. But she was also filled with dread as the work week came and went. It would be better to be honest, and he would know what to do. She was anxious about his reaction as she planned to tell him about the whole horrible incident. She worried that he would see the shimmer of guilt, shame and betrayal she felt throughout her entire body. They walked along the harbour at Circular Quay. It was another sunny day and seagulls floated on air currents above, occasionally diving to rescue a chip a tourist had dropped and then proceeding to fight amongst themselves, in a loud squabble. They made their way to the Opera House, where they sat on a sundrenched bench, close to the blue water of the harbour. Mia decided it was now or never.

"Wolfie, if I had something really bad to tell you, that involved me. You'd want me to tell you, wouldn't you?" she asked apprehensively.

He smiled wanly, "Of course, I want you to be honest."

"Even if it would really hurt you, Wolfie? I don't want to hurt you, but I think it would."

"Of course, you can tell me anything. What is it?" He was sounding a little concerned.

She faltered, “I am so sorry Wolfie. I don’t know how to tell you. How to say it.”

“Just tell me. It’s okay. What is it?” he asked warily.

“I’ve had an affair.”

Wolfie looked stunned and hurt. He fell quiet. He was looking down at his hands in his lap. Mia felt awful.

“I’m really sorry. I’m so sorry. Please forgive me. It was a mistake.” Mia was upset too. She was crying.

“Who was it with?”

“Norman.”

“How long has it been going on for?”

“It just happened, and I didn’t want it to, and I don’t want it!” she replied, becoming more upset.

He wanted to know every detail and kept probing her with questions. “How many times?”, “What positions?”, “Did you go down on him?”, “Did he go down on you?”, “Where did it happen?”

“Twice. The first time, I had some drinks, and was feeling tipsy, and didn’t expect that to happen and the second time, I just lay there. I promise I didn’t do anything. I didn’t want to! I said no but he just helped himself. I never wanted to have sex with him!”

“But you did it twice, not once but twice,” he replied in a surly manner.

“The second time, I just lay there. I didn’t participate. I didn’t want to be there.”

“Do you love him?” he asked with a sneer.

"No, I don't love him. It was just sex, for him, another notch on his belt. I never wanted this!"

He wasn't listening! He wanted her to resign, but Mia was worried about doing that now that they had a mortgage. She thought it would be easier to find a job whilst still employed and agreed to start looking immediately. Meanwhile she would just avoid Norman. Eventually, Wolfie agreed to move on if she told him that it was never going to happen again. She promised him.

The first thing Mia did on Monday was to visit Norman in his office. She knocked on his door, which was already open. He looked up and gave her a big smile.

"Hey," he said, happy to see her, "come on in."

"How was your break?" she asked, so everyone could hear. He rattled on about his holiday, but she was not interested. When he finished, she said in a lower voice, "I've told my husband everything, and that's never going to happen again." She felt strong and empowered now that her husband was standing behind her.

A week later, Mia lost her job. She was still in her probationary period, so it was easy for them to let her go. One of the partners called her in and told her that it was not working out. She was sure it was something Norman had said. Mia, though relieved, felt under financial pressure but she was glad they had made the decision for her. She left and never spoke to Norman again, or anyone else from that office. It did not take her long to find another job. She was young and there were plenty of jobs around for junior accountants. They both settled back into their daily routine, though for a while he was aggressive towards her in their love making sessions. He fucked her hard at every opportunity. She felt as though he was reclaiming what was rightfully his, like a dog marking its territory.

I'm so sorry that I hurt you, Wolfie. I feel dreadful. Should I have just quit and not said anything? If I'd done that you wouldn't be hurting and suffering now; maybe that would have been better. I'll be a good wife, the best wife you've ever seen and make it up to you.

Wolfie had warned her that if it ever happened again, he would leave her. She had never wanted this to occur in the first place and knew in her heart it would not. She would be more alert to subtle signs and not so trusting of men in the future. She would never again be as naïve. She was certainly wiser, but at such a high cost!

They had talked at length about what had transpired between herself and Norman. He forced her to relive her ordeal by repeatedly asking her for every detail, until she had had enough of trying to make him understand that she had never wanted this. In the end, she let him go on and on and would just sit there quietly. Neither of them reached the conclusion that it was actually a rape. Sometimes when they would fight about small things that got on each other's nerves, he would turn to her venomously, "Well, at least I'm not going around fucking the first person that comes along. I'm not classy like you, you slut! Fucking in a stairwell." She had had enough of his constant slights.

When he was calm, she said, "Look, you have to stop bringing it up all the time, slut shaming me and rubbing my nose in it. If you truly have forgiven me like you say, then we don't talk about it anymore. It's not going to work if we can't get past it. If you can't let it go, then we will have to go our separate ways."

Wolfie agreed and neither of them mentioned it again. He eventually stopped fucking her angrily, and tenderness returned to their lovemaking. Their lives were returning to normal. Mia secretly ached for years about what had happened to her, not truly realising the enormity of it, that it had been rape. Torn inside because she felt guilty for cheating yet at the same time feeling innocent of having had an affair. She had not deliberately snuck out to have a romantic liaison, but she had been friendly, kind and had trusted Norman. She had enjoyed his attention and had accepted it as harmless office banter. She thought that someone flirting with you just meant they liked you. Should she have read the signs? She wondered how she could have.

On the other hand, Norman had not physically attacked her and dragged her into a dark alley, so something just never sat right with her and it festered in the pit of her stomach like cancer. The guilt and shame gnawed away at her insides. Around that time, there had been the ongoing debate in the media about abortion and if women should be allowed to abort at least in the case of rape. She had been astounded by some of the comments made by male politicians that she had read:

"Rape is like the weather. When inevitable, relax and enjoy it … In a legitimate rape the female body has ways to shut itself down. If a woman has the right to an abortion, it's only fair that a man be free to use his superior strength to force himself on her." She hoped never to be alone with this delusional politician.

"When life begins with the horrible situation of rape, it's something God intended to happen. Rape victims should make the best of this inauspicious situation." She wondered how they were supposed to do that exactly.

Times were different then. There was nothing in the news about date rape or that "no meant no". There had even been a court case at the time, where a judge had ruled that "no" meant "yes". This had caused outrage in the community amongst women's groups when this prominent judge had ruled in favour of the defendant.

No wonder Mia did not realise that she had been raped!!!

Norman had wanted sex, and she felt obligated to give in to him because she had put herself in that dangerous predicament. She had been friendly with him, and he felt entitled to her body. For nearly a decade, she did not think of it as rape. She thought of it as something she had caused and that Wolfie could not understand. He could only judge.

Happily Never After
Chapter 10

After spending Saturday afternoon at the hairdresser, Mia came home with a new haircut. She excitedly buzzed the intercom, and exuberantly bounded up the two flights of stairs two at a time, full of anticipation. She was prepared for his compliment. The door opened and Wolfie appeared. Her smile broadened from ear to ear.

"That's disgusting! To think you're my wife!" he growled.

Mia laughed but was appalled. "What do you mean? I think it looks trendy. I love it!"

"It's revolting! It's not feminine at all."

Mia had her hair cut very short. The length of a man's but it suited her. When she was back at work, she received many compliments from her work colleagues, her family, even Wolfie's family. Many asked, "Have you lost weight?" Many commented, "You look like a model," and "WOW! You look taller," as well as, "That haircut makes you look like a supermodel."

Though disappointed by his remarks, she also did not take them seriously. He had been the only one to give her negative feedback. It was her body, and she could do with it as she pleased. Mia's drastic new hair style was symbolic of the resurrection from her tragedy and was reflective of the confidence she felt in her new work role. She thrived there. She loved the dynamic environment of this second tiered chartered firm, the diversity of her role, where she experienced all facets of accounting. It was a firm of forty-five staff, and they behaved like a big family. There were often social drinks after work, or dinner and on the weekend games of badminton and tennis.

Mia had made friends with a girl in the IT department called Michelle, born in the Philippines and grown up in Australia. Mia found her to have a contagious spirit and quickly caught the Pinoy laughing bug from her. Michelle made going to work more fun. They went out for lunch every day. Mia blossomed there. Michelle was five years younger than her and looked up to her like a big sister. Mia seemed so wise and in control of her life, being married and having a career. Michelle had been dating her high school sweetheart for the last five years, and there was a common expectation that she would marry him, but that was not what she wanted. Michelle would often ask Mia for her advice on affairs of the heart. It was like they were kindred spirits, sharing the same mindset, energy and beliefs and always giggling and chatting.

There were six partners in the firm who were all meek and reserved, except for her team's partner, Kevin Moore. Kevin was loud and gregarious. He would take the whole team to lunch, every time there was a birthday, and at Christmas he invited the team to his house for a BBQ, including their spouses. Mia and Wolfie arrived at Kevin's sprawling property in a gorgeous leafy suburb. It was a modest five-bedroom house on a large block.

Mia was the only female on the team and had a pleasant afternoon mingling with her co-workers. Wolfie was relaxed and getting to know them too. He was having no trouble as she had spoken highly of all of them. They sat in the garden, eating snags and coleslaw salad on their laps, enjoying their typical Australian barbeque lunch.

Dirk said, "You should come and try paddle boarding with us next weekend, Mia. We have the boards and take them out to a little bay where it's calm and flat."

"No way. That looks like hard work. Don't you need good balance and core strength? I don't think it would be my cup of tea."

"Why don't you come and give it a try?" asked Brock.

"Look, thanks, but it's not something I can see myself doing."

Wolfie interjected, "You'll get to see her big white, flabby arse." He laughed loudly and though this was meant to sound light-hearted and jolly, it did not hide the vindictiveness beneath it. She looked at him horrified; where conversation had flowed, there was now a deafening silence.

"Why on earth did you say that?" asked Mia.

"Because it's true, they'll get to see your big white, flabby arse." Wolfie laughed raucously, and when he started to laugh, it was the ultimate insult.

Mia's three colleagues were sitting there gaping at Wolfie, appalled and dumbfounded. She felt awkward and hurt. It was the first time that he had directed his piercing sarcasm at her in such a public forum. Mia would point out how pathetic he looked when he publicly humiliated her, let alone how hurtful it was. It was not the best behaviour of a loving husband! She was noticing his nasty streak more and more. He did have a very unpleasant sense of humour and would often make fun of people, in a cruel way. When they got home and he seemed in a relaxed mood, Mia asked, "So why did you say those horrible things about me in front of everyone at the BBQ? What was that all about?"

"Well, they're true, aren't they?" he said sourly, not even looking at her.

She felt her stomach clench, "No!" she snapped, glaring at him. She took a deep breath as she said, "Do you think that's the behaviour of a kind and loving husband, to publicly humiliate his wife?"

"Don't exaggerate, the truth can hardly publicly humiliate you." His mouth remained in a thin, firm line.

She could gladly have strangled her husband at that moment. "We've already established that it's not the truth, and I certainly think it makes you look like a right dickhead to put me down like that, so if that's the way you want to come across, knock yourself out!" He was looking at her like a wolf with its leg caught in a trap. Wolfie continued to sneer and swipe at her until it blew up into a row, then he would have the excuse to storm off into the other room for the rest of the evening. When he left the room, Mia just rolled her eyes and shook her head in exasperation. It now seemed that he was spiteful by nature and could quickly become the personification of mockery, scorn and blame, whilst she was quicker to laughter than anger. In spite of this flaw, she still loved him with all of her heart and believed that together they would figure it out.

***

Wolfie had a change of role with his company. He was now based in the Sydney office, and rarely travelled. This also meant that he had lost his company car. Now that Wolfie was home, he never let Mia study, always wanting to spend every spare minute of the day with her. He would continually interrupt and distract her with, "Come watch TV with me." "Let's go get something to eat." "Let's go get a hot chocolate." "Do you want to go see a movie?" and on weekends, "Let's go for a walk; you can study later." His walks were never short and before she knew it, the day had gone, and she was too tired to take out her textbooks.

They had fights over this, with Mia screaming, "You never let me study!"

"Is there anything wrong with me wanting to spend time with my wife?" In the end she relented as she always did.

He was selfish not to let her have time for herself, especially since there seemed to be different rules for him. If he wanted to take two hours to read the Sunday papers from front to back, in sequence, first section first and then the next, and folded back knife-sharp when he was done, then that's exactly what he would do. It would be Mia's role to bring him as many cups of coffee and tea as he desired. The rules for him and those for her seemed to be getting further apart each day.

Mia finally completed her degree, much to her father's delight. He had looked forward to her graduation, and the black cape and mortarboard ceremony. Her parents had clapped loudly and proudly to acknowledge what their child had achieved. Now, her employer expected her to complete her professional year or PY. It was only a year of study and once complete would mean more money, which was something Wolfie always seemed to worry about. It was no surprise that she failed her first exam. She tried to cram the week before, but it obviously was not enough. Though no one in her office passed, she remained disappointed with herself. She reluctantly enrolled in the next module to please her manager.

One day, Wolfie suggested randomly, "Why don't we move to Germany? We could get jobs there. It would be a great experience."

Mia laughed. "What …?", she laughed again. "You're not serious!" She was surprised by this random escape plan that he seemed to have formulated on sheer impulse.

"Yes, I'm being very serious. I miss my country and family, and I think it would be a great opportunity."

Mia could never comprehend how someone who had spent most of their adult life in Australia and was basically Australian could pine so much for the so-called Motherland.

"We've just completed our degrees and have very little practical experience. I don't speak the language, and you said yourself that your German is about the same standard as that of a primary school student. What kind of jobs could we get there?"

"I'm sure we could find something."

"Probably as cleaners or working in supermarkets. I wouldn't be able to work as an accountant. I don't speak German, nor do I know their accounting rules and regulations, and what about your Mickey Mouse degree? … Sorry, sorry… I mean your marketing degree. What kind of job could you find there? I don't see how it would work. We would be on minimum wages." She waited for him to pounce on her glib remark.

He chose to ignore it, as he replied, "We could take night classes and learn German there."

"What about our apartment?" asked Mia.

"We could rent it," he suggested.

"That's not something that I'm interested in doing. I've just started my career here. We've bought our first place and you want to uproot us to go on some adventure, for what? We're fine here. I'm not going."

"Come on, Mia. It would be fun. Just the two of us," he pleaded.

"If you want to go so badly, then you go. I'm not stopping you. You can send me money for your share of the mortgage every month, but I'm staying here. I'm not moving to Germany!"

He would regularly mention it, trying to wear her down, even accusing her of destroying his dreams, though this was the first she had ever heard of them.

Finally, his Uncle Louis in Germany explained, "In Germany, you will not do as well as you are doing in Australia. You will have difficulty finding work in your chosen careers without being fluent in German, and it would take you a long time to buy a home." After that, he never mentioned it again. Her question was whether it was as a result of a man offering him advice.

It was the start of a new day and Mia awoke suddenly, not feeling rested. Her mouth was dry and then she remembered that it was her birthday. She felt a flutter of excitement in her belly, knowing that Wolfie would fuss over her. She could hear him in the kitchen, getting mugs ready and putting the kettle on. She got up excitedly.

On the table marked "To Mia" was an envelope. She eagerly ripped it open. There was a card with an animation of a girl in a flowered pink dress with a Peter Pan collar and a large pink bow in her hair, arranging flowers in a vase. It read, "Be a good girl on your Birthday!" She opened the card, "Or would you rather have FUN?" He had written:

Happy Birthday my darling Mia,

Here are a few words from your hubby.
Poems you like, and a poem you will get,
Like the ones when we first met.

I love you sweetly, I love you still,
Even now what a big thrill.

Sometimes I see glimpses of the past, like a book,
Yes, that's right, it's the plaits and that schoolgirl look.
Don't go red, don't blush,
Just hug me with all that mush, mush, mush.

Our future together is woven as one,
Let's be joyous and have lots of fun!
There are some chores like work & PY,
But study, be diligent and it will pass right by.

You have much to look forward to with your hubby,
Such as career changes, bigger homes and bubbies,
I want two but Mia wants four,
Who'll be right? – I don't want to end up poor.

I will do my best as husband and father,
Not to forget best friend and lover.
This I know is important to you,
Without love, you just wouldn't be happy, would you?
Happy Birthday it's your 24th today,
Let's shout from the rooftops,
Hip, Hip, Hooray!

He loved her and she adored him; wholly and unconditionally. "Happy Birthday! My birthday girl!" he said as he affectionately put an arm around her and softly kissed her lips. He then took her on a shopping spree where he doted on her all day.

***

City prices had exploded. It was Wolfie who decided to sell their apartment because they could double their money, and then look in the suburbs near her parents so that in the future, when they had children, Mia would be close to them. They bought a cosy two-bedroom red brick townhouse in a small complex in the suburbs, surrounded by greenery. About three months after moving in, interest rates hit a record high of 18%. They could not meet their loan repayments. It was "the recession we had to have" as famously described by the then Prime Minister, Paul Keating.

Luckily for them, they were able to lease their townhouse for a year whilst they lived rent free with Wolfie's father in his terrace house. Sam and Tammy had downsized, so that there was less gardening and maintenance and more time to indulge in travel.

Mia knew that Sam was particularly difficult to live with, seeing the way he treated Tammy at times, always expecting her to do his every bidding. He worked full-time, and Tammy stayed at home and kept the house. He never did any domestic chores. He reminded Mia of some fat maharajah sprawled out on his satin daybed, cooled by women fanning him with giant feathers whilst he barked orders at the lowly women. Tammy was his maid, his servant, his slave. Mia would never let Wolfie treat her like that!

He disliked odours and forbade Mia and Wolfie from cooking. They were only allowed to boil water, so they often ate pasta or ate out. Somehow, they managed to live there for a year. Tammy looked after the cleaning, but they had to take extreme care of the furnishings which were his father's antiques. Their own belongings were in storage.

One evening, after a Chinese meal, Mia felt nauseous. They had just arrived home and it was late. Wolfie began badgering her for a blow job. She had started to give these to him as he was relentless in his requests.

"Wolfie, I feel sick, like I'm going to heave."

"Come on! You hardly ever do it." He continued pestering her until she gave in.

He lay naked on the bed and she knelt over him as she commenced her "mouth work." He gave her instructions, "Hold my dick firmly at the base like this with one hand and cradle my balls in the other and stroke them. You can also lick them if you want."

"What!? Gross! That's disgusting!"

"Okay. Okay. Just stroke them ... mmm, that's good, wait, wait, not too tight. Not too tight."

He offered some suggestions; "Can you glide a little more with your mouth up and down my cock? No need to suck so hard, though it feels nice. Yeah, that's good. Can you try a bit more of that?" and "You're doing a good job. Do you like it?"

His eyes rolled back into his head as he closed his eyes, pleasure taking hold of him. Then, in a panic, "I can feel teeth, I can feel teeth." After a while, he exploded into her mouth.

Mia felt the vomit rise and expel itself, no longer being able to hold it in.

"Oh, that's warm," he chuckled as it ran down and spread all over him like a small blanket. They had a towel with them, so he scooped everything up and ran to the bathroom. She lay there feeling very ill.

Two weeks later Mia was having her period and suffering with her usual three-day migraine. She felt like she was being stabbed in the head with a dagger and was sitting next to him on the sofa watching TV, having just swallowed two headache tablets.

"The muscles in my neck and shoulders are locking from this migraine. I feel so sick. I'm going to bed."

"Already? But it's only 8.30pm. Why don't you stay with me and watch a movie?"

"I can't, Babe. I don't feel well. I need to lie down, besides, I've just taken something to help me sleep. Any chance you could give me a five-minute massage before I'm unconscious, please?"

"What's in it for me? I'd like a blow job."

"What!? But I have my period, and you normally avoid me during this time, plus I have a pounding head, I feel like throwing up! You don't want me to puke all over you again. Do you?"

"Your mouth isn't having a period."

"Don't be a pig!" She slammed her glass of water down so hard that it slopped over a pink floral cushion. She swung her legs to the floor and stood up with her eyes sparking fire, her head pounding and her nostrils wide, as she said, "You can't even give me a five-minute massage?! I'm suffering!"

"Alright. Alright. Just wait for the ads, I'll give you one during the ads, but only for as long as the ads, and not a minute more." He gave her a quick knead and said, "There, I'm done. I've got sore fingers and I'd better not hear any complaints."

When she menstruated, he treated her like a leper, and hated touching her. No hugs, kisses, caresses of any kind, and would hardly talk to her. It was as if he could catch her ailment. Sometimes she would deliberately say, "Oh my breasts are sore and tender. Aunty Flow must be on her way." She would then watch in amusement, as he went out of his way to avoid her. She occasionally used this as her weapon for some peace from him.

The next day she rang her mother. Their relationship had changed significantly since Mia had moved out and was now married. The way her mother treated her these days was more like an adult than a child. They had become closer since she had left home; she saw her mother, not just as her mother, but as a close friend and trusted confidante.

After exchanging pleasantries, she said, "Mum, he always wants me to give him blow jobs and to swallow. I don't like it. It makes me want to vomit!"

"Oh, that's disgusting. I'm lucky your father has never asked me to do anything like that."

"I never did that before we got married but now, he asks for it all the time!"

"Your father and I never liked him. We thought you marrying him was a mistake."

"You never liked him? I had no idea. Why didn't you ever say anything?"

"It's your life, and we didn't think you would listen."

Well, that's great! What am I supposed to do now? I'm stuck with him.

Once Mia hung up the phone, Wolfie suggested they go for a walk, looking at the little cottages that lined the streets. Strolling along, Wolfie said, "Isn't it funny how we are all born from a cunt, and then spend the rest of our lives trying to get back into one?"

Mia was astounded by his crude comment, but she laughed it off, as she said, "What …? I don't think you could be more obscene and vulgar if you tried!"

"But it's true. Think about it."

"Well, I can assure you that I'M NOT trying to get back into one!"

"I was never like this until I met you!"

"What are you talking about?"

"I was never this coarse until I met you! You've made me the way I am."

"What a load of crap! Just because I like the odd dirty joke. I am not, and I will never be as crass as you!" If anything, she loathed his ribald vernacular.

1991

First Born
Chapter 11

Saturday morning, Wolfie had gone to work, and Alex sat cooing in his bouncer. She was dusting the bookcase. In the sunlight, she watched the dust particles swirl, caught in a current and for a moment she floated as if separate from the room, higher than her thoughts. She reminisced about the time Alex had joined them …

They had finally moved back into their townhouse. Interest rates had come down and the economy was starting to pick up again. Mia had still not completed any of her chartered accountancy studies. She could not motivate herself and would always defer, a few weeks before the exam. She had been feeling unwell, queasy in the stomach, tired, and lately her nipples had started tingling. At the doctor's surgery, her family doctor, Dr Knight asked, "Has anything out of the ordinary happened? Have you travelled overseas recently?"

"Yes, I've just come back from a six-week holiday to Europe with my husband."

Wolfie had organised their wondrous trip. He had said, "I have to go to Germany. It's been six years since I've been back." They had stayed with both sets of his grandparents, and she had also visited her godmother and one of her aunties, who had not seen her since she was four. With Mia speaking fluent Italian and Wolfie a little German they had managed to travel around Europe relatively easily. They did get lost in Rome looking for ruins. At the time, this had been stressful as they had missed their connecting train back to Switzerland, but now they laughed about it. Mia saying, "If I didn't speak Italian, I think we would still be wandering the streets of Rome today." It had been a magnificent vacation; everything had been perfect.

"You wouldn't happen to be pregnant, would you?"

"No," Mia answered, a little exasperated, as every time she went to a doctor, that would be his first assumption.

He asked her to urinate into a small jar. He then dipped a paper stick into it and watched it change colour.

"Congratulations, Mrs Schmidt," Dr Knight said, "you're pregnant."

Mia sat there dumbfounded. "I am? How far along?"

"From what you've told me, I'd say about six weeks."

Mia was stunned. She left the doctor's office and headed into the city to go to work. As she walked along, she caught a glimpse of herself in a department store window. I don't look any different, but she no longer felt the same. A car driving past honked its horn and the driver wolf whistled.

That's disgusting! Perving on a pregnant woman!

Mia was excited and could not wait to share this good news with Wolfie. She was ready to be a mum. He picked her up after work, and as they drove to a nearby mall to do their grocery shopping. He happily chatted about his day then asked, "So how was your day? "Well, I went to the doctor this morning, to see why I'd been feeling sick."

He interrupted. "Let me guess. Everything's fine. See I told you it was nothing."

"Well actually, it turns out that I'm pregnant," replied Mia sourly.

"No, you're not," Wolfie replied quickly, chuckling nervously.

"Yes, I am."

"No, you're not."

"I'm being serious. I'm pregnant," replied a slightly frustrated Mia.

"No, no. You can't be."

"I'm telling you, that I'm having your baby and I'm apparently six weeks along."

Wolfie appeared flustered. Mia could not understand why he was not jumping for joy. She had expected him to whisk her up in his arms and twirl her around, like they did in the movies. Almost from the first day he had met her, he had always said that he longed to be a grandfather. She had naturally assumed that this had meant that he would like to be a father first. Wolfie eventually accepted that Mia was carrying his child. What choice did he really have? It was the fear of the unknown, the new territory that he found daunting. He began to relax as they discussed baby names. He said, "I like the name Alexander for a boy. That was my uncle's name, the one who was killed in a tragic skiing accident at the age of 35. He was such a kind, gentle man." He began tearing up.

"It's a good name but could we shorten it to Alex? Don't forget that we also need to consider girls' names." They had decided not to find out the gender of their baby, wanting to keep it a surprise.

In the third month, they telephoned their parents. Natalia and Nonna had the best reactions and screamed their excitement. All were pleased at the impending arrival of the first grandchild. Everyone seemed delighted at the news of an upcoming birth, but she would never see any expressions of joy from him. She was bitterly disappointed.

Wolfie stressed about finances and having another mouth to feed. This was not something he had planned or anticipated, and felt it was too soon. He worried that they did not have savings of at least $10,000, his baby budget, and safety net. They did not have any savings, especially with the expensive worldwide trip they had just had. It seemed like the perfect time to start a family, having been happily married for four years, had a glorious break overseas, and then moved back into suburbia. True, it had been unplanned, but she was sure that many others who had found themselves in similar circumstances had successfully managed it.

Her mother told her, "We only had $100 in the bank when your brother came along, and we managed just fine. You learn to tighten your belt."

At about four months into her pregnancy, she lost her job. Wolfie worried. Mia took it in her stride. The job market, though slow, was picking up. She applied for many positions and noticed quickly, those she told she was expecting, she never heard from again, and those that she kept it a secret from, always gave her an interview. She eventually found a job as a part-time bank teller. She did not tell them that she was expecting nor that she had an accounting degree. To make ends meet, Mia also took a part-time job at a fruit market where they paid her in cash.

Wolfie was very pleased, "That's fantastic news! Cash in hand means the tax man won't know about it, so it's worth more. I love your gumption, Mia. I could never do jobs like that."

Yes, I know you have your limitations, Wolfie, and you're too much of a snob!

She thrived in her role as teller, and particularly enjoyed the branch competitions that allowed her to express her creative side. Staff were encouraged to decorate their branch to promote new campaigns, such as the no fee chequing account, or the latest insurance product. Prior to Mia's arrival, they had never won. Now they won every single time, thanks to her creative ideas and catchy slogans. Mia loved it! She felt inspired, stimulated and productive.

She began suffering greatly from morning sickness and thought a more apt name would have been all day sickness but soldiered on. As her pregnancy progressed, she became very fatigued as both jobs required her to stand on her feet all day. She was able to hide her growing belly from both parties until she was six months gone. The bank was unimpressed that she had kept this concealed, but she assured them that she would work until the day she went into labour and then only take six weeks maternity leave. She had already lined up a long day-care centre for her unborn child. She eventually quit her job at the fruit market, having almost fainted several times. As they had still not purchased a car, Mia had to catch public transport which took her an hour and a half each way. The connection between the bus and train was poor. If she had had a car, door to door would have taken her about forty minutes.

Wolfie marvelled at Mia's burgeoning belly. He constantly took photos of her. "Can you please stop taking photos of me looking fat!"

"I think you're beautiful and it's amazing watching your belly grow, knowing there's another little human in there." He would take great delight in annoying his little bub, by gently pushing or rubbing on what felt like a foot or an elbow, just to watch their baby stretch across her tummy, moving to get away.

"Initially, I was nervous about becoming a dad. I didn't think I was ready but now I can't wait and I'm looking forward to meeting the little guy or gal."

Mia's belly grew and the more it expanded, the more his libido decreased. Hers, on the other hand, had not waned; it had probably intensified! Particularly in the last month, when he avoided any contact with her, worried that he might poke the baby in the head. *Don't flatter yourself honey! You're not that big!* But she uttered some supportive platitudes instead. She took to teasing him by dancing around the house, singing Jo Jo Zep & the Falcons hit, *"Shape I'm In"*, hamming it up as she rubbed her belly, until he banned her from singing it, not appreciating her humour.

She thought it was important that they both have an idea of what they were in for, so she enrolled them in prenatal classes. After all, they were in this together. He said, "I don't know if it's a good idea that I attend the birth. I mean, I'm going to be thinking of that each time we have sex and it's going to put me off."

"Don't be ridiculous! I need you there. Just stand at the other end away from the action if you're too scared."

They had started the countdown to their baby's imminent arrival, and they were ready. They had purchased a cot, a pram and all other incidentals. One

Wednesday evening after work, she came home with a cold. Her nose was running, and she felt miserable. That evening she went to bed earlier than usual, thinking she had just been overdoing it. At about 1.30am, she awoke to pain in her abdomen, and realised she was having contractions.

"Wolfie, Wolfie. It's time." Mia whispered as she gently shook his shoulder.

Wolfie a little sleepy, "What?"

"It's time. The baby's coming, it's time to take me to hospital." They had recently purchased a car for the pending arrival of their baby.

"No, no," he answered, waking suddenly. "It's too early. Are you sure? This can't be right. It's too early. You still have two weeks to go. Are you sure?"

Not this crap again!

She got up, dressed and reached for the overnight bag she had prepared four weeks earlier. Wolfie had no choice but to get himself dressed. At the hospital, Mia changed into a gown and was made comfortable in a bed. Wolfie sat beside her looking nervous. Her contractions grew closer and stronger. She found the pain unbearable. As a particularly nasty one gripped her, she held her breath. The nurse said, "Breathe, breathe. Don't hold your breath."

With every contraction, Wolfie would say, "Breathe, Mia, breathe." Then in panicked tones he would add, "Are you okay? Can I get you something? Can I do something?" He was getting on her nerves. Finally, at the end of one particularly excruciating contraction, Mia sucked in a huge amount of air as she yelled, "Shuuuut up!"; she'd had enough of his helplessness.

The nurse asked Mia if she would like a mirror.

A mirror? I don't really care how I look right now.

The nurse explained it was to see the baby's head crowning. Mia declined. She was happiest in denial and just wanted the baby out! She finally agreed to an epidural, although she had wanted a drug free birth. She could not take the pain any longer and this baby was reluctant to make an entrance. Eventually, the doctor placed a little cap on her baby's head and suctioned it out. After 21 hours of labour, they welcomed their son, Alex, into the world. He was 55 centimetres long and weighed 3.5kgs. He had black curly hair and the darkest blue almond shaped eyes.

She lay in the hospital bed feeling like she had just been run over by a freight train, whilst two nurses fussed over her, and a doctor stitched her up for what seemed like an eternity. She wondered why women would have more than one child. Wolfie sat in a chair against the wall in front of her, cuddling their first-born. He was proud and radiant. She watched in sheer amazement as his face lit up, and for a few seconds he looked 20 again. All the love she had for him raced once more to the fore. The hurt and the neglect were all forgotten as they both shared the miracle of their first son. She had never seen him so euphoric. She enjoyed the look of pure happiness on her husband's face. It was so rare these days. He was speaking to Alex in hushed tones.

"Hello, son. I'm your father," he purred to the tightly wrapped bundle. "I'm going to make sure that you have a good life and that you'll have lots of brothers and sisters to keep you company."

Mia was mortified. *No, he won't! Not unless you get a surrogate. There's no way I'm ever going through that again!*

Mia was 25 years of age, and one month away from her 26th birthday. Wolfie was 27. Later that evening, when she was alone with her son, and he slept quietly in the crib beside her, various thoughts flooded her mind.

I've been looking forward to meeting you and giving you a cuddle for nine months, but now that I've done that, what am I supposed to do with you? Take you home and care for you for the rest of my life? It was a daunting thought.

The nurses showed her how to change Alex, who had finally pooped. Mia opened his cloth nappy to find a very large, black sticky deposit. It was meconium, which she had never seen before. She started to wipe his bottom with a moist cotton cloth as instructed by the nurse. It was like tar and stuck well to his tiny buttocks. Mia started to retch.

"For goodness' sake, it's your son," said the nurse.

"It's still shit, and it's revolting!" she answered defensively, gagging as she said this. She managed to clean Alex without vomiting.

Guess I'm going to have to get used to this.

Alex was jaundiced, which was not uncommon for a newborn, so he lay beside her under Bili-light lamps in his crib completely naked, except for some goggles worn over his eyes for protection. He looked like he was sunbaking in a solarium. Mia's breasts were engorged from her milk having come in, and they pinned her to the bed like anvils. Each one at least three times the size of her son's head! A nurse gave her some cold cabbage leaves to line her bra, and this offered her some relief. The nurses showed her how to attach her son to her bosom, but it was not easy. He was still very sleepy and not interested in being fed. When he did suckle, Mia felt pangs of pain. The nurses explained this was helping her uterus get back into shape.

One morning, as she sat in bed with her son suckling, he swallowed a couple of big gulps of milk. His little hand opened and rested on her bosom. He was perfect, she marvelled. From each little fingernail on every tiny finger to his plump rosy cheeks, to the cutest part of him, his little feet. Precious blobs, soft and squishy, yearning to be covered in a thousand kisses. She gently stroked him as he fell asleep, and she had just settled him in his crib when Wolfie appeared. He walked over to his son, his face full of warmth and appreciation.

He leaned over to give her a kiss and she ripped open her hospital gown, "Check out these puppies!"

"WOW!" he exclaimed in appreciation, "Dolly Parton eat your heart out." They both laughed.

***

Natalia was ecstatic at the birth of her grandson. Mia's older brother, Nino, was too busy serial dating and not ready to settle down. Her parents continuously hounding him with, "When are you going to get married?"

Her other siblings were too young to wed. Nonna was also thrilled at being a great-grandmother. She was ready to impart a lot of her wisdom, "You must wear a girdle for six weeks after the birth. This will help you get your flat tummy back." Mia did as she was told.

"You must also wrap your baby's belly for the first three months. This will ensure that his belly button becomes an innie rather than an outie."

"Wrap his belly?" enquired Mia.

"Yes, firmly with a bandage."

Her mother whispered, "Just do as she says, it'll keep her quiet. Just don't let your doctor see it, he'll think you're crazy. Nonna is full of old wives' tales, but she means well, and some of them really do work. I bandaged the four of you, and all of you now have innies."

Mia's mother and grandmother would have liked to spend more time with her once she got home, but Wolfie's mother had already invited herself to stay with them for two weeks to help with the baby.

Sabine had a unique outlook on life and her dream was to one day build a house of mud bricks. She spent quite a bit of time reading, anything and everything, pouring over every inch of the newspaper, trolling for a good conspiracy theory.

With her eyes full of wonderment and her brown pupils dilated, she exclaimed, "They've discovered water has feelings."

"What? Feelings?" Both Wolfie and Mia enquired.

I'm amazed you turned out so normal, Wolfie, with a mum like that, and poor Sam and what he would have had to put up with.

"They've done studies with two identical glasses of water filled from the same source, and then placed a photo of Mother Teresa under one and Adolph Hitler under the other. Within weeks, the glass of water with Adolph Hitler's picture had gone off, causing algae to grow and it was no longer drinkable. The glass of water with Mother Teresa's photo remained pristine."

"Is that so," replied Mia. Wolfie had left the room. Sabine kept excitedly talking to her about water's feelings for the next hour. She thought her mother-in-law was a bit of a kook, but never vocalised this to Wolfie.

When Wolfie came back, Sabine said, "The whole country is being listened to, spied on and monitored by the government using the clouds in the sky." Mia found it difficult to keep a straight face.

Wolfie whispered to Mia, "My mother is killing me with her crazy ideas. She has too much time on her hands and reads and believes such drivel."

"You don't say."

"Yes. Haven't you noticed? Once she gets an idea in her head, she's like a dog with a bone, and won't let it go. She's really hard work." She listened to him but did not comment, never speaking ill of his family like he did of hers.

Mia began amusing herself, "Sabine, did you hear? They say that man never really walked on the moon," she asked conspiratorially.

Sabine could not stop herself, "I know. That video of Neil Armstrong placing the American flag on the moon, shows it flapping in a breeze. There is no wind in space, so how could it move like that? People are saying it was filmed here on earth! In a studio!" Mia pretended to fuss over Alex as she picked him up and left the room, but not before throwing Wolfie a knowing look. He understood what she was doing. He gave her a look as if to say, "Thank you very much!" She left the room with a smirk on her face and Wolfie was his mother's captive audience for at least the next hour. It was too easy. Though Sabine sometimes burdened them with the viewpoints she shared, she was still helpful to Mia and a distraction to her adjustment to having a newborn.

She went back to work exactly six weeks after the birth of her son, as she had promised. She found this extremely tiring because Alex was not sleeping through the night yet and it was Mia who got up for him because she was breast feeding.

She found a long day-care placement and would drop him off and pick him up every day. Her parents never offered to help and rarely babysat, and Nonna was too elderly to drive and too frail to care for her great-grandson on her own. Her mum once said to her, "We didn't have any help when you were all growing up, and we managed. We did it hard, so you can too." Mia had been stupefied by her mother's remark but was too stunned to reply. This annoyed Wolfie. "The reason we bought here, was to be close to your family, so they could help us when we had children." He continued, "Your parents never help us out, but they're always happy to come over for a free feed." That was untrue and besides, her parents were younger than Wolfie's and both still working. They also had three children still living at home, the younger two approaching their teens. When she invited her parents for dinner, they always came, but there was an open invitation to their house. Every Saturday night, the three of them went there for dinner, and Wolfie never complained. Whenever they saw Alex, they fussed over him. They were still involved in their grandchild's life. Mia rejoiced at having a night off from cooking and devouring a hearty home cooked meal that someone else had prepared. If Alex was sick, then Mia's mother, who now only worked on weekends, would take care of him so that Mia could go to work. There was still some support.

Wolfie's father and step mum were also delighted to be invited for a "free feed" and never declined. They also never babysat or reciprocated by having them over for a meal and certainly never cared for Alex when he was sick.

Wolfie said, "It's because my parents got divorced. Things might have been different if Sam and Sabine were still together. Let's face it, Sam isn't very paternal, is he? I don't have a close relationship with Tammy, so they aren't going to be interested in babysitting. People should never divorce. They should always try and work it out. It's never that bad, and it's just not worth all the damage it does."

Mia had not anticipated motherhood to be so demanding. She was still recovering physically from the birth, and now had sore nipples. She was exhausted from the sleepless nights and had added to her burden by returning to work. After another exhausting night, Wolfie stretched as he woke up refreshed and exclaimed, "Alex was good last night. He slept through."

"Not quite," replied Mia, "I had to get up several times for him. He kept falling asleep at the breast and when I tried to sneak him back to bed, he would wake up every single time, without fail."

"Really?" he replied, surprised. "I didn't hear him."

"I know. I don't know how you can block him out. I hear every little gurgle he makes."

Sometimes, out of sheer lassitude, she would bring Alex into their bed. She would lie on her side so that he could continue suckling, and she could rest. There were nights when they could not settle him. It was Wolfie's idea that they all go for a car ride as the gentle rocking motion always lulled him to sleep. In the car, Wolfie drove as Alex cried from his baby capsule.

"He's sure got a good set of lungs on him," he noted, amused.

"Where are we driving to?"

"Let's just drive around and see if we can get him to fall asleep."

Sometimes, Mia would also fall asleep and would be startled awake by the sound of the radio.

"What are you doing? You'll wake him," she said, turning down the volume.

"It's a good song."

Wolfie enjoyed cuddling his son, and would make comments like, "He looks like an alien," and "When he wrinkles his forehead, he looks like a wise old man," as well as "He looks like a fat Buddha," and excitedly, "He's holding my finger!" When he soiled his diaper, he would pass him to Mia, pulling a disgusted face, "I think he's done something."

"Can't you change him? He's your son," a weary Mia would ask.

"No, I told you. I don't change nappies," and he never did.

It had been another particularly difficult night with Mia being unable to settle Alex. It was now daylight, and she knew that she wouldn't be able to get to sleep even though she felt like she needed toothpicks to keep her eyelids open. She decided to jump in the shower to wake herself up. A few hours later, Wolfie woke up. From downstairs, she heard a commotion in the bathroom. He was screeching profanities in English and German. She went to investigate, and as she reached the landing she heard, "FUCK ME DEAD!"

She appeared in the doorway, "No thanks. I think I'll pass." He threw her a dirty look., "NOW what's wrong?" she asked.

He answered with animosity, "The bathroom floor is soaking wet! I've told you before, open your eyes before you leave the bathroom and don't leave the floor soaking wet! I'm tired of getting my feet wet because you can't clean up after yourself!" Her towel was lying in a massive puddle of water.

"What are you talking about?" she asked, and continued stoically, "It wasn't me."

"Well, who the hell was it then? There's no one else here and it certainly wasn't me."

"I'm telling you that there was no water on the floor when I finished my shower this morning. I don't know what's happened; this has only started happening recently, but why are you always throwing my towel in the dirty puddle? It's unhygienic! Use your own!"

"You silly cow! I'm sick of this fucking shit! Just look before you leave the bathroom!" he thundered; his face stretched in an ugly grimace.

"I've already told you. It wasn't me, and don't start calling me names or it's not going to end well … I think you should quit while you're ahead!"

"Oh, I'm ahead now, ahead of what?" he snarled.

"You're always the one that starts with the swearing and name calling. How hard is it to be polite to me?"

"YOU ALWAYS START!"

"No, I don't. I'm never the obnoxious and immature one, that would be you!"

Wolfie disregarded her and kept stomping and slamming cupboard doors. Once he was in this mood, he saw injustice and inconvenience everywhere in his life, and it would take him hours to calm down and be pleasant again. Mia had seen Sam behave in the same way.

"I feel like you're disrespecting me when you throw my towel onto the floor like that."

"Respect has to be earned," he replied disdainfully.

Mia was outraged, "What!? What's that supposed to mean? I'm your wife!" She felt like a wild animal about to pounce. "How dare you say that to me! Do you think you're better than me? Do you think you're superior? I should be your equal!"

She continued loudly, "You should respect me for all that I do around here, especially compared to you who does fuck all but bitch, day in and day out. I also don't know if you've noticed, but I've just had your baby. Your son. Which I'm pretty sure is another reason why you should be showing me some respect."

He was no longer listening to her, reclined in the armchair reading his newspaper, barely acknowledging her. He asked with exaggerated composure, "Do you have to scream? You can never discuss things calmly, can you?"

Can you hear yourself? You're the one, that always said "communication is important". Where has that guy gone? Because I don't know who you are. Can I have my husband back please?

Eventually, he did admit that it had been a "bad choice of words", that he had not meant it, only because she would not back down. He had referred to her as a "ball breaker", but she sometimes perceived no other option. If she did not stand her ground every so often, she felt he treated her like a boot brush hedgehog and she regularly felt his feet. Mia wondered how a person like her, a person who had so much love in her heart and soul, had ended up with a man she was beginning, at times, to despise.

Later that evening he suggested, "Why don't you sleep in tomorrow? I'll get up and bring Alex to you in the morning so you can feed him."

"That would be lovely. Thank you, darling," she replied in appreciation, impressed that she had not had to ask him for his help.

The following morning, after bringing her the wrapped little bundle, he jumped into the shower. Later, she entered the bathroom, stepping into a puddle in the middle of the floor.

"Wolfgang? Can you come up here a minute please? I want to show you something."

He begrudgingly stamped up the stairs, knowing that he was in trouble since she had not used his nickname.

She said tauntingly, "Look at the bathroom floor, it's soaking wet. So, what did you do?"

He was flabbergasted. "But I didn't do anything."

"Should I believe you? Do you think that's an acceptable answer considering the way you carried on with me? Maybe I should also yell and call you names? What do you think?"

"I don't know what to say. It wasn't me."

"Really? Is that so?"

He looked bewildered but didn't offer her an apology. He seemed incapable of recognising the way he was behaving and the fact that such outbursts had debris that needed cleaning up. Something he seemed to think was HER job.

She called a handyman; the shower tray had a leak, and it was just normal wear and tear. Wolfgang never admitted fault.

She did get tired of his exploits and the way he sometimes treated her, but what could she do? Mia felt she had him on a behaviour modification program. She ignored his flagrant egregious actions and tried to compliment and praise the good.

It was finally Wolfie who one day suggested, "I really think we could benefit from some marriage counselling. We just seem to be fighting all the time and it wasn't like that before. I think we need help. I've actually booked us an appointment. Will you go with me?"

"Marriage counselling you say, that's a bit extreme, isn't it? The problem is I talk but you never listen. Surely, if we sit together, we can sort out our differences."

"Look at what you're doing now, you're blaming me. Let's just give it a go and see if it helps. Come on, Mia, I really want our marriage to work."

How could she say no? Besides, the sex therapy had turned out not to be so bad, so she decided to attend counselling with him.

Heed the Warning
Chapter 12

The sign on the door said Karen Whitmore Marriage Counselling. Mia turned the handle with a sense of trepidation. Wolfgang was so close that she could feel his breath on the back of her neck. As she turned her face to look at her husband, he smiled at her, and she briefly saw the handsome young man who had filled her heart with warmth and happiness all those years ago.

"Good morning, I'm Karen Whitmore, please come in and take a seat."

Karen was in her late thirties, with a modern pixie cut and pink glasses that framed her brown eyes with their long lashes. She had the kind of eyes that instilled calmness and trust. Mia felt instantly relaxed, as she smiled back at her. Mia sat on a chair opposite the desk with her legs crossed and laid her hands in her lap. Wolfgang took the chair next to her with his legs splayed and his arms akimbo. Light streamed in from the large windows.

Karen asked some initial background questions from behind her enormous desk, things like, how long they had been wed, their ages, their ethnicity, and whether their parents were still married. It was their first couple counselling session after four years of marriage. Not many people did that in 1991.

Their session was well underway. Wolfie had the floor.

"She's very black and white and has no shades of grey," he said in an accusatory tone.

Mia looked directly at him as she replied, frustrated, "I've already explained that you're looking at things the wrong way. I'm not black and white, I'm passionate, there's a difference. I do everything passionately. I love it or I hate it. I know what I want and there's nothing wrong with that."

She turned to Karen and added with conviction, "Besides, I've asked my girlfriends if they thought I was black and white and ALL of them … basically scoffed …and said, 'No not you. Never! You have so many shades of grey,' so I really don't know what he's talking about."

Adjusting her notepad, Karen asked, "What's an outcome that you would like to achieve here today, Wolfie?"

"I'd like to spend some alone time with Mia. I'd like to have a date night at least once a week."

"Is that something you would be interested in, Mia?"

"Yes, but I worry about the expense. We don't have any family that will readily babysit, so we would have to pay a sitter. We can't afford to pay someone once a week and then, on top of that, eat at a restaurant or go to a movie or whatever it is that would please Wolfie. Alex goes to bed at 7.30pm every night, so we could watch a movie at home together for free."

"I need to get out without Alex around. Just you and me," he whined.

Karen had just taken a sip of water. "What about a compromise and say once a month? Would both of you be happy with this arrangement?" After thinking about it, they both nodded their heads in agreement. Karen continued, "So, what's brought you here today, Mia?"

"Well, Wolfie has," she said with a giggle. "He thought we needed help. He said our relationship had gone off track. I think we're just both adjusting to our first born, Alex, who's still a baby. I don't see why we can't simply discuss things and work them out, instead of airing our dirty laundry publicly."

Karen maintaining her professional decorum continued, "Is there anything you'd like to achieve today, Mia?"

"Well, if I really think about it, I would like him to help me more around the house. With the baby, I find I am so busy. I do everything for him, as well as everything at home. He hasn't even changed a nappy yet. I just feel like it's more work than it should be."

"I told you that I would never change a nappy and I'm not going to."

"Why won't you change a nappy?" asked Karen.

"I told her from the beginning that I would never change any dirty nappies. She wanted a kid. She can do it!" He brushed his hand through the air as he said this as if he was swatting a fly towards Mia. His gesture reeked of dismissiveness.

With his demeanour souring, he added, "It's disgusting and I'm not going to do it! I'm not changing nappies and that's final! She didn't discuss having children with me. She just went ahead and decided to have one!" he said as he pointed his finger angrily at her.

"I fell pregnant accidentally," Mia interjected in her defence. "We were on holidays overseas, and I missed a pill or two with the time zone difference. I got confused. I didn't think I'd get pregnant that easily. I'd been on the pill for seven years."

Karen looked at Wolfie expectantly, "Was it an accident?" and then turned to Mia, "Did you discuss contraception? Were you using condoms? It does take two." Wolfie threw her a disapproving look but did not respond.

"He doesn't like to use them. He says the sensation isn't as good with them on and refuses to wear them." Mia continued, "I find I'm just exhausted. Alex isn't sleeping through the night and I was only home for six weeks after his birth, before returning to work because Wolfie was stressed about finances. Plus, I'm doing all the cooking and cleaning. He never lifts a finger to help!"

Karen looked at Wolfie expectantly.

"We have very traditional roles. She does everything inside the house, and I look after everything outside … the garden and so forth. I do the finances. She never touches them and doesn't even take an interest in them."

Mia rolled her eyes and shook her head as she said, "He asked me to take over the finances because he was sick of them. I told him that I would be very happy to if he would be willing to swap roles. I would happily take them over, if he did everything else that I do." She paused as she added sarcastically, "but for some strange reason, he didn't seem to be too keen."

He said sternly, "Well, I know that you would only do them for a little while; I would then have to take over when you would stuff them up."

Mia did not respond even though she was seething mad. Karen looked perplexed. Mia was sure she had seen Karen's professional mask drop for a moment and a look of utter incredulity take its place.

"Is there anything you would like to add, Mia?"

"I don't see why I would stuff up. I mean, I'm the fully qualified accountant here, not him."

Their session continued in this fashion. Wolfie would ask Mia to explain something that had occurred, and promptly interrupt her with, "You're telling it wrong and too slowly. We haven't got all day." He would then take over, adding, "Let me do the talking, people listen to men."

Comments like "You don't know what you're talking about," and, "In what world did buying that make sense?" peppered his dialogue and were very familiar to Mia. At the conclusion of their session, as they were leaving, Karen pulled her aside.

"Excuse me, Mia, one moment please." Wolfie waited in the hallway.

Karen said quietly, "I think you should leave him."

Mia was completely taken aback. She gasped, "What …? Why?"

"I can see that he's difficult, rigid in his outlook and won't change. I suggest you leave him for your own good. He can't be reasoned with."

Mia was speechless. "I mean it, Mia. Don't stay with him. You'll be better off without him."

This interaction with Karen left Mia rattled. It filled her with doubt and annoyed her. She had only seen them interacting for an hour, so how could she possibly draw this conclusion so quickly? Did she want to destroy Mia's life? How could she be better off raising a child on her own? Karen's role was to save their marriage, and not to take the pin out of the grenade and detonate it.

In the car, Mia told Wolfie what Karen had said. He chortled loudly as if he had just heard a good joke. "She was such a stupid bitch. She was hopeless." He also did not believe her diagnosis of their relationship.

"I was surprised. I couldn't believe it! Fancy saying something like that to me! What a nerve! I thought marriage counsellors were supposed to save marriages at all costs, and that service was affiliated with the church as well. Unbelievable! I never expected her to drop that bombshell. I'm sure it's uncommon for a marriage counsellor to dole out that kind of advice. I'm sure it's unheard of!"

"She should be reported. She was so unprofessional. Don't worry. We'll find another marriage counsellor, a better one."

Mia had loved him, trusted him. She had now made a child with him, and she knew that he loved her too. After all, it had been his idea to seek counselling and he would now find a "better one". She still believed they were both willing to dedicate the time and effort required to make their marriage work. On the other hand, Karen was the marriage expert. Had she become so adept at her profession that she could tell in one session that couple counselling could not save them? Had she seen something irrevocably broken in Wolfie? Was she an exceptional judge of character? Mia wondered if her marriage was really in such trouble, and if she should leave. Could it be fixed? Could it be saved? Was it even true? If so, when had it started to unravel?

The following day, Mia called her mother from work during her lunch break, wanting to confide in her about their marriage counselling session with Karen. It went straight to voicemail; she was screening calls. Mia started to playfully leave a message, waiting for her to answer.

"Bonjourno mamma! Ciao mamma sono io. Ciao! Ciao! Mamma ci sei? Rispondi al telefono! Raccogliere!" She always spoke to her family in her native tongue so as not to lose it.

Her mother answered the phone breathlessly. *"Bonjourno, bonjourno Mia. Come stai?"*

"Bene, bene, e tu mamma?"

"I'm good. I'm good. I was putting the shopping away, I just got home. You make me run, what's up?"

"I went to see that marriage counsellor, Karen, with Wolfie yesterday, and you're never going to guess what happened?"

"What?"

"At the end of the session, she pulled me aside and said I should leave him!"

"Did she say why?" Natalia asked warily.

"She didn't think that he could be reasoned with, and that in the long run, I'd be better off without him. What about Alex? I don't think he would be better off without his father."

Natalia sounded perturbed as she replied, "That's strange. What a weird thing to say, but then I don't know what they're supposed to do. Your father and I never did that. We just talked things over, but then he never acted like Wolfie. He wasn't difficult like him."

"I know what you're saying. He has a temper, and he's got an odd sense of humour where he stirs people all the time, but I still think he's a decent guy. He does have his good points, and he's not like that all the time, because then, yes, it would be a problem. I've just had his baby and I love him. There's no way I'm going to leave him. I don't think she knows what she's talking about! He obviously loves me too, or he wouldn't be dragging me to see a marriage counsellor as soon as he thinks our relationship is in trouble."

"How much is all of this costing?"

"Yeah, it's not cheap, Mum, but he needs it. I think he's still getting used to having a baby around. If it was up to me, we never would have gone either, but he says you get your car serviced every six months to avoid major repairs, you maintain your house when something breaks down, and he says it's the same with a relationship. It's like getting a service. It makes him happy. He doesn't want to see Karen again and he's going to book a different marriage counsellor."

They talked some more before they hung up. When Natalia got off the phone, Gino asked, "Who was that?"

"Your number one daughter."

He chuckled, "How is Mia?"

Natalia gave him a rundown of their conversation, and added with a sense of foreboding, "I think one day he'll leave her. I don't think he's the husband type. He's too selfish and immature."

Gino's Italian temper rose. "He better not hurt her! I'll kill him! She wasn't lucky picking him. I hope it works out for her."

A week later, Wolfie organised another counsellor, Yvonne. Her office was sterile and clinical. Wolfie sat next to Mia on the sofa with his legs touching hers. She had a sense of trepidation.

What is this one going to say to me?

Yvonne was of slender build with long brown hair tied into a braid that reached her behind and wore a natural pout. After the usual introductions and background questions, Yvonne stood in front of them near a white board. It felt like they were at school again.

"I don't know if you've heard of Glasson's theory, also known as choice theory?" They both shook their heads.

"It states that all we do is behave, and that almost all behaviour is chosen, and we are driven by a desire to satisfy our five basic needs." She drew five cups on the whiteboard. "Glasson states that everyone has five basic needs, which are represented by these five cups." She pointed to each one: "Love and belonging, power, freedom, surviving and the fun cup or recreation and learning cup, as some people find learning fun." She paused before continuing, "To give you an example, everyone has a love and belonging cup or love cup. Some need this filled to the brim and others don't. If you're the type that needs it filled to the top, but you're always giving love to others and not getting any in return, then one day you might become miserable because your cup is half full or completely empty." She scribbled over the love cup so that it was half full, with arrows leaving it in every direction. "If this situation were to occur, that person would then change their behaviour to try and replenish their love cup. They could look to do this in two ways. Either positively, by say, getting a puppy, or they might do something a little more unsavoury like have an affair. In both instances, they are trying to replenish their cup. That's how it works."

Mia realised immediately that her love cup needed to be filled to the brim by her family. Despite always filling his and others' cups, she did not receive much in return, just an occasional drop to keep her going. Her choices were influenced by her need to be loved, but what about Wolfie? Which cup motivated him to make his choices? Why did he choose to lose his temper and yell at her? Why did he not go for a walk instead, and come home when he was calm? Why did he not join a gym and exercise his frustrations away? There were always alternatives to the way he chose to behave. How could she not have seen this before? How could she not have known the selfish, mean, immoral man beneath the façade? Even she had to admit, when the façade had thinned and she had seen glimpses, she had dismissed them.

I loved him. I looked the other way so many times because I loved him, because he was my husband and now because he is the father of my son.

They saw Yvonne a few more times before things settled down between them. Wolfie became more relaxed as they started their date nights, and he began showing Mia more affection and respect as he had done when they were first married. He was listening to Yvonne and realising that Mia needed love in return. Mia was happy that their issues seemed to have been resolved and that Wolfie was keen to make things work. She also never received any private recommendations from Yvonne, like the one she had received from Karen.

Cause or Cuss I Can!
Chapter 13

Wolfie decided that he would be better suited as an accountant as he liked working with numbers and enrolled himself in a conversion course at university. He had simply come home one day and decreed that he would be changing careers and that was that. Mia was too busy to argue and let him be, but this now meant that he would spend weekends upstairs studying in the bedroom and Mia would be on her own downstairs keeping Alex quiet. She resented this because he had never allowed her to study when she had attempted her professional year, which in the end she had given up. This left her with no choice but to move into the commercial sector. However, she found the mix of people there more interesting, and less conservative, which suited her. She continued supporting him and even completed his financial accounting assignment because he had found it to be too complicated. He had earned 19 out of 20, thanks to her.

When Alex was three months old, Mia stopped breast feeding him. Now that she was back at work, sleep-deprived and feeling the strain of managing everyone's needs around her, her milk supply had become inadequate. Once Alex started on formula, he was a more settled baby, but his reflux worsened. Both were amazed at the amount of foul-smelling vomitus that could come out of such a tiny human being. He reminded her of the small girl tied to her bed in the Exorcist film, possessed by the devil who could rotate her head three hundred and sixty degrees and projectile vomit everywhere. Alex seemed to have this skill too. The stench of regurgitated milk was overpowering. It almost made Mia retch.

If Wolfie was cuddling him and wanted to pass him to her, she would yell, "Wait!", almost catapulting from her chair, her left hand up in the air like a stop sign. Before promptly covering her right and left shoulders and her lap with cloth nappies, protecting her like shields, she would then say, "Okay, I'm ready. Hand him over."

Regardless, they both loved him dearly. Wolfie could not relate to the baby stage and longed for Alex to be able to speak and interact more with him. He was a very happy baby and always had a big toothless grin for them.

They were settling into their family routine and townhouse. They bought new curtains, some furniture and some art for the walls. It was beginning to look and feel like a cosy home. Mia was pleased with her decorator skills. However, the existing carpet was obviously of poor quality. Mia was sure that if she ran her clean finger through the shag pile, it would somehow leave a stain. Ever since bringing Alex home, the number of marks on the carpet had increased ten-fold from his ongoing reflux. Wolfie howled every time he found a new stain and Mia would apologise, subserviently dropping to her knees to clean it. She was becoming fed up.

He came home from work one evening wearing a glowering face.

Geez, he doesn't need to wear a mood ring. His face says it all!

He bellowed, "FUCK! There's another stain on the carpet."

This time Mia snapped, "Is there? Well, I haven't seen it yet because I've been nursing your son ever since I got home! So, since you saw it first, and you're always the one to find them! Why don't YOU get down on your hands and knees and clean it?!" Wolfie never mentioned the stains again, nor did he ever help clean any. She shampooed the spot later that evening. She had had enough of his constant angry outbursts. He was always the first to see what needed to get done around the house, but also the last to do anything about it. Little things like this seemed to make him angry, but afterwards he would not even remember that he had become enraged.

Despite working part-time, she found she had little time for herself due to travel time, housework, and being Alex's primary caregiver. It had been an enormous adjustment for her. She realised that he was not giving her the unconditional love or the support she needed as he had done before the mortgage, before the son she had borne him. She gave this to him all the time, but he did not reciprocate.

Why do you have to act like such a jerk? I feel like you don't love me or value me when you always come home in a bad mood, and when you scream and yell at me, because there is a new stain on the carpet. You always seem to be able to find something to get angry about. Why can't you give me unconditional love, the same as I give to you?

***

Something new had been bothering Mia, and she wanted to discuss it with him. He appeared cheerful, so she thought it would be a perfect opportunity to sit down and have a chat. She approached him with a mug of coffee in each hand. He was sitting at his desk reading a finance magazine.

Mia said, "Hey, Babe, got a minute? Here, I've brought you a cuppa."

"Thanks, Babe, come sit next to me," he said as he removed papers from the chair.

"I just wanted to mention something that I don't know whether you've realised or not?"

"Sure, what is it?"

"Well, I think you're swearing a lot more than you used too. Why is that?"

"Fucked if I know."

"Can you please be serious for a minute. Every second word that comes out of your mouth is 'fuck'. You're using the expletive as a verb, adverb, and noun. You never used to talk like that before."

"I'm fucking talented then, aren't I?" he said with a grin.

"As an adjective now too. Really? Your language these days has deteriorated so much so, that you would make a sailor blush. I think that group of yobbos in your last role, were a bad influence on you."

"Fuck those fucking fuckers!"

"I imagine you talk like that at work. It's offensive and disrespectful to carry on like that, not to mention the blaspheming and your increased use of the 'c' word."

"Cunt?" he asked facetiously.

Mia sighed in frustration. He added, "What about you? You're no angel. You swear as well."

"Look, Babe, I don't swear half as much as you. I don't blaspheme and you never hear me use the 'c' word. A lot of people find this offensive, especially women. If I were you, I would never use that profanity when women were present. I was just trying to make you aware of changes to your pattern of speech, but if you want to be known as Mr Fuckity Fuck, then go for it. I obviously can't stop you! But just know that it does reflect quality of character."

Wolfie sniggered. They heard Alex cry out from his cot.

Mia said sweetly, "Sounds like Alex just woke up from his nap. Would you like to get him?"

"No, thanks. I'm fine sitting here. You can go." His earlier buoyant mood seemed to have vanished. She turned and stalked off; her expression stony.

His vocabulary did not improve. She had seen him rage and shout, calling her "fucking bitch", "cunt", "cock-sucker", and "arsehole". Yet he could go outside to drop something in the bin, see a neighbour and talk to them over the fence as if nothing had happened, and he would be amiable, for half an hour or more. He would then come back inside and continue denigrating her, picking up where he had left off.

On one such occasion, as he entered the foyer, she asked, "Is this for real? Are you really angry or just pretending?" She was glad his eyes were not machine guns as she surely would have looked like Swiss cheese.

He exploded, "FOR FUCKS SAKE! Now what are you on about you stupid bitch?!" He was behaving like a tempestuous child.

"Oh, I'm a stupid bitch? I'm not the one behaving like a schmuck, acting angry towards his wife, then going outside and being sweet and friendly to the neighbours." She paused as she grimaced and added in a sarcastic, high-pitched voice, 'Hi Henry, how are you? How's your week been?' and come back inside and rant and rave like a demented lunatic. Obviously, you can control your temper if you want to."

He roared even louder, "You stupid mother fucker! ..."

"I've told you before, don't call me names! And um, technically, you are, because I'm a mother!" Her witty ripostes were hilarious, but he looked at her menacingly as he became further incensed and now swore in German as well as English. *"Dummes stück scheiße! Was für ein dummes Arschloch!"*

When he was in this state of mind, she did her best to avoid him, but he would seek her out and continue with his belittling comments.

Wolf by name and wolf by nature!

She had seen him punch a hole in the living room wall when he was in one of his moods, causing his knuckle to swell and making him think he had broken it. His wrath had been aroused by a visitor. The son of one of their friends, with intellectual challenges, had rifled through his desk and taken his lotto entry. He never found it and was sure it had been the winning ticket. However, after injuring himself, he never punched the wall again. She had seen him pick up a chair and fling it across the room, breaking it. Another time, he stormed off to his study and slammed the door with such fury that an antique mirror fell from the wall and shattered into pieces.

"Well, that's seven years of bad luck!" Mia had called out, unafraid of his vengeful anger, but his mood had changed. He was saddened because it was a gift from Oma. She noticed that these days he took better care of his possessions. She was too exhausted to grasp that he had become unable to move beyond his own problems and that he believed it was acceptable to project his own weaknesses onto others. She never recognised that it was his own fears and vulnerabilities that he was not acknowledging.

As Alex grew, Mia relaxed more into motherhood, and began to find it less daunting. When Alex commenced eating solids, Mia gave him rice cereal, mashed banana with a couple of drops of freshly squeezed orange juice and then eventually started cooking for him as well. She would puree his food and try to get him used to tasting different flavours. She found the preparation of meals at dinner time daunting. Mia had grown up in a family where everyone ate everything. Often, Wolfie would not even taste something and declare that he did not like it and would not eat it. She was preparing three different meals every night. One night, she reached her threshold of tolerance. As she brought the dinner she had cooked to the table, she said sternly, "This is the meal I've prepared tonight. If there's something you don't like, pick it out or don't eat it. If you're still not happy, then make yourself a sandwich!"

Wolfie, being a sloth at times, and not wanting to strain a muscle making a sandwich, decided not to complain and gave Mia's cooking a try. Before he knew it, he started to appreciate her culinary skills. His list of acceptable foods grew which made things a lot easier for her. With his dietary requirements now in line with the rest of the household's, Mia wondered where Wolfie got the notions that came out of his mouth. Just like his declaration that he hated certain foods that he had never tried, he would randomly blurt out things that seemed to come from nowhere. She thought his strange ideas were because of his unusual upbringing. For instance, he also told her, "I don't want my kids to call me Dad. I want them to call me Wolfie. I've always called my parents by their first name, and I want them to do the same."

"No. I don't agree with that. They will call you Dad or Daddy as a sign of respect."

"No. They can call me Wolfie."

She really need not have worried about this because, since she always referred to Wolfie as "Daddy" when talking to Alex, in no time at all, his first word had been "Dada".

A few months later, Wolfie admitted, "You know, I actually like being called Daddy."

"Of course," came Mia's triumphant response. "It's nice." And she left it at that.

Chloe...1994
Chapter 14

When Alex was about two, Mia longed for another baby. She pined for a daughter. Wolfie stressed about finances and even though it had been difficult financially, they had managed to make ends meet. She had been on the pill since the age of 19, stopped briefly when she fell pregnant, before resuming it again and was still on it at 28. She told Wolfie that it was his turn to take care of contraception, and he would have to use condoms. He flatly refused. "If I get pregnant, then don't blame me," she sang sweetly. Mia did everything she could think of to entice him, stopping short of naked cartwheels. She was pregnant in no time. Wolfie was again angry. For years to come, he would blame her for deliberately getting pregnant not once but twice. She would simply respond, "It takes two."

Early in their marriage, prior to them having children, she remembered that she would randomly be woken in the middle of the night by him, kissing and groping her. He would then mount her, have his way, roll off and turn away from her sound asleep. The first time this had happened, she had asked in the morning, "What got into you last night?"

"What are you talking about?" he asked blankly.

"We had sex last night. Weird sex, but we had sex."

"We did? Why was it weird?" he asked confusedly.

"Don't you remember? You woke me up kissing me and being all touchy feely. You climbed on, did the deed and rolled back over to your side of the bed fast asleep."

"No. I honestly have no idea what you're talking about. I don't have any recollection of that at all."

"Listen, I've heard of sleep walking, but I've never heard of sleep fucking." If she had wanted to, she could have fallen pregnant so many times.

Mia's pregnancy progressed, and again she had all day "morning" sickness during her first trimester. She was conscientious, still going to work, dropping off and picking up Alex from long day-care, and still doing all the cooking and the house chores, coping with her increasing workload. When it came to Alex, she truly did everything for him, having changed every single one of his nappies, except for one when she had left him in Wolfie's care. Mia had come home just as Wolfie had finished cleaning a hearty mess. Alex had smeared poo all over his pram as he played with the handfuls that had leaked from his nappy. Wolfie appeared agitated.

Mia calmly said, "Obviously, you left him too long in his dirty nappy."

You were waiting for me to come home and change him. Guess you waited too long. Sucked in! Feels like karma to me, for all the times you refused to do it.

Mia was working for a large international insurance company in their finance division. With her due date not far away, she had worked again throughout her pregnancy. One day, her team leader, Nick, handed her about ten customer insurance portfolios for her to work through. She took the folders and plonked them on her desk and thought she would duck off to the toilet quickly before getting stuck into her new task. In the bathroom, she noticed a thick mucus like substance on her underpants and realised it was the show, or mucus plug. It had begun. She was in labour. The same thing had happened to her with Alex, and come to think of it, she also had the sudden onset of a nasty cold. Remembering how long it had taken with the first, she did not panic but knew that she needed to move quickly. She collected the folders and went to see Nick.

"Excuse me, Nick, but I have to go, so I need to give these back to you," she said, handing them to him.

"It's okay. Just hang onto them and look at them when you've got time. There's no rush," he said, handing them back to her.

"No, no. You don't understand I need to go NOW," insisted Mia, still trying to return the folders to him.

"You mean now? You have to go now?" with understanding and panic starting to fill his eyes.

"Yes, now. Don't say anything I don't want everyone to know," whispered Mia.

"Let me get you a taxi." He was panicking.

By the time Mia was leaving the office, everyone was wishing her well. She had the taxi take her to her mum's place. It was five in the evening so she was unable to reach Wolfie because he was at night class, and they did not have mobile phones yet. Her older brother, Nino, was picking Alex up from long day-care. Mia was in a bean bag in her parents lounge room having regular contractions and was crying, "I don't want to do this. I remember what happened the first time. It hurts."

Natalia said, "Well, it's a bit late to worry about that now. You should have thought of that nine months ago!" But she was half joking, her way of coping with any fraught situation was to use this kind of humour. Natalia, who had started dinner, looked over at Gino watching TV. He was oblivious to what was going on around him. She said, "Gino, look at her contractions and the way she's acting. I think we had better take her to the hospital. The baby is coming."

"Now? But my footy match is tonight. It's about to start." He then added with a smile as he looked over at Mia, "Don't worry, my darling daughter, anything for you, I'll get the car keys."

Mia, curled up in foetal position in the bean bag, was unaware of what was going on around her. The waves of pain towered over her and then pulsed through her. She could feel the muscles regrouping, preparing for another onslaught. The absence of pain, never again would she take it for granted.

Natalia replied, "You can just drop us off and then come back to make dinner for the younger two. Nino is working tonight."

In the delivery room, in a gown and safely in bed, the midwife, Agnes, an older and professional looking lady with short grey hair and quick, friendly eyes, gave Mia a small plastic mask so that she could administer laughing gas to herself as required.

She sucked wildly on it but felt no relief. Asking, "Is this working? Is it switched on?" as she continued inhaling desperately. She felt the urge to be on all fours. They had told her in her birthing classes that it would be her choice as to how she would like to deliver, but Agnes kept making her lie on her back which was extremely uncomfortable. The baby must have been lying on her spine. She changed her position to all fours a couple of times, and each time Agnes would make her lie down on her back again. After enduring a couple of hours of contractions, Agnes offered Mia a stronger pain killer, some Pethidine. She agreed.

Natalia said, "No, don't give it to her. Look at her. The baby will soon be here."

Agnes responded, "No, it will be hours before she delivers."

The medication given intravenously instantly dulled her pain, so much so that Mia lost interest in what was happening around her. She was completely spaced out.

"Are you alright darling?" asked Natalia concerned.

Mia moaned.

The midwife said, "Oh my gosh! The baby's crowning. It's coming. Push Mia! Push!"

Mia tried but nothing happened. Her body was unresponsive.

"Come on Mia, give me one big push," encouraged Agnes.

Natalia took umbrage at her comment, "She can't push! Look at her, she's completely zonked out!"

Mia tried again but could not command her body to move. Agnes placed her hand on her swollen abdomen and started to apply pressure. Mia groaned in pain. Agnes was sliding her hand vigorously along the length of Mia's belly propelling the baby forward. She continued repeating this forceful stroking until the baby popped out with a gush of fluid.

"Congratulations, Mrs Schmidt. It's a girl." Mia was rapt.

You poor thing. One day, you'll have to go through this too.

The baby was whisked away to another room to have her mouth suctioned as she was distressed and had pooed in the womb. Natalia wanted to follow them, but Mia who was holding her hand said, "Stay with me, Mum," as she squeezed Natalia's hand. Mia had torn again, and this was currently being stitched up. Her daughter was handed to her snugly wrapped in a blanket. Mia could only see the top of her head and her face peering from her cocoon. Those familiar almond-shaped dark blue eyes looking up at her with that mop of curly black hair just like her brother before her. Mia counted ten fingers and ten toes, all was well, and it was over. She now had the daughter she always wanted.

"Hello, Chloe", she whispered, "I'm your mum."

Natalia was bursting with pride and joy and could not wait to embrace her first born granddaughter. It had been significant for her to have witnessed her birth. Chloe had been in a hurry to enter the world and arrived in three hours and eighteen minutes. Exactly forty minutes after the Pethidine had been administered. Natalia had been right again.

Shortly after nine, Wolfie walked into the delivery room. Mia was resting as she waited for hospital staff to finish preparing her room. He spoke gently to her.

"Hello, Mia, how are you? How far along are you?"

"What? She's over there," pointing to the bassinet at the foot of her bed, "it's a girl."

"What? You've already had her? It's a girl?" Wolfie was catching up.

"We couldn't get hold of you. We tried."

"I had class tonight. I only realised something was up when I got home, and no one was there, and all the lights were off." He walked over to the bassinet and started to coo and talk gibberish to his daughter. She watched him for a while and then closed her eyes.

The next day Wolfie brought Alex in to visit them.

"Look, Alex, this is your little sister, Chloe, and she's bought you a present." As she said this Mia handed him a huge box wrapped in brightly coloured wrapping paper. She had kept this ready in her overnight bag. He excitedly ripped it open and loved the plastic tool set! Mia had read up about sibling rivalry and was prepared but she need not have bothered, for Alex had immediately fallen in love with Chloe. He had not needed any gifts. He thought she was terrific.

Mia's mother-in-law, Sabine, came to stay with them for two weeks to help with Chloe. One afternoon Sabine suggested, "Why don't I pick up Alex from day-care while you nurse Chloe?"

"I think it'd be better if I picked him up. I'm trying not to disrupt his routine, as I don't want Alex feeling neglected, unloved or jealous of his little sister now that she is taking up so much of my time. Besides, Chloe is fast asleep, and I won't be gone long." She said as she picked up her handbag and keys.

On another evening Sabine said, "Why don't I look after the children so that you can get dinner ready for Wolfie?"

Aren't you supposed to be helping me? Why don't you give me a break and you get dinner ready? This isn't a bloody resort!

Mia found herself looking forward to Sabine leaving. Despite still recovering from giving birth, dealing with cracked nipples and feeling exhausted, she was determined not to let anything drag her down; especially now that her family was complete. Little did she know that life was about to throw a seemingly insurmountable roadblock into her path.

Present Day

... 1995

Tribulations
Chapter 15

The Spastic Centre social worker lent Mia a video of the seven stages of grief. She asked Wolfie to watch it with her, but he declined, "I've got better things to do with my time. You'll let me know if there's anything worthwhile, I need to know."

Mia was very aware of the grief she was experiencing. There had been shock and denial at what Professor Fourrier had proclaimed Chloe's future would be. She had gone through the pain and guilt stage.

Is it my fault? Did I eat soft cheese? Did I drink before I found out I was pregnant? Did I take aspirin or something else before I knew? Could I have done something differently?

She called out to the universe, "WHY!?"

She asked God, "Why Chloe? When she has seen no evil, done no evil and heard no evil. Why her? Why our little family?"

There had been anger and sadness. She mourned the loss of her perfect, normal child. They had no idea what they were in for, but a vague inchoate sense of loss was beginning to take over. Mia knew in her heart that she would do what was best for her child. She had experienced the first four stages of grief in quick succession and looked forward to stage five which was the upward turn. Anything, that would help her not feeling like she was lost. She did not feel calm but thought Wolfie had skipped straight to stage five. Stage six was putting the pieces of their life back together and moving on. Mia thought they were a long way from this. The final stage being hope and acceptance. How can anyone accept?

She thought it was interesting, that when Wolfie told his family about Chloe, they did not seem concerned. Sam had actually said, "Don't worry. She'll grow out of it." Mia felt enraged by his ignorant comment as she clenched her fingers into tight fists.

What an odd thing to say? How will she grow out of it when the damage is permanent? Why is everyone so calm? Why is no one angry, yelling, screaming or crying? These people are devoid of emotions. They're like ostriches hiding their head in the sand hoping everything will go away, but it won't.

None of them could cope with a tragedy or a crisis. This rigid, emotionless behaviour baffled her.

Eventually, Mia went back to see Dr Tucker who torpedoed her into a very different, strange new world, of endless medical appointments; now she would see physiotherapists, speech therapists, occupational therapists and numerous doctors. It became apparent that Chloe's therapy sessions would be during office hours, which meant that Mia would be unable to return to her job after her three months of maternity leave. Mia rang Vivienne, her boss, to resign. Vivienne, also a mother, and valuing Mia as a team member, offered her the opportunity to work evenings from 7pm until 10pm. This was a relief for them both financially, but an extra strain on her. She again took on the burden of dealing with all of Chloe's needs, a weekly hourly appointment for hydrotherapy, physiotherapy and occupational therapy; as well as performing endless exercises with her and becoming adept at using the equipment that she needed. She found the possible implications that stretched into the future hard to face.

At one of the weekly physiotherapy appointments, Mia asked, "Will Chloe be able to wear stilettos?"

"No. She'll be able to wear them but will find them uncomfortable and difficult to walk in, so she'll choose never to wear them," she answered honestly. This had crushed her. Mia had had visions of shopping with her daughter for these girly things in the future. Her little dream had filled her with happiness, but just like that, it had been abruptly quashed. Mia relayed this story to her long-time friends, Josephine and Ezra, who also had a disabled son. He was confined to a wheelchair and could not speak.

Ezra had replied, "I did the same thing. I asked the specialist if Blair would ever be able to bike ride. I had the same reaction when he told me he would never be able to." Ezra was a keen mountain bike rider and had hoped to do this activity with his son. Ezra continued, "When we were in the doctor's office, and were told that Blair had cerebral palsy, the doctor said, 'With a lot of love and support from your family you will be able to get through this.' I said, 'Oh well, we're fucked then, aren't we?!' The doctor looked a little surprised and said, 'No. Not necessarily', and I said, 'Well, if you're telling me that I have to count on love and family support, then there must be no other options available, so we're fucked!' "

This had amused Mia; though not a funny story, Ezra's delivery had been entertaining, and like her, he was a realist.

Natalia worried about Mia, as she watched her daughter spiral down into an abyss of darkness, filled with sorrow. She had started gaining weight, something she had never done before, as she ate chocolate every day. She was beginning to fit snugly into her size 12 clothes when she had previously been a 10.

Finally, Natalia said, "What are you doing? Are you trying to look like me? You're putting on weight. Stop it! Otherwise, it will be too hard to lose!" She listened to her mum.

Mia realised that Wolfie was struggling too with the news concerning their daughter. His mother, Sabine, had just moved to Queensland, and rarely visited. His brother, Thomas, was also living overseas, and his father, Sam, was often travelling abroad with Tammy. He was not getting the support he needed from his family. He did not have a network of friends he could turn to, having never bothered to keep in touch with his university friends, and he saw his best friend, Stephen, maybe three times a year. Just when the rough spot in their marriage had smoothed out recently, now it seemed they had hit another bumpy patch.

I think it's about to hit the fan again! He's about to fall apart. I'm going to need to be strong for everyone, Alex, Chloe, Wolfie, and myself.

She took the colander from the cupboard and a bag of green beans and sat at the dining room table. She snapped the ends off each bean and tossed it into the colander as her mind began to wonder. She quietly studied Wolfie who was watching a documentary on TV, lying on the couch. He was so still she could not make out if he was even breathing. He was moodier than usual, quiet and withdrawn. He had stopped talking to her. She knew a storm was brewing inside him, slowly taking over.

She prayed again, like she had done so many times before, *Please God, give me strength! Who knew my life would become so tough? They say love is blind. Who knew that Wolfie would be so difficult? Was he always like that and I just didn't see it?*

***

Wolfie was working hard at his job and was also still studying at university. Mia was displeased at the friend he had made. Lisa was in her early twenties and obviously enamoured of him, the older man. She proceeded to call him most nights to talk about her boyfriend problems. Mia did not appreciate this one bit! He would be sympathetic and listen to her tales but had completely shut Mia out, leaving her feeling isolated and hurt.

One day, Mia was drying Chloe after her bath on the change table. She was now five months old, and they had just returned from a week's holiday in Queensland. Mia thought Wolfie must have been feeling better since he had organised the trip. Maybe he was finding his way back to her. Wolfie walked into the room and spoke clearly and calmly, "Mia, I'm leaving you. I don't love you anymore and I haven't loved you for the last year. It's best that you get on with your life, and me with mine."

"What are you talking about? How can you say that? That's news to me! Is it Lisa? You're happy talking to her and offering her a shoulder to cry on but what about your wife?" replied Mia, overwhelmed, but he walked away picking up his wallet and car keys, heading for the door.

She yelled out after him, "That's right, walk away! Do what you do best, with your tail between your legs, you coward. Don't worry about your children, I'll raise them on my own and give them a good life, because that's the difference between you and me. I'm not chicken shit like you!" The door slammed and he was gone. She knew he would be back. Like her, he had nowhere else to go.

Mia was reeling from her husband's cruel words and had not yet told her family or her friends what was really going on. His daughter's dire prognosis had obviously been a shock to him too. He had been keeping his feelings in a tight knot inside himself and was now, finally, reacting. It seemed surreal to her and she hoped that he would soon come back to his senses.

The following day he left work early and dropped in on her parents. Natalia was home alone watering the garden. As he'd been married to her daughter for seven years, with two children, she was naturally pleased with his impromptu visit. She waved to him as she turned off the tap and walked over to greet him. He said, "Mia and I are breaking up. I don't love her anymore and I haven't loved her for the last year."

Natalia burst into tears and was unsure what to say, "Are you sure?"

"Yes. If I don't leave her now, I'll leave her in the future. So, I might as well do it now; that way we can both get on with our lives. It's for the best," he said, composed.

He suggested, "I think it would be a good idea if you built a granny flat in the backyard, then Mia could live there with Alex and Chloe …" Natalia continued to openly weep.

He then proceeded to tell all their friends that he was leaving her, that he no longer loved her and had not loved her for the last year. He told his family the same story. Things deteriorated further between them.

One day, Julie had called Mia for a chat. Wolfie answered the phone. "Hello."

"Hey Wolfie, it's Julie, how are you?"

"Hi Julie, I'm good. Listen, there's something you should know. I'm leaving Mia. I haven't loved her for the past year." He seemed happy to spread his news to anyone who would listen, and each time he did, Mia felt a flutter of anxiety in her stomach.

"What? Are you sure? What's happened?"

"I'll put Mia on, she can explain it to you." Mia was in the bedroom nursing Chloe.

"Here, it's Julie. I've told her." Mia looked at him disapprovingly as he walked away. She felt her voice trembling and becoming a wall of water as she sobbed on the phone to her friend. Julie was surprised to learn of the difficult time she was going through. She had even tried to call Wolfie back to talk him out of it, but he was adamant. He was shouting his news from the rooftops. Kikki, a friend of theirs from their university days living in England, called for a chat. He picked up the phone in the lounge room, "Hello."

"Wolfie! It's Kikki. It's lovely to hear your voice! How are you?" Kikki always sounded excited. Again, he shared his intentions of leaving. His news was now international. Kikki also called him weekly for more than a month, trying to talk him out of it, concerned that he was making the biggest mistake of his life. She eventually gave up when he started getting abusive towards her.

Despite being separated for four months, they still lived under the same roof. His mother came to visit him from Queensland to support him, and snubbed Mia. The children were asleep upstairs in their beds. She deliberately spoke in German, so Mia could not understand, but would sometimes add in English, "She's so stupid," so that Mia knew exactly who she was talking about.

Sabine had sat down at the dining room table with Wolfie, and then turned to her and said, "Why don't we all sit down and see if we can't work this out?"

Mia felt herself erupting, "This is between Wolfie and me. It has nothing to do with you! How dare you come into my house, speak only in German, and occasionally add in English, "Oh, she's so stupid." This is still my house. So kindly show some respect or you can leave."

Sabine got up abruptly and walked towards her with her hand in the air like she was about to hit her, as she angrily muttered, "I'll show you some respect."

Mia stood there without fear.

Lay one finger on me you stupid bitch and I'll pulverise you. Just give me a reason. Go ahead. Do it!

She waited unflinchingly for the blow. Sabine's hand stopped short of her face. Mia threw her a triumphant look. She then turned to Wolfie, "You'd better control your mother! If she lays a hand on me, I'll call the police and have her charged." She could see that he had been taken aback by his mother's hostile behaviour. It had been unnecessary, but he had not intervened.

A few days later, she received a letter penned by Sabine.

Dear Mia,

You are a member of our family just like Wolfie is. So, I will tell you exactly what I would tell him. Life has not turned out how you had hoped, but nevertheless, you have created your life the way it is. Nobody else is to blame.

You've both decided to buy a house you can only afford on two salaries, and you've decided to have children. There's never any guarantee that our children will be the easiest and healthiest. When we decide to have a child, we say we want to be responsible for their souls no matter what. It's tough to come to terms with the fact that YOU have produced a child with a problem, but it happens to a lot of people, and they manage. The sooner you can let go of the guilt, the outrage, the despair, the sooner you can concentrate on doing what's best for them.

Now the way you came at me that other night was unnecessary when I was trying to help. I'd been considering ways of enabling you to stay at home. You destroyed that. I still want to do everything possible for Alex and Chloe, but I feel the connection between you and me is broken. It will take some time for that to heal again. Respect is something you earn; it can never be demanded.

Anyway, if you're going through a tough time in your life, accusing and damaging others will not make things easier. It'll erode whatever support there would've been and you'll end up alone and bitter. I hope that maybe soon we can have a talk together and start rebuilding our relationship.

Sabine

Mia was incredulous. All the things Sabine was accusing her of, were things that Wolfie was doing. He was the one abandoning them. She had only ever blamed herself secretly, and no one else. So, this was where Wolfie got his stupid idea that respect had to be earned. More pieces of the puzzle were falling into place and creating a worrying picture.

When Mia saw the way Wolfie's family were ignoring her, she decided to write to Oma to tell her what was happening and about Chloe's condition. Mia believed she had a right to know. She had always come across as a loving, caring and warm individual, unlike the rest of them. Sabine was furious when she realised what Mia had done. Sabine did not want Oma to know, saying she was too old and frail and "the shock would be too much for her". Oma was outraged by her daughter's meddling ways and was glad that Mia had come to her for assistance. She asked Sabine to stop interfering. In her next letter to Oma, Mia took delight in enclosing a copy of Sabine's offensive letter.

Mia felt caught in a chaotic vortex. She was still coming to terms with what had happened to her daughter. She was uncomprehending of Wolfie's family so readily accepting his decision. She could not understand why they were not appalled by their son's behaviour. Her husband was leaving her because he was a perfectionist, and did not want to be associated with his disabled daughter. She worried about what her future would look like, raising two children on her own, and continually caring for this helpless individual. Would she be able to work full-time? If she did, how would she get Chloe to her daytime appointments? Would she be able to manage on her own financially? She tried not to dwell on the worrying thoughts that kept entering her mind.

It was during this time that her friend at work, Aston, came to her rescue. He was a good friend and was disgusted with the behaviour and attitudes of Wolfie. He was determined to be there for her and sent her a huge bunch of flowers at work to cheer her up. She took the flowers home and placed them in a vase in the middle of the dining room table. They looked spectacular.

Wolfie, walking past, asked, "Who are the flowers from?"

"Wouldn't you like to know!"

Aston would console her when she was upset. Slowly their friendship turned into something more. He worked out at the gym, and it looked as if his rippling muscles would burst through his shirts, like the skin of a ripened nectarine. He was tall and dark and had warm green eyes and always make her laugh with his sense of humour. Their personalities were almost identical, and it was as if they had been friends for years.

Their work Christmas party was coming up and Aston was on the social committee. The theme was Hollywood movie stars. Mia was looking forward to dancing the night away and releasing some tension. The event was being held at the Convention Centre in Darling Harbour for more than a thousand staff members. Mia dressed as Audrey Hepburn and looked sensational. She wore a tight full-length black gown with her hair gathered on top of her head in a loose messy bun with a sparkly tiara. She accessorized with long gloves and pearls around her elegant neck. She danced with Aston, enjoying the festivities.

By the end of the evening, they were both tipsy. As they were saying their farewells, he leaned in for a peck. It turned into a long, passionate French kiss. Mia quickly pulled away. She was surprised at how easily it had happened. When they saw each other at work the following Monday, it was as if nothing had happened. He always worked back and their desks were side by side. They easily slipped into conversation as they always did. It was not awkward at all. One day, Mia was home alone, and Aston came over for lunch. They ate together and when he got up to leave, he grabbed Mia and kissed her passionately. She fell into his arms. They were naked in no time, ravishing each other's bodies. She needed to be loved, but he unexpectedly pre-ejaculated all over her stomach. He apologised profusely. It turned out that he was experiencing problems in the bedroom with his wife. He was either having trouble maintaining an erection or he would ejaculate before they had even begun. This made Mia realise that an affair was not what she needed or wanted. When he left that day, she cut him off and never spoke to him again. Besides how many complications in life could one person handle?

About a week later, she received a card from him. It had giant sunflowers on the cover.

Dear Mia, I'm sorry that I took advantage of our friendship and of you. I know you're vulnerable and I should've been a better friend. I'm truly sorry. Aston.

As she tossed his card in the bin, Mia realised that she had not had an affair seven years ago. She felt the guilt lift slightly from her shoulders. It was a much-needed relief. She finally understood that what had happened was rape and began forgiving herself. Although Natalia thought Wolfie was a coward, she was grateful that Mia was finally beginning the climb up from her dark chasm of despair. His betrayal had made her fighting instincts kick in to get her back to the surface.

A few weeks later, Wolfie suggested that they go to mediation to work out the division of their assets, which basically consisted of their home.

Mia said, "I can't go with you. Look at me, I'm a mess. You can only mediate if you're in agreement, which I'm not. That's not what I want. I would rather hold your hand and go to counselling."

"Do you want to give it another shot?" he asked gently.

"Yes."

She never told Wolfie what had happened with Aston. Wolfie also never asked why Aston and his wife were never invited for dinner. Shortly after this, Mia was also made redundant. The company decided to outsource their financial services to India, and she never saw Aston again.

Mia then found a job in a pathology lab, all night on Wednesday and Thursday. Wolfie was impressed. "You're so good at finding jobs, and a night shift. I don't know how you do it! I don't think I'd be able to do that."

"We can't survive on your salary alone. If I could find a night-time accounting role, I'd take it. If I can find a decent childcare facility for Chloe when she's a bit older, then I'll put her into care and find a part-time accounting job. Until then, I'll take what I can and this way I can still take her to appointments."

"You've got balls, Mia. I wouldn't be able to do half the things you do."

Why not? Save me the praise, please. It would be nice if sometimes you pulled your finger out and just did it, like I do. If I can do it, then you can too. I'm not some super woman!

Mia was still confused about her feelings.

Did I have an affair with Aston? We got naked together, cuddled and kissed.

She looked up the definition in the dictionary. "An affair is a romantic affair, and refers to sexual liaisons among unwed or wedded parties. A casual relationship which is a physical and emotional connection between two people who may have sex without expecting a more formal romantic relationship. An affair is by its nature romantic."

Interesting. I don't think what I had was the slightest bit romantic. It was a fling that lasted about 30 seconds, but you accused me of having an affair the first time, even though I told you that it happened against my will! I guess that makes us even.

She was clearing the plates from the table one evening after dinner.

"So, what made you decide to come back?" she asked.

"Well, I thought you would have no trouble finding someone else, and I didn't want my kids calling someone else Dad," came his quick reply.

"Well, if that's the only reason you've come back. You can fuck off again!"

"Oh, and I love you too," he replied matter-of-factly. She looked and listened for signs of sarcasm. There were none!

Are you being insincere? Is that the best you can do? Me Me Me! What about us?

Though this was not the way she would have liked him to answer, she accepted it and decided to give it another go. She had loved him, and still did. She remembered the charming, young man who had taken her breath away and longed for his return. She knew she had looked the other way so many times because she loved him. She wanted her marriage to work, and divorce to her, would mean failure. She wanted a successful life. She wanted to try because he was the father of her children and wondered if marriage counselling would be a feasible option with these types of responses from him.

Nevertheless, they tried it again. Wolfie organised it. Yvonne had changed jobs and moved on. Their new counsellor was Michael. He was an older gentleman in his late fifties and showed the effect of Melanesian admixture in the thickness and protrusion of his lips, the flatness of his nose, and his widespread nostrils. He was still married to his first wife, which Mia thought was a good sign, obviously being able to preach from experience. He let them talk about their issues. Mia said, "He can't accept that he has a disabled daughter. That she's not perfect. He is ashamed and embarrassed."

Wolfie squirmed in his chair, his hands clutching his thighs, his knuckles white. "That's not true. It was just a shock. Family is important to me. It's everything."

Mia complained that Wolfie did not help around the house, whilst she did all the cooking, cleaning, child rearing, worked and dealt with anything else that required attention.

"What about if you cooked dinner once a week on a Sunday night to give Mia a break, Wolfie? And what about if you also took over the laundry. You should also be participating and contributing as a member of the family."

Mia agreed, as did Wolfie.

"Is there anything else you would like to discuss, Mia?"

"I've had enough of his temper! He's always flying off the handle at the smallest thing. And when he is working back, he never calls me to say that he will be late, and I go to the trouble of making him dinner."

"Why can't you give her a call?"

"I honestly don't think about it," he answered with a sheepish grin on his face. Michael threw him a disapproving look.

"I don't mean it like that," he continued. "I just get bogged down with what I'm working on and time flies by. I don't even realise the time. I'll try harder to remember to call her."

"Anyway, one night that he hadn't called, and I had again made dinner. I realised he wasn't coming home so I was putting everything away, when he walked through the door at 9.30pm to ask, 'What's for dinner?' I said, 'Nothing. The kitchen is closed.' "

"Fair enough," said Michael.

"Exactly. I said, 'You couldn't be bothered to call me to let me know that you would be running late. Dinner is done.' There was a plate of pasta on the countertop. He asked, 'What's that?' I replied, 'Nothing.' He took the plate and hurled it to the ceiling. It smashed into a thousand pieces and rained spaghetti all over the kitchen. There were stains from the pasta sauce on the ceiling!"

"What happened next?"

"I said, 'I'm not cleaning that,' and went to bed."

"I will try to control my temper. I haven't done anything like that since."

"Did you clean it?" asked Michael. Wolfie nodded.

"Though not very well. I ended up scrubbing the ceiling! He always makes things harder than they need to be. I don't know how many times I've asked when he comes home to say 'Hello' and give me a kiss. HE CAN'T BE BOTHERED TO DO IT! NEVER!"

Michael looked at Wolfie, "Come on, Wolfie, it's common courtesy."

"Exactly!" huffed Mia.

Wolfie laughed nervously, "Okay. Okay."

Wolfie had been romantic, exciting and fun. Now he was childish, mean and petulant, using arguments and picking fights to take his frustrations out on her, which was wearing her down, but he seemed to be listening to Michael and to her. Maybe there was still hope for them to find their way back to each other.

Life goes on ...
Chapter 16

Putting this good advice into practice was not easy, but eventually they started to function as a family. Both were still committed to their relationship. Mia attempted to shield Wolfie from any further problems by continuing to handle Chloe's needs, knowing she could never lean on him. Though she found it tough at times, she accepted it as her life and dealt with it.

She dragged Alex along to his sister's appointments. He would sit in the corner distracted by tasty snacks and colouring activities.

As they drove home, Mia talked to him and asked him questions, "What colour are the trees?"

"Green!"

"What colour is the car?"

"Red!" he yelled without hesitation, enjoying this game.

"What colour is Chloe's hair?"

Mia watched him in the rear vision mirror as he hesitated while studying her hair, before finally yelling in triumph, "Lellow!"

Chloe did now have a head of blonde curly hair and it amused her even more that Alex could not say the word yellow properly yet. He was adorable with his round spectacles, mop of brown hair and big smile. He was Mia's joy. She could not understand why Wolfie did not seem to enjoy these precious moments with their young children like she did. Especially, when she could see that he was still grappling with this life, so she decided to join them into a coffee club organised by parents from the Spastic Centre. She thought it might do him some good to talk with other dads in the same situation. It proved successful as Wolfie looked forward to the monthly social gatherings. Everyone took turns inviting the group to their place (adults only), no children, for either a potluck or themed dinner, or whatever else they desired. They both made some real connections with these people. After all, they were all dealing with the same problem.

Mia also found it comforting to talk to these mums. They were very informed on every aspect of living with a physically or mentally challenged child. As their children were older than Chloe, they had much more experience and knew about the services available. They also gave insights into what could happen next and how best to handle and overcome whatever it might be. Mia considered herself lucky because she thought Chloe was one of the least affected children in the group. It was also helpful for her to talk to these mums about how she was feeling, as she had no one else in her circle who could understand firsthand what she was going through. One of the mums in the group gave Mia a poem by Edna Massimilla called, "Is Heaven's Special Child" which offered her some peace. She found any kind words soothed her aching soul.

Mia was close to her mother and rang her daily, usually in the evening when the children were entertaining themselves and Wolfie was still at work. It was only to her mother that Mia felt comfortable venting about how things were at home. She was sickened by Wolfie's behaviour and did not want it influencing the children.

After dispensing with pleasantries, Natalia asked, "How are the children? How's Wolfie?"

"The kids are well, but Wolfie's been driving me up the wall!"

"Now … what has he done?" asked Natalia, sounding frustrated.

"I was in the kitchen peeling potatoes when I could hear this click, click, click noise coming from the dining table."

Natalia sounding curious, "What was he doing?"

"He was sitting there cutting his toenails. Bits of nail were flying everywhere in the kitchen, flicking all over the floor, in every direction."

"Oh yuck," Natalia chuckled.

"I asked, 'Do you have to do that here?' I was furious. He said, 'It's more comfortable.' Then I realised he was using my kitchen scissors! I flipped. I went over to him and snatched them out of his hands. I said, 'Gimme those!' "

"Men can be such pigs," Natalia replied with disgust.

"I said, 'Do that upstairs with the toenail clippers. That's what they're there for.' He went upstairs sulking. He can be so sickening! I swear sometimes, he acts like a child! When people ask me if I'm married with children, I say, yes, I have two, but I also have a husband, so that makes three!" Natalia was laughing.

"He can be so vile, Mum. Sometimes when we're driving in the car, he thinks I don't see him picking his nose, and making snot balls that he flicks out the window. He can be absolutely nauseating."

Natalia again said disgustedly, "A lot of men pick their noses."

"Thankfully, he doesn't eat his harvest in front of me and I make sure he doesn't touch me with that hand either." Natalia laughed harder.

***

As Alex grew up, he wanted to spend more time with his father, but Wolfie was always too tired. Mia would start singing *"Cats in the Cradle"* by Harry Chaplin, about a father and son's relationship. As the child grows up, their relationship changes from a busy father neglecting his son to a busy son neglecting his father. Wolfie would throw Mia a disparaging look. He would then play ball with his son. It would inevitably end in tears as it would not take long for Alex to receive a ball to the head or the face and the fun would be over. Alex's ball skills were not yet fully developed and Wolfie could never bring himself to play to Alex's level of ability because he lacked patience and was competitive. He would go through the motions of playing and could then claim, "Well, at least I tried."

Before Chloe arrived, Mia had liked nothing more than rushing home from work to collect her son. She would play with him, helping him put the shapes in the matching slot in the container, stacking blocks and driving cars around on his mat that looked like a city. She adored spending time with him and reading to him, and he loved the attention. One day they were looking through a picture book together, and he said, "Awful Tower?"

Mia repeated puzzled, "Awful Tower? What's that?"

He turned the page in the book and pointed to the Eiffel Tower. Mia laughed. When it was time to get dinner ready, she would say, "It's time for Mummy to go do some cooking." Alex would repeat, "Ga-goong! Ga-goong! Ga-goong!" This always made her laugh. He was bathed and quietly gurgling by the time his father got home.

With two children, she found she had less time, as she had to bathe them both, usually putting them in the tub together to save time, do Chloe's exercises and sterilise bottles. Even though the list of tasks was endless, she did it all unfazed and before Wolfie had walked in the door.

When Alex was a toddler and cried because he was upset, Wolfie would say, "Stop acting like an old woman."

She loathed this expression, and would correct him, "You mean, old man".

Wolfie would continue, "He's acting like an old woman."

Mia would persist, "How do you know an old woman behaves like that? Does Oma? I think it's definitely more old man's behaviour." He knew what she was getting at, but he would continue arguing with her.

Eventually, he would turn his wrath on her, as if it was her fault, because she had dared stand up to him. She knew he would, but at times she'd had enough of his constant criticism, bullying tactics, verbal abuse, invalidation and cruel behaviour. His father had also treated his family in the same way and this had obviously become learned behaviour. She did not want this pattern to be repeated with their son. It was to stop HERE and NOW.

Mia never badgered him, thinking there were better ways of making him behave appropriately. She avoided deliberately picking fights with him as he did with her. She ensured that things ran fluidly in the home, never realising that by intentionally avoiding confrontations, she was handing power over to him. This was the price she paid to keep the peace.

Wolfie, though better with the toddler phase of his son's life, could not cope with injury or sickness. If Alex fell over and scraped his knee, Wolfie never picked him up to comfort him. It was always Mia. One evening, even though he had been wearing anti-slip socks, Alex had walked into the kitchen and slipped on the tiled floors. His legs went out from underneath him, and he fell back, his head hitting the floor with a gut-wrenching thud. He let out a blood-curdling scream and started to cry. Wolfie stormed away in an angry fit. It was Mia who ran to help him. She soothed him, ensuring he was uninjured.

It was a new day, and the smell of freshly made custard wafted through the house as it sat cooling on the bench, forming a skin that when pushed created folds. Wolfie came to find Mia to proudly announce that he had passed his last exam and was now a fully qualified accountant. Mia was thankful that it was finally over and that she could have her husband back. He then announced that he would be commencing his Certified Public Accountancy studies. Again, this meant that he would be spending all weekend studying upstairs and not helping Mia around the house. She felt like a single mum; he never spent time with them, and it was up to her to entertain the children and keep them quiet so that Daddy could study in peace. She had also not yet completed her own CPA and needed to do so for her career. But he always did what he wanted when he wanted! Whilst he banished himself upstairs, she would bring him cups of tea and snacks and would find him sitting in the reclining armchair, feet up on the Ottoman, notes opened on his lap staring out the window.

"Are you actually studying? Each time I come up here, you're staring out the window daydreaming. Are you actually getting anything done?"

"Yes, yes. I'm thinking about my notes, making sure that I understand what I'm reading." Mia would sometimes sit and chat with him for a minute before making herself scarce. If she stayed too long, he would ask her to leave because he needed to study. Despite feeling that she asked for little, she felt again like she was not receiving much from him.

Out of Sync
Chapter 17

Mia organised for her little sister, Sophie, who was now in her teens, to come and babysit so that they could have SOME time together. They sat in a modest restaurant, studying the menu. After a while, Wolfie said, "Check out the something sweet section. This place has some sweet- sounding desserts, excuse the pun!"

Mia chuckled, "I was just looking at that too. The chocolate mousse and the sticky date pudding sound divine."

"I was eyeing the crème caramel and the black forest cake. What do you think? Should we indulge?" he replied, a smile curling his lips.

"That's extremely decadent!" replied Mia, trying to sound responsible.

"Come on, Mia, once in a while won't hurt. I'm thinking entrée, main and dessert." They ordered three desserts each for their dinner. They both enjoyed their sinful and gluttonous meal.

The next time Mia booked a German restaurant. She was looking forward to having as much fun as they had the last time they had dined out together. Their lederhosen-attired waiter took their order, Albondigas meatballs and for their main they both had schnitzel with potato rosti. For dessert, they both settled on an apple strudel with vanilla ice cream. She had decided to try and spice things up a little. They were about halfway through their main, with Wolfie happily digging into his schnitzel. Mia leaned in and whispered, "I'm not wearing any panties."

"What …?" he asked looking at her as if she had sprouted a second head.

Again, in whispered tones, and accentuating every word, whilst keeping eye contact with him, she whispered, "I'm not wearing any knickers."

"What …?" replied Wolfie in astonishment, and in the same breath, "That's disgusting!"

Mia watched Wolfie's face; it was riddled with bewilderment and genuine disgust. He repeated, "That's disgusting!" his eyes darting to the left and the right, as if to check that no one seated close to them could overhear.

"Why …?" asked Wolfie, perturbed.

"Why not?" shrugged Mia. "It's liberating."

Wolfie let out a small nervous chuckle and proceeded to make cat crying noises for the rest of the evening. "Meow. Meoooowwww. Meow. Is pussy saying meow?" The meaning of his response was unclear to her, and she was disappointed that he did not have the sudden urge to whisk her away somewhere private and ravish her. She never bothered again.

Years later, Mia was at work, sitting at her desk in an open plan office when her colleague, Hannah, would tell her about her evening. "I took Bill out for a romantic dinner last night. Halfway through the meal, I leaned in and whispered, "I'm not wearing any underpants." Hannah laughed as she said, "Well, he couldn't get me out of that restaurant fast enough!"

Mia thought she was very fortunate but kept quiet, never telling outsiders what it was really like.

***

When Alex was four and Chloe was one, they moved into their own five-bedroom home with a yellow timber picket fence and plenty of curb side appeal, after Wolfie decided they had outgrown their townhouse with two children. Mia thought that everything was going well in their lives, their family, their relationship, and that the worst was behind them.

One evening, Mia went to the pantry and took two onions and some garlic cloves from the metal basket and placed them on the chopping board as she pulled out a knife from the drawer. She heard his keys jangling at the door, and went to greet him, as she often did. She could picture herself as a Labrador, being as gleeful as one when her beloved came home. She ripped the door open before the keys could finish turning in the lock. As he stepped inside, she threw her arms around him, and stood up on her tippy toes to give him a kiss. He pulled a face of repugnance as he stooped down and offered her his cheek.

"Hey, what's with the cheek! Have you got cold sores?"

"No," he replied, shaking his head.

"Well then, stop pulling a face and pucker up!" They pecked on the lips. On one such occasion, he said to her, "It would be really nice, if sometimes when I came home, you would drop to your knees and give me a blow job."

Mia was aghast, but chose to laugh off his comment. "Don't be so feral! You make me wanna barf!"

"I'm not. I'm just saying that sometimes it would be nice. I've had a hard day at the office. It's been a long, exhausting day, and it would be nice to come home, and have you drop to your knees and give me a blow job."

"Yeah, well, that's never going to happen. When you walk in the door, I'm busy in the kitchen getting dinner ready for you, and there are kids about. What about them? And what about having a shower?"

He continued, "I'm just saying. It would be nice."

She shrugged her shoulders and stalked back to the kitchen to finish making the home-made pizza for tonight's dinner. Had he forgotten that she had also had a full day at work? She had not stopped since she had walked in the door, having picked up the kids from after school care, and long day-care, and then sat down to help Alex with his reading and find out about his day. If he had any extracurricular activities after school, it was also Mia who taxied him to them.

Have you forgotten who you're talking to? I'm your wife, not your sex slave! I'm a human being, not just a series of orifices for your pleasure! You disgusting pig! Surely you must be joking. I couldn't think of anything worse than sucking on your unwashed penis that's been sweating in your office pants all day! Cheese dick! Gross! I always have to shower before any action, but you don't. I don't think so.

Although she found his comments offensive, she did not pick a fight and chose to laugh it off. He had once said, "Sometimes your words cut like a knife," but so could his. He would complain a few more times, about his need for his homecoming blow job. He was acting like a child again, and Mia did not have enough energy to deal with that kind of behaviour on top of everything else. He quit mentioning it after realising that it would never eventuate.

What was he thinking? What about Alex and Chloe in the next room? Did he want his children to witness this exchange? Did he want them scarred for life?

When they moved into their new home, Wolfie started talking about a threesome. The first time he had just mentioned it in passing, the same way he would have said, "I'd love a cup of tea please," but he had said, "I'd really like to have a threesome one day with you and another."

Mia though shocked, had just laughed this off, "That's never going to happen."

When she rang and spoke to her mother the next day, making sure that Nonna was out of ear shot, she said, "Mamma, you know what he said to me last night, and don't tell Papa or Nonna. Okay?"

"Okay," Natalia laughed.

"I'm serious, Mamma. Don't tell them. Especially Nonna. I hate the way she says things like, 'He's your husband. He should be treated like a king,' and all of that other rubbish! Last night, he said that one day he would like to have a threesome. He said he didn't want to die having only been with me."

"He's sick," Natalia replied with revulsion in her voice.

"His words hurt me, because I always thought it was romantic that we were each other's first. I don't know if he was kidding or not, but it's never going to happen! There is no way I'm ever going to do that! He also always wants a blow job! I'm sick of hearing about it."

"Oh, that's disgusting." Mia could hear the nausea in her voice, as Natalia continued, "I'm lucky, your father has never asked me to do anything like that."

"You're right, you are lucky, Mum, to have found such a nice man as Dad. I find I'm continuously fighting with Wolfie about the stupid sex stuff that he wants. He can be such a pig at times!"

When Mia hung up the phone, she sat on the sofa and resumed her knitting. Outside, a dog barked, and a lawn mower started. Inside, the washing machine finished its cycle and beeped twice. Her knitting needles made their soft clicking noise whenever they met. Mia noticed that Wolfie was again struggling emotionally. He had taken a break from his studies and told her that he felt suicidal at times.

She once again took pity on him. "Why don't you take it easy? Relax, Babe, did you want to watch some TV? I'll look after the children." She brought him an endless supply of beverages and ran him hot baths to help him relax.

He said tenderly, "I love you, Mia. I love your caring, nurturing side. It's one of the nicest things about you. It makes me feel loved when you bring me cups of tea and coffee." She smiled at him as she always did.

She emphasised all the blessings that he had in his life. "You've got so much to be thankful for. You have a wonderful life with your gorgeous wife, family, and comfortable home."

He replied nodding, "I know."

"I know I've said this before, but why don't you go get some help? Why don't you make an appointment with Dr Knight and see if there is something he can help with? Review your medication. Recommend a new therapist."

"Yeah, maybe." He never did, and she did not know what more she could do.

His libido was low due to his depression and exacerbated by his anti-depressants. He had been taking them for years, and they had not made love in a while. Although she made him aware of her availability, she never pressured him. Because his rejection hurt her, she had learned to let him be.

Finally, one evening, he was in the mood. Mia was grateful; maybe he was starting to feel better. Looking deep into her eyes, he pulled her close as he kissed her deeply. She frantically returned his kiss, her soft lips melded into his and his tongue excited her and sent shock waves through her entire body. Why did his kisses feel so good? Why did he only kiss her like this when they made love? Her desire was insatiable, she felt as if she was about to self-combust as she arched her back and surrendered to his touch. His hands all over her, worshipping her body, finding every hidden nook of pleasure. She pressed herself against him, feeling his hardness, "Fuck me please! Just fuck me!" she heard herself moan. He came quickly, shuddering as he gave one last feral thrust inside her, collapsing onto her breasts, spent, their bodies pressed together. Both of their hearts beating hard. Though he did not bring her to orgasm, she still loved having sex because she felt close and connected to him. It was not the sex that she wanted but more comfort and reassurance of his love. Afterwards, they lay on the sheet, damp bodies spooned together, naked and fitting together like two pieces of Lego. She loved the skin to skin contact that sex afforded her. She craved it. As he held her in his arms, he said, "Sometimes, I feel like I've got nothing to live for. Sometimes I just want to kill myself."

Mia felt the familiar surge of exasperation and simply exploded, "Then why don't you just do it! "I'm sick of hearing about how you want to kill yourself! That you've got nothing to live for! Then just do it!"

"Fine! You'll get your wish. If that's what you want, then I'll DO IT!"

"How can you say you've got nothing to live for? What am I? Chop Suey? What about the children? Your beautiful home? If you honestly believe that you've got nothing to live for, then do it. I'm sick of you holding that over me! Don't try to guilt me by telling me I'll get what I want. It's what you want not me!" She continued as she tossed the bedding aside and got out of bed, "And however you choose to do it, don't make a mess because I'm tired of cleaning up after you!" She left the room fuming.

Oddly enough, after this exchange, he never mentioned it again. Had she called his bluff? Or had he decided to never share his dark thoughts with her again?

Fissures
Chapter 18

Outside, the magpies warbled. Inside, there had just been some drama. Mia rang Wolfie excitedly.

"Hey, Wolfie! Guess what? I've got great news! The kids have just had their first fight."

"Hey, Babe, what are you talking about?"

"Chloe took one of Alex's toys and wouldn't give it back. She watched amused as he screamed and cried. She had such a devious, cheeky look on her face. It was great!"

Wolfie laughed. "That's good news, is it?"

"Well, it's so NORMAL! They've never had a fight before. That's what siblings are supposed to do, and I never thought they would. I never thought they would interact with each other. It's fantastic!" Alex was five and Chloe about two. Though Mia was pleased, the novelty soon wore off!

Since the age of one the Spastic Centre had periodically plastered Chloe's right leg and alternatively her arm to get them into the correct position. To get her to weight bear and eventually stand on her own, they then started plastering both legs. They would plaster her in such a way that it would look like she was wearing wide open-toed boots. They were bulky like moon boots, the idea being that, with a solid wide foundation, this would give Chloe the confidence to stand. On one such occasion, Mia had Chloe in her stroller and was out shopping. Chloe was cute with her curly locks poking out from under her red tartan hat. She had on a matching dress with both her legs plastered in bright pink plaster. She was a very happy child. Always bright-eyed and smiling. They entered the lift and a couple in their fifties joined them. Chloe smiled up at them.

"What a little sweetheart!" exclaimed the wife. "What have you got there? That's a cute little piglet. Is that your friend?" she cooed. Chloe beamed at her as she snuggled the little bean bag pig that she carried everywhere with her, under her right arm.

"Hello, little darling. How are you? What's happened to you? Have you broken both your legs?" asked the husband. He then turned to Mia, "What happened to her?"

Mia was fed up with the invasion of privacy, continually being asked this by strangers. She also resented the tone and implication that often came with a stranger's query, maybe there was child abuse going on at home. The lift doors opened, and as Mia exited with Chloe, she said through gritted teeth and in a deadpan voice.

"She wouldn't eat her broccoli."

At first, the gentleman looked stunned, and then quickly regained his composure. "Oh, good one! You had me going for a moment there!" He was laughing. The lift doors closed behind them. She could still hear them both laughing as they walked away.

When it came time to removing her plasters, Mia would be filled with dread. Chloe would scream as if her limb was being amputated, terrified by the noise of the electric saw. It was safe as it would stop on contact with skin, but it would take three of them to hold her down and keep her still, the physiotherapist and Mia as well as the OT who would come in to help. Chloe's cries echoed into Mia's soul and she worried that her daughter would go into cardio arrest from her hysteria.

They loaned her a large, sturdy wooden frame. It looked like a lectern. Mia would have to strap Chloe into this wearing her artificial foot orthotic, or when she was in her plasters for extra support. A large wide black Velcro strap held her firmly in place, pulled tightly across her bottom. She would be locked into a standing position and would have to stand there for an hour a day. As soon as Mia strapped her in, Chloe would begin howling. It sounded as if she was being murdered. She would try with all her might to wiggle out of her strap. Mia would retreat to the kitchen and make dinner. She would hide there, unable to watch and hear her daughter's screams. Without fail, she would eventually go quiet. Mia would tiptoe into the lounge room to find her asleep in a standing position but convoluted with her head resting on the small tabletop in front of her; dummy still in her mouth, a crayon still clenched in her hand and a big puddle of drool in front of her, all over the picture she had been drawing.

Mia would diligently practice Chloe's exercises with her at home. One was picking up small items with her hand and dropping them into a metal tin can. Chloe could easily do this with her "good" hand but would completely ignore her affected side. Mia would tap her right hand and ask, "What about this lovely hand here? Can this lovely hand have a go?"

Chloe would concentrate, her left hand making an involuntary fist as she tried to command her right hand to do the task at hand. It was difficult for her to clutch the peg, let alone hang on to it, lift it and then move it forward to drop it into the can. Since she could do the task with her left hand then that's what she would choose to do.

Mia could see that Chloe was clever. If she was asked to open something that would require two hands, one to hold the object, and the other to twist open the lid, she would pop the jar between her legs and squeeze her legs tightly, holding it in place and then turn the lid open with her good hand. Mia started to believe that her daughter could have a future.

Finally, at nearly three years of age, she could stand, and this was when Mia had decided to get Chloe baptized as she had done for her brother before her. On the Sunday of her baptism, her parents, brothers and sister, along with Wolfie's father and step mum attended the service. Chloe looked like an angel in her long flowing white dress which tied at the back with a large silk bow and her shoulder length blonde wavy locks. On her feet she wore bulky red leather boots. They looked like Doc Martins for a toddler, and they were very expensive but gave Chloe the ankle support that she required to enable her to stand. Chloe could still could not speak, yet she understood perfectly, and she could make herself understood as well.

Chloe was standing on the pew next to Natalia. She leaned on her grandmother as the priest approached her, said his prayer, dipped his finger in the holy water and marked her with a wet cross on her forehead. As he walked away Chloe looked at Natalia as she pointed to the priest, then pointed to her forehead and angrily crossed her arms with a "Hmmmmpf!" Natalia and Mia, who had witnessed this, tried to stifle their laughter.

"Did you see that?" whispered Natalia to Mia. "She's smart."

Chloe started walking and talking when she was nearly four and was far from the "vegetable" that Professor Fourrier had predicted. Mia could see her future would not be as bleak as originally foretold. She was an alert and very jovial little girl. Whenever they approached her mother's house, from the backseat Chloe would pipe up, "Go Nonni house?", absolutely adoring her grandmother.

When Chloe turned six, Mia started to grasp the depth of Wolfie's betrayal at wanting to leave her because of Chloe. She had not been able to respond or properly process all that had happened at the time, putting her needs aside as she focused on her daughter. Now, as the clouds parted, and she was no longer functioning on autopilot, she began to breathe and feel what had happened, how he had acted, and the wound cut deeply. She begrudged the fact that she did everything. She was juggling her career with the expectations of motherhood, but now even more so with Chloe's special needs.

Mia had been resourceful because she had to be, acting as the sole carer for the children, caring for Wolfie, organising tradespeople, even painting the house internally when required. All he could do was criticise. He had complained about her painting and the poor craftsmanship after he had examined it scrupulously, almost with a magnifying glass.

On one occasion, Mia was tidying up some of the children's toys in the loungeroom whilst Wolfie lay on the sofa watching television, as she said, "Wolfie, that English oak tree in the front yard is preventing the lawn from thriving. If we trim the bottom branches, then the sun will get in, the grass will grow, and we'll stop trudging mud through the house when it rains. What do you think?"

"That's a great idea. You always have amazing foresight and vision. I'll get round to doing it, probably on the weekend when I'm not so tired."

He did not trim the tree that weekend nor the following nor the one after that. Mia did not nag him. She again found an inexpensive tradesman and got him to remove the lower branches so that one could easily walk under it. Mia was at the sink, washing the dishes, when Wolfie came home, strolling in with his usual arrogance and started shouting, "Jesus fucking Christ! What the bloody hell have you done to that tree?"

"Must you blaspheme? You know I hate it."

"God damn it! It looks fucking terrible!"

"I got someone in to cut the lower branches and take the rubbish away. I thought I would help you, since you're always tired. He worked for about four hours and was very affordable at $175."

"You and your hair-brained ideas! I'm sick of it!"

"What are you talking about? You agreed that it was a good idea!"

"You're such a stupid bitch! Can you never discuss things with me first!" he continued, shrieking.

Why didn't I ask your permission? I pay half the bills around here and do all the work! You impossibly narky, bumptious and opinionated fucktard!

The grass grew back under the tree as Mia had predicted. One Sunday afternoon he came indoors from mowing the lawn.

"The grass is growing nicely under the oak tree; it's easier to mow now that I can walk under it. It's so much better than it was before and looks lovely and green."

Mia ignored him.

Another one for the keeper!

When things got tense, she dodged conflict or made jokes and laughed to diffuse the situation, but it was hard work. At times, it felt like a relentless machine gun shooting at her. His unpredictable temper was so violent. He could not tolerate being contradicted or challenged, and therefore, they all walked around on tiptoe, talking in hushed tones, and waiting for the moment that he would explode into anger, causing untold aggravation to everyone in his orbit.

They were going through an ugly period again, hardly speaking and avoiding each other. The wounded had little chance of succour. She finally told him she wanted a divorce. She could not forgive his behaviour, and she was aching.

That weekend, Mia got up early to attend a self-help seminar. Her girlfriend Petra had recommended it. After this course, she was assured that she would know the meaning of life. Before leaving home, she stood patiently in the foyer, with her mobile to her ear, listening to the automated female voice instructing her on how to top up her account. Outside, the weather had turned; there was torrential rain accompanied by thunder and lightning. Mia ignored Wolfie who said something to her as he walked past. Taking offense, he started yelling and calling her names; she turned her back to him, as he raged.

Suddenly, she felt a blow across her head. Shocked, her ear ringing, Wolfie shouting and screaming, followed up with a second hard slap. Her phone went flying and hit the tiled terracotta floor with such force that it broke into pieces. As she bent over to pick up the fragments of her phone, he grabbed her by the back of the neck and pulled her into the kitchen. She tried to resist, but he was too strong. Mia tried to pull his hand off, to prise open his fingers, but he held her fast. She continued struggling, trying to break free as his right hand gripped the back of her neck, holding her at arm's length, so she could not retaliate.

"What are you doing? Let me go!" Her resistance was futile against the rage that had seemingly given him superpowers.

He violently threw her face down onto the kitchen counter. She felt the warm blood gush out of her nose, and she could taste the metal in her mouth. Glasses flew in all directions, shattering into smithereens. Chloe, who had witnessed this horrific event, began screaming and crying hysterically as she ran upstairs. Alex opened his bedroom door to her cries. "What's wrong?" he asked genuinely concerned.

"Daddy's hurting Mummy! Daddy's hurting Mummy!" sobbed Chloe uncontrollably.

Mia heard Alex exclaim, "Oh, crap!"

Wolfie continued yelling insults at Mia, now having her pinned to the kitchen counter. Despite her efforts, she could not free herself from his grip. He was too strong and completely out of control. Pulling her by the hair, he wrestled her to the ground. She flopped helplessly like a rag doll.

After that, he sat atop her, squashing her face down into the cold tiles. She tried to get up but was wedged firmly beneath him. She stopped wriggling, as she understood, submissiveness was what he wanted from her.

He stood up. She was crying.

"That's right cry. What are you crying for?" he snarled belligerently. She tried to walk away, but he followed her like a shadow, continuing to hurl abuse. She had no idea what he was so upset about.

Finally, she got away and went upstairs. On the landing, Alex met her, as he whispered, pulling out a long knife from under his jumper, "Don't worry, Mum. If he hurts you, I'll protect you."

Mia knew this had to stop. Alex did not deserve to go to prison for protecting her. She called the police. She comforted the children and asked them to stay in their rooms knowing they would be safe there. Mia remained calm on the outside, even though she felt like she was trembling all over and was in shock over what had just happened. She knew that if she said little and did not raise her voice or appear to challenge him in any way, she would be safe. She had to survive this moment.

She came back downstairs, where Wolfie was, still ranting and raving. She felt scared and vulnerable.

"I've called the police," she said calmly.

"Oh, that's right. Call the police. You can never take responsibility for your own actions, can you?" he roared.

I NEVER TAKE RESPONSIBILITY for my actions! Have you looked in the mirror lately?

The police arrived. Mia had stopped bleeding, and she felt that they were not taking the matter seriously, even though he admitted to having assaulted her. However, they did suggest that she think about taking out an AVO. She decided to take this course of action, to send him a clear message. His behaviour was unacceptable! That night Mia was terrified. She slept downstairs on the sofa with the door locked but lay awake frightened most of the night. Every sound made her break out in a sweat as she thought he was coming for her. She had ensured the children were safe in their beds. Alex had barricaded the door to his room.

On the day of the hearing, standing outside the Court House, some ladies from a group, "Violence Against Women", ushered Mia into their office and offered her coffee and sanctuary. They were very welcoming and advised that often before proceedings a spouse would try to coerce their partner into dropping the charges. They had seen it all before, the begging for forgiveness, the endless apologising, and the numerous promises that things would change. Exactly on cue, Wolfie appeared at their door, wanting to speak to Mia. This protective trio shooed him away, their only concern to shield and protect her.

One of the policemen who had come to her house that horrible day, said, "You should think about leaving him because it's been my experience, that once they start hitting, they don't stop." Mia was worried.

Should I leave him? Will he attack me again?

She wanted to save her marriage and Wolfie was promising her that he would change, that he would never hit her again and that he would help out more around the house and with the children. He told her that he loved her and that his family was important to him, that it was everything to him. She could see in his eyes that he meant every word. He was her husband; she trusted and believed him.

In the Court room, a court-appointed solicitor went through his motions, the judge sat listening intently. Wolfie had decided to represent himself. When it was his turn, he spoke eloquently, "Your honour, I'm sorry that I did this terrible thing to my wife. I don't know what came over me that day. I promise that it was the first time and that it will be the last. I'll never raise a finger against her again." He continued as he looked directly at Mia, and said with sincerity, "I'm so sorry."

The Judge then turned to Mia, and asked, "Is there a chance for reconciliation?"

"Yes."

She saw the relief on Wolfie's face and knew that he was back to his old, rational self. He was listening to her. She had his attention. Despite his negative actions, she knew they were fuelled by a desire not to lose her. She still had his heart. Once again, she forgave him. Her hope was that they would work out their differences and start being a proper family. Their marriage and their little family were worth saving, as was he.

Once they were home, Wolfie confided, "I was so relieved when you said there was a chance for reconciliation. I thought you were going to leave me. I love you, Mia, and I'm truly sorry, and I won't ever hit you again. I promise."

Mia was disarmed by his vulnerability and knew she had made the right choice.

He again organised for them to see Michael their marriage counsellor.

Michael greeted them, "Here they are, that handsome couple, the Schmidts. How have you both been?", adopting a casual off-the-cuff tone, the right balance between warm and professional.

Wolfie replied sheepishly, "Hello, Michael, as I explained on the phone, we've had some issues again. I've also enrolled myself in the anger management course your office has. I took my temper out on Mia and I never want to do that, or hurt her again. Ever!"

"Yes, I saw that. Good on you, Wolfie, that's a step in the right direction. How are you, Mia?"

Crossing her arms, and looking up at the ceiling she said, "I've been better. I hate that we are back here again, especially since we agreed on certain changes last time, which Wolfie has stopped doing or hasn't even bothered to do!"

"Like what?" he asked curiously.

She sighed loudly, "Something as simple as giving me a kiss when he walks in the door. He still doesn't do it!"

Michael gave Wolfie a disapproving look. Wolfie squirmed in his chair; he knew he was in the wrong and about to be told so by Michael. Their session continued.

Mia complained that he had stopped cooking on a Sunday night and resorted to getting take away. He would often get pizza and ask her to make a salad. She did not feel like he was honouring his part of the agreement, but she complied, as she always did. She also mentioned that it seemed easy for him to abscond from his chores, simply announcing that he would no longer be doing the laundry because "there's a dog's hair on my sock! and it's bloody disgusting!" His task of doing the laundry had not lasted long, nor had he picked up another chore instead. Being a submissive and devoted wife, she washed everything. If she had not done so, the dirty clothes would have simply piled up. He also requested that his items of clothing be stowed away in the following fashion: underpants folded into little squares, his socks rolled up together in their matching pairs, so that his draw looked like a box of bonbons. His business shirts and trousers were to be hung neatly in his closet. If she failed to comply, he would be furious.

She explained to Michael how she had bought a laundry basket for their room to encourage him to stop leaving his dirty clothes lying on the floor, which seemed to work, until he crammed in as much as he could to the point where she no longer used it. She had said, "Since you're the only one using the laundry basket. Could you please carry it down to the laundry for me?"

"No problem," he had replied, but he never did. She would ask again and again. One day he was furious, "I've run out of clean undies and socks."

"Did you bring the basket down for me like I asked? Like you promised you would."

In a huff he took the basket down and left it outside the laundry.

"Well, I've finished doing the washing for this week, so if you want any of that done, you'll have to do it yourself!"

He went out and bought himself new underpants and socks for the week.

Michael looked at Wolfie. "I don't need to tell you that you haven't been trying, do I, Wolfie." Wolfie was adamant that the dog hairs were disgusting! He then mentioned how frustrated he was in the bedroom. He complained that Mia never swallowed when she gave him blow jobs. Michael who always seemed to side with her asked, "Why does she need to swallow?"

"Because it's nice."

"I don't want to swallow it! I don't like it! It makes me want to throw up, and I don't see why it's so important! He's finished by then, so why does it matter where it goes? I suggested going down on him, letting him cum in my mouth, giving him a kiss and depositing the contents into his. If he could swallow it, then I would be more than happy to do it too." Michael looked amused, entertained by the turn in the conversation. She continued, "But, you know what? He was outraged by my suggestion, saying it was disgusting! I said, 'It's not good enough for you, but it's good enough for me.' Mia was fuming. Wolfgang was sitting there not knowing where to look.

Mia paused to throw Wolfie a dirty look as she resumed her dialogue, now irate, "He then said, 'That would be like me going down on myself. How would you like me to make you go down on yourself!?' I said, 'You do that to me all the time!' He's always like, 'Give me some mouth work first, then I want to fuck pussy for a while because I love to fuck pussy, and then you can finish me off.' WELL, HELLO! I CAN TASTE MYSELF ALL OVER YOU AND I FIND IT VERY UNPLEASANT!" She had screamed the last sentence looking directly at him.

Michael turned towards Wolfie. "She doesn't need to swallow. Does she? If she says she doesn't want to do something, then you shouldn't be forcing her. You're done, so it makes no difference, whether she swallows or not. Does it?"

Wolfie reluctantly agreed. "Okay. She doesn't need to swallow." Mia felt a tiny victory.

Mia said, "Whenever I suggest something, which I think might be fun, like trying fluffy handcuffs or taking turns tying each other up with silk veils or ties, he says no. He doesn't even want to try it. I respect his wishes and don't continually hound him. He never takes no for an answer! I'm also fed up with him continuously annoying me to have a threesome. He wants this with the two of us and a prostitute. Yuck! I'M SO NOT INTERESTED! He's like a broken record, he stops asking for a while and then starts up all over again. It's never going to happen! It's the same with anal sex. I'm not interested in that either!"

She had tried anal sex with him, after he had continued pestering her. The first time it did not work because she was anxious and there was no way he was getting in. The second time, he got in part of the way, but she suddenly felt the most excruciating pain.

"Stop! Stop! That's enough. It hurts and I'm done!"

A couple of days later he said, "Let's try it again."

"I don't want to! I've had a sore behind for two days, and I've had trouble going to the loo, so thanks but no thanks." She said this as she gathered the dirty clothing from the second floor, throwing it into the laundry basket and making her way downstairs, as he trailed behind her like a puppy.

"Actually," he said in whispered tones, "I was reading about it online last night, and we were going about it all wrong. Next time, you need to fast the evening before, preferably for the whole day. That way I won't have any faeces on my dick."

"Are you listening to yourself? There won't be a next time. Why should I fast for the whole day?"

"It will be better."

"You can't even fast for ten minutes! Thanks, but I'll pass."

"But we didn't really give it a good go," he protested.

"Are you gay or something?" She hoped to shut him down.

"No, but I would like to try it."

"I gave it a good go and I'M NOT INTERESTED! I tell you what, if you try it first and you don't have a problem with it, then I'll give it another go."

"What do you mean?" he asked puzzled.

"You fast for a day, and I'll find the biggest carrot, and fuck you with it. If you like it, then I'll be keen to give it another go. By the way, I won't be gentle."

"No, I don't think I would like that."

"Why is it okay for you to want something, and even if I say no, you can never let it go. But when you say no, it's the end, there's no room for negotiation. It's all about you and what you want. Double standards, Wolfie. Double standards."

For months after this, when taking her from behind, he would hungrily say, "You're ready. I can see that you're ready. Can I try? Can we try anal?" This would be an instant turnoff for Mia. He had also, on so many occasions, nearly entered her "accidentally" from behind. She had to be vigilant.

Michael addressed this issue quite simply. He looked at Wolfie and said, "If she tells you that she doesn't want to do something, or is not comfortable with it, then you have to respect her wishes. You can't force her into doing something she doesn't want to do. You have to listen to her." Just like that, it was the end of the matter. Why could he not hear her when she said NO!? How could he not understand her?

She had discussed his need for a threesome with him. He had said, "It's every man's fantasy and I'd like to know what it would be like before I die."

"Wolfie, there is no way that I can watch you fuck another woman. It would make me crazy with jealousy, and I'm likely to get a kitchen knife and stab you both to death!"

"It's also every woman's fantasy too," he replied with his infuriating smile.

"It is not! It's certainly not this woman's fantasy. I have never been interested in being with another woman. Never!"

"Never? Really?" He sounded genuinely surprised.

"Definitely! It's not something that I would EVER want to try. I like men and I like penis."

"How do you know unless you try?"

"I know myself. I just do. I might be tempted into trying it with you, me and another guy." She of course had no intention of following through on this either.

Wolfie replied, in a panicked tone, "That's not the way the fantasy goes."

"How do you know unless you try?" she replied smugly. "You could then also have anal sex; he would enjoy it more than I would." Her husband was quiet.

Fissures Torn
Chapter 19

It was the weekend after their last session with Michael. Wolfie was once again putting in more of an effort and was more present with her and the children. The children were growing up quickly. Chloe was a pretty girl who understood humour, and, like her mum, was very quick-witted and sharp. She could talk, and she could walk, though she did have a slight limp on her right side and her right arm usually hung listlessly by her side. She was about seven years old, and they had been watching a documentary on volcanoes as a family. Copious amounts of molten lava and black heavy ash were spewing from the mountain top, and they referred a lot to Mother Nature. Chloe turned to her mum and asked, "Who is Mother Nature?" Mia did her best to explain.

After a slight pause, Chloe asked pensively, "Is she God's wife?" Mia laughed. She could see that her daughter had common sense and intellect.

It had not been easy. There had been countless hours spent attending doctors' rooms, hospitals and various therapists, but Mia never gave up on Chloe. Like everyone else, Mia thought Chloe had a maximum potential, and she would assist her in reaching it. She had dragged her daughter to every clinic she could think of and seen every specialist who might be able to help. She did everything in her power to support her. Not just through therapy but tried encouraging her to make friends and develop her social skills, getting her to join girl guides, gymnastics classes, and regularly having friends over for play dates.

One evening, when Wolfie and Mia were sitting in the loungeroom chatting, and the children were playing in their rooms, Mia said, "I nearly died today. Your daughter came home from school, to tell me that a boy had told her how babies were made!"

Wolfie chuckled, "Why? What did she say?"

"She said, he told her that the boy puts his penis down into the girl's vagina. I didn't say anything, so she asked, is it true? I quietly nodded, and then she squealed in disgust. 'EWWWWW! You let Daddy do that to you?!' I replied, 'Yes, but only twice' and then I said, 'That's disgusting! You're never doing that to me again!' "

Wolfie was shaking his head as he quietly sniggered, "Why did you tell her that? She's going to have the wrong idea about sex."

"She was judging me! She knows that I've done it twice, since I have two kids, so I thought it sounded plausible. Besides, she has time to learn about sex, she's only in primary school."

Alex who had walked through the loungeroom on his way to the kitchen, at the wrong time, was softly chuckling. Mia smiled at Alex, as she said defensively, "What was I supposed to say?" He laughed harder as he left the room. She had a good relationship with him, having ensured to forge a strong bond with him, always taking an interest in what he was doing. He liked to read fantasy novels, so any book he recommended to her she would also read, then they would discuss the characters and plot twists at length. When he expressed an interest in playing soccer, Mia enrolled herself in a soccer coach course and became assistant coach to his under-eight's team. When he took up Karate, it was Mia who attended with him. There were plenty of father and son teams, but theirs was the only mother and son team. Alex was also doing well at school. He was clever and becoming more handsome by the day, with the thickest and longest dark eye lashes she had ever seen, his very full and symmetrical lips and his chiselled face. Mia was amazed at how different the children were from each other, considering they had come from the same gene pool.

Mia sometimes felt they were growing up too quickly. Chloe was now nine and Alex was twelve. Late one morning, Mia sat in the rumpus room, sewing her cross-stitch embroidery as Alex foraged for food in the kitchen. He was always hungry. He had been watching his mum as she talked to him.

"You're the glue," he said.

"What?" she asked, not grasping what he had said.

"You're the glue."

"I'm the goo? What are you talking about?"

"You're the glue that keeps the family together."

"Oh."

What an insightful young man. I'm so proud of him. He is already so wise at twelve! He's such a caring, sensitive young man.

A sound escaped deep from within Mia's stomach. It sounded like she had swallowed a kitten. Alex, standing by the refrigerator, laughed as he imitated it. Mia chuckled too.

"Guess I'd better feed it. It's almost 11am. I'm going to make some cheese and tomato paprika grills. Would you like some, Alex?"

Alex gratefully, "Yes please! Could I have four?"

"Four! You must be hungry. Okay. No problem." Chloe entered the kitchen.

"Would you like some cheese grills with tomato and paprika, Chloe?"

"Yes please, but could I just have one."

Mia called out, "I'm making some cheese and tomato grills with paprika for lunch, would you like some, Wolfie?"

"No thanks, but I'll take a toasted sandwich."

Mia walked through the formal dining room and found the newspapers spread all over the table, but he was nowhere to be seen. She found him in the study on the computer. With hands on hips, she said, "I don't recall offering you a toasted sandwich. Would you like a cheese grill?"

"But I don't feel like a cheese grill. I want a toasted sandwich. It won't take you much more effort to make me a toasted sandwich."

"Well, if that's the case, then feel free to make it yourself. I'm making cheese grills. Now do you want one or not?"

"Alright. Alright. I'll have two."

She walked away muttering, "Ingrate!" under her breath.

"I heard that!" he called out amused.

Good for you! It's a shame your attitude isn't as good as your hearing!

Even though their relationship seemed to be getting back on track with Michael's help, Wolfie did not realise that his attempts at displaced humour only exacerbated an already strained relationship, causing new fissures to tear open. The constant behaviour he displayed did little other than to blight the good times somewhere deep inside her.

Mania
Chapter 20

Mia won the employee of the year award at her company. It was satisfying to receive recognition as at times she felt like she was walking a tightrope, balancing all her commitments on her small frame, and although she found her life challenging, she was resilient and excelled in all that she did. At the annual company Christmas dinner, Mia was presented with a framed achievement certificate and a $5,000 gift voucher to be used with the firm's travel agency. It was Mia who always won awards and accolades at work, never Wolfie. She dashed home to proudly share her good news.

Wolfie was delighted. Their 19th wedding anniversary was approaching, and he suggested a family holiday to New Zealand. Mia spoke to Jodi at Ramsay Travel who organised their itinerary for a two-week trip to the South Island. They would arrive in Christchurch, spend a couple of nights there before collecting their hire vehicle and drive around the island. Every second day, they would arrive at a new destination, just the four of them. It was brilliant!

They went to Dunedin, Wanaka, Queenstown, Hamner Springs, and Milford Sound. Mia particularly liked Hamner Springs. It was nestled in the mountains and reminded her of a small European Alpine village. Their hotel had been the most luxurious accommodation they had ever stayed in. The children also enjoyed their own separate wing. They all had a wonderful time!

Mia had to drive because Wolfie had lost his license for six months, due to his speeding fines. In Australia, he was always taking risks, chopping and changing lanes at high speeds and weaving in and out of traffic. Mia hated it! She had even sacrificed some points for him on more than one occasion, claiming that she was the driver at fault. She refused to do this again and wanted him to learn his lesson. So, he finally had to give up his license. However, he still believed the police were singling him out.

As a red sports car overtook them and zoomed off into the distance. This took Mia back to the time Wolfie had come home from work to tell her about the red sports car he had to have. With his voice full of excitement, he explained the car's redeeming feature, "It can go zero to 100 in 3.5 seconds."

"That's fast, but when will you ever be able to reach that speed, considering that you're usually stuck in peak hour traffic, and the most you can do is 40km an hour?"

He increased their mortgage to purchase it. When they went out together on the weekends, he had a need to speed. The more she asked him to slow down, the more he would accelerate. It was best if she sat there quietly. She would close her eyes and rest her forehead lightly against the cool of the window, pretending to doze, but the truth was she did not want to die. She often just kept her mouth shut because it was just too hard. She was always happiest in denial. She remembered when he took her out in his fancy sports car one evening and they had stopped at the traffic lights, their windows down and a warm summer breeze sweeping in to find them. Wolfie had grimaced, his face full of disgust, as an offensive odour like fermented fish guts and rotted durian wafted into the car. Turning to Mia he'd said, "Yuck! Is that you?"

"Fuck off! Why would that be me? That person there has obviously spread fertiliser in their garden."

The light turned green. He accelerated. She jerked forwards and placed her hand on the dashboard to steady herself. They drove in silence. He looked over his shoulder, jerked the car right and accelerated past an old lady in a blue mini.

"Get off the road love! Where'd you get your license from? A packet of cornflakes?"

"Babe, I don't like it when you speed and drive like a maniac. Can you please slow down?"

"Relax, it's safe," he replied with a maniacal grin.

"If a cop sees you, you'll get booked! You're currently doing 80 in a 50 zone."

"I'm keeping an eye out for any pigs!"

The car lurched right. In the car ahead, sat two young boys, one with his lips squashed against the back window, the other frantically waving.

"Statistically, I'm sitting in the death seat. If you swerve and hit something, then chances are I'll die. Do you think I have enough death cover? I mean you're going to need a lot of money for someone to cook, clean, look after the kids and then there are those extra services that you're fond of, which you currently get for free. What do you think?" As her words sunk in, he eased off the accelerator. It had worked this time but she knew that it would be short-lived.

Mia was glad to be having this mini break with her family. She hoped that Wolfie was over his midlife crisis and that this was a new start for them. She hoped that Wolfie would start to control his temper, now that he had taken those anger management classes. Even though Mia admired the rugged beauty that surrounded them, she was looking forward to a break from driving. With towering mountains positioned on the edge of the lake they approached Queenstown, the hub of adventure, thrumming with adrenaline and an omnipresent sense of fun. Their anniversary fell on the day they arrived there. Wolfie organised to take Mia to a very expensive French restaurant, *Le Petit Chat Noir*. As they sat together, sipping red wine, he looked lovingly at her. His eyes were warm, and he had a tranquil look on his face.

"I can't believe that we've been married for 19 years. It's amazing and look at the great life we've had together. Our nice home, and our beautiful family. I know we've had our ups and downs and been through a lot, but I think this has only made our foundations stronger."

Mia sat quietly watching and listening but keeping her own counsel.

What …? Stronger foundations? I see the columns having irreparable damage from the pointless battles. Even castle walls give in to battering rams over time.

He continued, "I'm looking forward to our children growing up and seeing what lives they lead, and to being a grandfather someday."

He had always wanted to be a grandfather but had never seemed keen on fatherhood itself. She had advised him on more than one occasion that you could not have one without the other. She had said jokingly that the thing about parenthood is that it's hereditary and if your parents didn't have any, then chances are you won't have any either. He had chuckled.

He continued, with a tender, sweet look on his face and a smile that made the corners of his eyes wrinkle, "I look forward to spending another 19 years with you and more."

What …? Another 19 years of this?

Mia was finding it hard to breathe, and there was a tightness in her chest. All she wanted was for him to stop talking. It was all too much. She took a sip of water as the food arrived. He was unaware of her reaction as she did her best to cover it up. She had never experienced such discomfort and wondered if she had just had an anxiety attack?

"I love you, Mia, and I love our children."

"I love you too," she mumbled, unsure if she was being truthful.

They continued their dinner without further incident. Their trip was coming to an end. Two days later, they were at the airport on their way back to Sydney. They were standing in a long, slow-moving queue with their passports at the ready. Wolfie was leading them, Mia stood behind him with Alex on her left and Chloe to her right.

Wolfie turned to look at Mia. She smiled lovingly at him.

Oh shit! What's with that face?

He looked like a coiled snake, and she knew she was about to feel the sting from his anger.

"You're a fucking bitch!" he hissed. "I'm sick of you! I've had enough! When we get back to Sydney, I want a divorce."

Mia flummoxed, "What …? What are you talking about? What's happened? I don't understand."

"Shut your mouth! I don't want to hear it! I'm telling you, we're through! When we are back in Sydney, I want a divorce!"

Staring into his eyes, the venom was there for all to see. She could feel the menace and swallowed down the retort she was longing to give. He continued hurling insults at her. The children were scared and uncomfortable, nervously looking at their parents and each other. Mia was completely taken aback. Where had this come from? She began crying. He was having another one of his manic moments, and all she could do was comfort the children and get them safely on the plane and back home. Though they both felt insecure in that moment, they knew that their mother would always protect and be there for them. They always sought her out when they needed support or guidance. Once again, Mia did not understand what was happening

Is this one of your manic moments again? I can't keep dealing with your shit! Enough is enough. If you want a divorce so badly you can have it!

Back in Sydney, she agreed. She could no longer be married to this crazy man! He had once again drawn up an Excel spreadsheet, with a suggested division of their net assets. He had also started throwing things away, including gifts she had given him. Amongst the items, she found an album full of explicit photos that he had compiled of her. In some, she wore garters and stockings, in others she was completely naked, legs spread. There were close ups of her touching herself and one with a vibrator inserted inside her. He had posed her in all of these. In some, she had semen on her stomach, her breasts, or around her neck. He had called this a pearl necklace. He had made her take the film to the local discount store to be developed. When she had collected these photos, the girl behind the counter had given her a knowing look and had a smirk on her face that read, "I know what you get up to, slut!" Mia had felt self-conscious and cheapened, and told Wolfie, but he ignored her feelings. "Don't worry about it. Everyone does it."

I don't believe you. What about using a Polaroid camera like I suggested, so I don't have to feel publicly embarrassed and humiliated? Who knows if these people haven't made copies and now show them to friends and family for a laugh? You're not being protective of me!

She destroyed the album and the negatives and any photos she found loose or on his computer. She decided then and there that she would never let anyone photograph her like that again. As Wolfie continued on the path of divorce, Mia could see that he would have moments of what she would call lucidness. During one of these, she said, "Wolfie, go to the doctor, please! You tell me on our 19th wedding anniversary that you love me, and you want to spend the next 19 years with me. Then two days later, out of the blue, you hurl insults at me and want a divorce. Something is very wrong. You told me that your doctor had changed your anti-depression medication before we left. Has he been monitoring you?"

"No. He told me to come back if I needed to."

"That's ridiculous! Please go back and see him; you need to! The dose or the medication is wrong for you. Something's not right."

In the end, Wolfie did visit his doctor who altered his medication, and he returned to a semblance of his old self. He calmed down and no longer wanted a divorce. Things went back to "normal" and Mia was left to handle this peculiar upheaval on her own, as usual. She knew he had a mental illness. The years of highs and lows were proof enough, along with the anti-depressants he required, and the manic mood swings that led to personality changes every several years. She still believed they were all better off together, stronger in their family unit. Her vows had also been, "in sickness and in health, for better and better"; she had made a promise. When he chose to have his illness managed, things were stable, and he would be reasonable.

There had been no "better and better" from him; she had experienced so much "worse and worse". Every five to six years he seemed to lose his grip on reality. There would again be major bedlam before things would once again settle down.

Perseverance
Chapter 21

Cockatoos swoop from the eucalypts; their usual morning racket. Inside, the four of them sat around the dining table having just feasted on fresh bread rolls and pastries that Wolfie had bought, along with the Sunday papers. Mia had turned 40. He presented her with a red velvet box. She opened it with delirious anticipation.

"Oh, my goodness, Wolfie, what a magnificent necklace! I love it." She was absolutely delighted with it.

"Happy birthday darling, I thought it looked Egyptian, and something that Cleopatra might wear," he said, helping her with the clasp.

"It looks like a road, Mum," said Alex.

"I think it looks like a gold paved, yellow brick road," replied Mia. The children laughed. She continued, "Oh, it's like kisses to my skin. I must say your taste has definitely improved with age."

"It's not that, it's just that we have a little more money than we used to."

"I absolutely love it! It's simply exquisite!" She threw her arms around his neck and planted a kiss on his lips.

He handed her a card, divided in two by a line down the middle. On the left, there was a cartoon drawing of a smiling woman with wild hair, looking meek in high heels with the title, "How to impress a woman." It read, "Compliment her, cuddle her, kiss her, caress her, love her, comfort her, protect her, wine and dine her, care for her, hold her, listen to her, support her, buy things for her, go to the ends of the earth for her." On the right, was an animation of a smiling man with open arms; it read, "How to impress a man … show up naked," and inside, "and bring beer! Happy Birthday!"

Dearest Mia,

You mean everything to me. Just as much now as 20 years ago. I love you, find you as attractive as ever and look forward to our future together, both with each other and our children.

Life begins at 40 and now you can begin a new chapter and restore your happiness. Let me help you, tell me what you need from me, talk to me, let me into your thoughts and life.

You've been carrying the load too much; I'm trying very hard to address this and help more as a caring and loving husband and father.

Have a wonderful 40th Birthday, my dearest Mia. My lovely, beautiful wife.

Love Wolfie xxxx

He also had the children sign the card. Alex had written: Dear Mum, Happy Birthday! I would like to thank you for raising me over the years. From when I was a tiny baby and had to do everything for me to now. Thanks Mum and Happy Birthday, love Alex xxxx

Chloe had written: Happy Birthday, Love Chloe. She had also drawn a flower.

Mia loved the card! Alex was growing into a sensitive young man and Chloe was copying his behaviour. He had been an excellent role model and they adored each other.

Reading his card, made her recollect when Wolfie had turned 40 and she had thrown him a surprise party. She had done this because he had never had one. As a distraction, on the day of his birthday she drove him into the city for his present from her. He tried to guess what it was.

"We're going on a bridge climb."

She smiled enthusiastically. "Good guess, and it would have been great weather for it, but no way. You know I hate heights. You would have to do that one on your own. You know I read an article the other day about the Sydney Harbour bridge climb; apparently, it has the highest number of proposals, with the highest number of acceptances, something like 75%. That made me laugh; I had visions of guys on bended knees and terrified girls like me, agreeing to anything to get down from that bridge! No wonder there's such a high success rate!"

Wolfie laughed. "Are we taking a helicopter ride over Sydney harbour?"

"Nope. That's another good guess, but again, I hate heights. I don't think you're going to get it."

He continued trying. She parked the car and led him to the pontoon. "We're going jet boating," she announced.

"Jet boating? Okay," he said, disappointed that he had not guessed correctly.

They were given ponchos to wear and placed their valuables away for safe keeping with the hostess and climbed into the jet boat. They were given some quick safety instructions and off they went. The sky was cloudless, and she had often thought that it was only in the southern hemisphere that it was such a brilliant blue. In all her travels around the world with him, it had always been most magnificent in Sydney, on a perfect day like today. They departed Circular Quay and headed towards Luna Park, the driver commentating as he took his guests under the Sydney Harbour bridge. He lunged and veered wherever he could, sending walls of ice-cold water crashing down on all his squealing passengers. By the time they were back and moored to the pier, everyone on board had been saturated. The ponchos had offered very little protection.

Wolfie stepped off, "That was great! That was awesome!" He wore a big grin. Mia shared his exuberance but was glad to be back on dry land.

"Let's go again! Let's do it again!" he enthused.

Mia laughed. "Don't be crazy, it wasn't cheap. Let's get some lunch, I'm ravenous. We can go again another time. And don't forget that we're going out for dinner tonight; my parents and the kids want to celebrate with you too." Reluctantly he agreed. They recovered their valuables and returned the soaking wet ponchos. They had lunch at a nearby café overlooking the spectacular harbour and could feel the salt drying on their skin. Both could not wait to have a shower and freshen up. It would be her next challenge to get him home, change, and to the restaurant in time for his surprise party. She had spent weeks planning and organising and, so far, he was completely unsuspecting.

She had booked an entire Thai restaurant, conveniently located about 15 minutes from their house. Wolfie had always said that he hated Thai food. When asked if he had ever tried it, he answered, "No. Never." Mia did not take his protests seriously. She knew him and his tastes and was sure there would be something on the menu that he liked.

Mia had selected a set banquet menu and organised a special birthday cake. It had taken a lot of effort to find someone who would make a cake to the design and specifications she wanted. It was made of Madeira and was of a three-dimensional woman, naked from the neck down to the navel, with an hourglass figure, laced in white icing with light pink nipples, her breasts full and over exaggerated. He would get a good chuckle out of it because if there was one thing she knew, it was that Wolfie loved breasts! The bigger the better. She had organised for her parents to be there, his parents, their dearest friends and his work colleagues. She had capped numbers at forty to keep costs down and had given everyone specific instructions on where to park so that Wolfie would not recognise anyone's vehicle. The children were in on it too and had not breathed a word to their father.

By the time they got home, they just had time to shower, get changed and go to dinner. Mia, as usual, was impeccably groomed and dressed to kill. She looked stunning in a soft pink, silk dress that flowed loosely around her ankles and flattered her slim frame. It was low-cut, which emphasised and displayed her ample cleavage. She wore a pair of red high-heeled peep-toe shoes and dripped in gold jewellery. She helped the children get ready. Chloe was beaming, wearing her favourite navy-blue velvet dress and Alex wore a chequered red collared shirt with shiny gold threading and a pair of jeans. When Wolfie came downstairs, she was alarmed by what he had chosen to wear. Dressed in a pair of beige shorts gathered at the waist by a drawstring that dangled from his waistband, a collarless shirt, in pale-yellow with horizontal black stripes, and was now bent over putting on a pair of white socks and his dirty old white sneakers. With as much decorum as she could master, she delicately asked, "You're not going like that are you?"

"It's hot and I want to be comfortable."

"But it's your birthday! Look at us, we've all made an effort, and dolled up."

"It's just dinner with your parents."

"It's still your birthday. What about throwing on a pair of jeans at least?" she replied, mimicking his nonchalance.

"No. It's too hot for jeans. This will do," he replied flippantly.

Mia could not press the issue any further without making him suspicious. They all hopped in the car and drove over to the restaurant. She casually looked around and was thankful that she could not spot any familiar cars.

"It seems pretty busy tonight," he remarked as he parked outside the restaurant.

"Where are we meeting your parents?"

"At the Ivory Kasalong."

"Not that Thai place," he whined, "I hate Thai."

Mia quickly replied, "Look, my parents wanted to go there. Just try it. You don't have to eat anything you don't want to."

The children ran ahead. Alex knew his job was to scout ahead on the pretence of wanting to greet his grandparents but secretly he was letting everyone know that the birthday boy was on his way. Mia and Wolfie walked in. All their friends and family stood waiting. In unison they chorused, "SURPRISE! HAPPY BIRTHDAY!"

Wolfie was stupefied. He threw Mia a glance and for a nanosecond she wondered if he was going to punch her in the face and run, but he embraced the moment. He was all smiles as he went around greeting everyone and shaking their hands.

"What on earth is he wearing?" asked Stephanie, a good friend of Mia's and now Wolfie's friend too. "He looks like he's about to go do the gardening!" she roared with laughter. She sounded like a foghorn but her laugh was full of infectious humour.

Turning to Mia, he asked, "Why didn't you say something?"

"Are you kidding?" asked a perplexed Mia. "I hinted that you should go and change more than once, and you refused."

"Well, you didn't try hard enough."

Whatever calm she felt had been replaced with agitation. "If I'd kept pushing, you would've become suspicious, so I tried and then let it go."

Stephanie, who was still so amused, was clutching her rib cage as she convulsed with laughter. Watching Stephanie laugh, Mia could see the tension leaving his face as he relaxed and decided to enjoy himself. Wolfie had a fantastic night! Their guests had a great time too. He was in his element being the life of the party! He was impressed at what Mia had been able to organise without him suspecting a thing. He loved the Thai food, and he especially loved his cake. He posed for the camera with his mouth open, hovering over a nipple. Mia felt self-validation and that life was more bearable having proven him wrong. She had chipped away at his steak and potatoes attitude, suspecting that he would like a new type of cuisine.

Driving home, he began listing all the people Mia had not invited.

"You could have invited the Dowell's and Liana and Murray."

"I was trying to keep costs down. I already spent over $1,000, so I decided to only invite our closest and dearest," came Mia's frustrated reply.

Listen ingrate! I was trying to be nice and throw you a party that you'd fondly remember for the rest of your years. Not stage a momentous event, even bigger than our wedding that would strain our finances!

She suggested, "When I turn 49 and you turn 51, we should have a combined birthday bash, and have a hundred-year celebration. We can invite everyone to our combined 100-year birthday party."

Wolfie laughed. "We'll talk about it then."

Mia could see that Wolfie appeared calmer these days. She was glad that she had stayed and tried to work things out, having always believed in the sanctity of marriage. Marriage for her was more than a contract between two people to ratify affections and provide for mutual obligations. Rather, for Mia, marriage was a vital institution for rearing children and teaching them to become responsible adults. She had done it for all of them, believing that her children would be happier and better off, not ever experiencing a broken home. She could finally see the rewards of her efforts in keeping her family together. The children were growing up. Chloe was now 14 and Alex 17.

Chloe had just changed high school and joined a mainstream school that did not have a special needs unit. She had better opportunities for her education there and was able to make able-bodied friends. Mia heard that the girls in her class had often invited her to join them for lunch and after school for a drink, but Chloe, who agreed to meet them, would never turn up. When she quizzed Chloe about this, she replied, "Why would anyone want to be my friend?" It caused Mia's heart to ache that Chloe could not see her worth. Regardless of her physical disability, she was kind, caring and considerate. Many would have been proud to call her a friend. Mia hoped that she would become more confident as she matured. She knew that staying with Wolfie and ensuring a stable home environment would go a long way to achieving this end.

Chloe required a lot of surgery in her formative years. Again, at 15, she needed her foot, knee and hip operated on. She had had a growth spurt and things were out of alignment. Mia knew that inevitably the responsibility would be hers again. It was at this time that Wolfie insisted on selling their home because he was fed up with the changing neighbourhood, with so many unregistered boarding houses having popped up in the area, as they lived so close to the university. None of the rest of the family had wanted to move, especially Alex who was in the middle of his final year in high school and sitting for his Higher School Certificate.

Mia asked, "Wolfie, if we move, will you be happy?"

"Yes," he replied unequivocally.

Alex said to his mother, "He won't be happy, Mum. He will never be happy."

They sold their home and moved into a rental property whilst they searched for a suitable home to purchase in a better suburb. They had unpacked most of their belongings when Wolfie announced that he was leaving for Germany for a three-week holiday. He needed a break! Every now and then, he would become restless and depressed, and his answer was to go visit his relatives overseas. He would come back refreshed, energised and untroubled. The first time he had done this she had been quite upset. Firstly, it was a drain on their finances. Secondly, why could he not wait for her to join him?

This time she pleaded with him, "Don't go now. Chloe's about to have surgery. I need you here. Just wait a couple of weeks and go when she's mobile and can move around."

"You don't need me," replied Wolfie. "You'll manage like you always do. I'll just be in the way."

"I do need you. Even if you don't do anything, it's still a help to me that you're there. You're still supporting me. Just wait until she's recovered and then go."

"I have to go now because of work. You'll be fine. You always are." He booked his ticket.

This cut Mia deeply, but she did not have time to dwell on it, having Chloe to consider. She would need help going to the bathroom and doing her physio exercises every day. Mia ensured that this went smoothly, even though it was physically challenging for her as they were now about the same height. For Chloe, it made no difference whether her father was home or not, as she always asked her mother for any assistance she required. Alex was also glad to be rid of him. He would be able to relax and be himself and not have to deal with his father's violent mood swings.

Mia continued working on the days following Chloe's surgery, but instead of going home at the end of the day, she would drive directly to the hospital and sleep on a foldout bed next to her. This way, she could help Chloe during the night if required, and make sure that she would eat at least one meal a day. The nurses were often too busy to cut up her food and give her the extra attention she needed. Mia would shower at the hospital and then drive straight to work, call home on her way, to check on Alex, and make sure he was managing on his own, and that there was some dinner for him that evening. She would grab a change of clothes and do it all again the next day. As the Company Accountant, Mia was in the middle of overseeing the implementation of the company wide new software program. There had been changes to processes that she had executed, and she had to test the new system in depth before taking time off to care for her daughter. Compared to Wolfie, she had greater responsibility and her job was much more stressful.

Once Chloe was out of hospital, Mia took annual leave. She had to be organised as it all rested on her shoulders. She also worked remotely to meet her work schedules. To add to Mia's stress levels, her employer wanted her to come in for two days whilst she was caring for Chloe. She would have to hire a nurse which would cost her more than her wages because Wolfie was in Germany. Upon his return, he had many gifts for her. One was an expensive black Ralph Lauren dress in a classic cut. He seemed to think that would ease his guilt. Rather than buy her anything, she would have preferred that he be there for her. That's all she had ever wanted. Him.

***

Eventually, they bought a house they could afford, but further than they had expected from the CBD. It was an architecturally designed modern home nestled in the bush. One afternoon, Wolfie lay in the sun on the banana lounge in the garden, like a capybara. In the foreground there was a gentle grassy slope to the hedge of Lilly Pilly. Across the road were patches of eucalyptus, their tallest branches dressed in olive, lit by the sun and a line of bush, the beginning of the national park that stretched as far as the eye could see in every direction. It was more spectacular than any painting she had ever seen. The only sound was the occasional call of a bush turkey that she thought sounded like an electric chicken.

Mia walked over to him carrying the cappuccinos she had just made. She placed his in the drink tray on his chair. "Thanks darling." He stretched his arms over his head and yawned ostentatiously as he sat up.

They happily chatted as they sipped their hot beverages. Chloe was in her room on her laptop and Alex was out with his friends. Mia loved these leisurely afternoons, spending quality time with her husband. He was talking to her about finances, one of his favourite topics. She was smiling into his handsome face, in the last touch of the sun on their faces, in the breeze that came out of nowhere and swept over their shoulders and stroked their cheeks and made Wolfie's prominent cowlick dance atop his head.

"If something happens to me, you should be okay. There's my super and my life insurance policy; that should be enough for you to pay out the mortgage and leave you some extra to keep any financial pressure off you."

"Do you think there's enough cover if something were to happen to me? I think you need to factor in that you'd need help cooking, cleaning, doing the running around and everything else that I do."
"Yeah, I know what you mean …", he continued, and talked at length about their assets.

Mia said, "If something were to happen to me, I've got no problem with you re-marrying. Just make sure that she's kind to our children and treats them right, otherwise I'll haunt you both!"

He laughed, "Nothing's going to happen to you."

"I'm just saying if it does, I'm okay with it. If something happens to you though, I don't see myself re-marrying. I don't think I could."

"I think you would throw a big party," he replied, with his irritating smile.

She ignored him. "I'd be devastated. I think I'd just raise the kids and be happy with them and our dog, Delilah."

"You would re-marry because your need for sausage is too great."

"You're disgusting!"

Though his comment made her laugh, she did still find him oafish. He liked to push her buttons to see how far he could go and to forget the futility and monotony of his life, so he often provoked her to see how she would react. As a result, they often bickered. On one of these many occasions, she was still annoyed with him, even after he had apologised, and he had wanted sex. Mia, being the obliging wife, had agreed though she was not in the mood. It was the first-time sex with him had been painful and uncomfortable.

Wolfie said, "Thank you, Mia. I could tell you didn't want to, so thank you."

You knew and still went ahead with it anyway? What's with that look on your face? Why do you look so pleased and so proud? Why thank me in that creepy way? Did you put your own sexual needs above mine again?

Soldiering On
Chapter 22

Wolfie would often seek her company for his amusement. Sometimes he would bring her a cup of coffee, if she was watching TV, and interrupt her, "Talk to me." In the car, he would turn off the radio when he had had enough music and talk back radio, place his hand on her knee and say, "Talk to me." That was her cue to dazzle him with her conversation. Mia did not mind this interaction with Wolfie, as it gave them the opportunity to connect in a way that was not immoral or dangerous. It was a way for her to keep the peace by distracting him with the gossip of her single girlfriends' lives. He loved hearing about the losers they had met online or the dramas they were having in the bedroom.

"That guy Melissa was seeing, turned out to be a religious freak. He bible-bashed her all night." Wolfie laughed.

"Oh, my goodness! Stephanie rang me the other day, and you'll never guess what's happened?" exclaimed Mia.

"What! What! Do tell?" He was mocking her.

She again disregarded his behaviour, "She's been going through a terrible time and hasn't told a soul. I guess she felt a little ashamed and embarrassed, but apparently Rob has run off with a younger woman! Ten years younger! Nerdy Rob! Can you believe it?!"

"Seriously?" He had stopped poking fun at her and was now listening intently.

"Apparently, she's some air hostess. A mutual client of theirs. I've seen a photo and Stephanie is much prettier."

"Sounds like a mid-life crisis."

"He's a bit late for one of those! He's 59!"

"Late bloomer." His comment made her laugh.

"I feel sorry for her. She didn't see it coming. I queried if things had been okay between them? She said, 'Yes.' I said, 'So you were having sex regularly?' and she says, 'Not often.' So, I asked, 'When was the last time?' She replies, 'About seven years ago.' I couldn't believe it!"

"Wow, really?"

"I said to her if the last time you had sex was seven years ago, then something was very wrong. She said he had started blood pressure tablets and was always tired, and she thought he was just getting older. Apparently, he is taking Viagra for his new bimbo, the home wrecker. Stephanie found it in his trousers when she was doing his laundry." Wolfie was shaking his head.

"He wanted to maintain the status quo, so he wanted to come home for dinner, see the kids, have her wash his clothes and then go have sex with the mistress. Originally, she agreed to an open marriage! She lasted six months before booting him out! Man! I would never put up with that! Anyway, he rocked up the other day wearing pointy shoes with shiny gold trousers, a thick gold chain around his neck and an unbuttoned collared shirt, exposing his chest. I said, 'You're not painting a pretty picture!' I couldn't stop laughing! It had her in stitches too."

Rob was an accountant, a tedious dweeb who lacked social skills and as Wolfie put it, "a boring dork!" He wore thick-rimmed black square glasses and a Beatles haircut.

"It's caused such upheaval at home. The three kids aren't talking to him and Stephanie is gutted. She's bitterly disappointed because she nursed him back to health when he was on his death bed last year with bacterial meningitis and now, that's how he repays her. It's such a mess. He's such a jerk."

"He's an idiot. I would never do that," he replied.

"She suggested marriage counselling and you know what he said, 'You can't improve on perfection'. I tell you he's lost his marbles!" Wolfie was still shaking his head.

"I've told her to let me know if there's anything I can do." Mia supported her girlfriends as much as she could. She was there for her friends to bounce ideas off, to get things off their chests and to provide them with a non-judgemental shoulder to cry on.

If Mia did not have gossip to share with him, she would talk about a book she had just read, something she had seen on television, or talk about a new hobby that she had taken up. Mia always had something going on, unlike Wolfie who liked to stay at home and remain glued to the television.

She would often tell him jokes. "There was a lady playing golf when she accidentally hit her ball into the bushes. When she went to retrieve it, she found a frog with its leg caught in a trap. The frog spoke to her. 'Please. I'm a magic frog. If you release me, I'll grant you three wishes.' The lady was suspicious, but since she had never encountered a talking frog before, she set him free. The frog sat there and asked, 'So what will your first wish be?' The lady stood there thinking, and was about to make her first wish, when he warned, 'There's just one catch, whatever you wish for your husband shall receive ten-fold.' She thought long and hard before saying, 'I'd like to be the richest woman in the world.' The frog replied, 'I'll grant you your wish, but be warned your husband will be ten times richer than you.' The woman replied, 'We're husband and wife. What's mine is his, and his is mine. That's not a problem.' The frog said a few magic words and hocus pocus she became the richest woman in the world. The frog then asked, 'And for your second wish?' Again, the woman thought long and hard before speaking, 'I want to be the most beautiful woman in the world.' Again, the frog warned, 'Your husband will be ten times more beautiful than you. He will be an Adonis. Women will flock to him.' Again, she replied, 'That's okay. We're married, and he has eyes only for me.' The frog uttered a few magic words and she became the most beautiful woman in the world. The frog then asked, 'What will your final wish be?' The woman thought long and hard before replying, 'I'd like to have a mild heart attack." Mia roared with laughter. Wolfie chuckled.

Now that the children were older, they were happiest being on their own. This meant that Wolfie and Mia were free to socialise kid free. They were relishing their newly found independence. He did not have many friends; she was his best friend. Being the social co-ordinator for the household and having many family friends, she would often entertain on the weekend at lunch or dinner. Those invited would then reciprocate with an invitation. "Hey, Wolfie, we've been invited to the Quails' place for dinner this Saturday. Do you want to go?"

Josephine and Mia had met when Mia volunteered to be a contact for an outreach program run by the Spastic Centre. It was to help new families meet those who had already experienced life with an older affected child and to offer support through advice and friendship. When she had called, Mia had invited her for a coffee and a chat, and they had immediately warmed to each other. They then had regular catchups after that. Their children being of the same age meant they played well together, and they had remained friends for over 15 years.

"But she's such a crap cook," he whined, accustomed to Mia's cordon bleu cuisine. She had honed her skills through the hours of solace spent waiting for him to get home from work, whilst her girlfriend prepared meals to the standard of a good bistro or café. Mia was thankful to have a night off from cooking and would have settled for eating sandwiches. She also loved catching up with her girlfriend, as she was such a down to earth and genuine person.

"Josephine said they would get pizza from up the road, that way you can have what you want."

"Do we have to go?"

"Yes. Don't be anti-social."

It was early Saturday evening and Mia could not find Wolfie. He was not in his usual places; the sofa was empty as was the media room and the study. She found him lying on the bed.

"What are you doing up here? Are you okay?"

"I'm not feeling that great."

"What's wrong?"

"I'm just feeling a bit down. I don't think I can go tonight."

"Don't you think if you get out, you'll feel a lot better? Once you've had a shower, put on some clean clothes and had a glass of wine. It'll change your thoughts. I mean, you've hardly set foot outside all weekend."

"I probably should have a shower. I haven't had one for the last three days."

"Gross! I thought there was the smell of dirty bratwurst!"

Wolfie laughed. "Very funny! But I just can't be bothered. You go. You'll have a good time without me." She knew there was no point arguing.

"I tell you what, how about I run you a bath and bring you a cup of tea? A good soak in the tub, is what I think you need."

Mia ran him a bubble bath as she had done many times before. Wolfie took off his shirt and threw it on the floor. His belly was round and slack, hanging over the edge of his waistband. Taking the rest of his clothes off, he stepped into the bath and slid down until his shoulders dipped under the soapy water, the bubbles popping gently against his skin. Mia came back in with a cup of peppermint tea and a plate of cheese and tomato slivers she had prepared on some crackers. As he relaxed in the tub, she could see the tension ebb away from his face.

"I love you, Mia, you're so good to me."

"I love you too, Wolfie." She smiled. It was a nice smile that warmed her entire face. She rang Josephine to let her know that Wolfie was sick and unable to join them and got ready.

She knocked on Alex's bedroom door. "Yeah?" He was lying on his bed reading a book.

"Hello, darling, I'm heading out in five to have dinner with the Quails. Your dad's not feeling well so he's staying home. I've made an eggplant lasagne. When you're hungry, you can just heat it up for yourself and your sister. Don't worry about your dad, he can fend for himself. Okay?"

"Yum! I love that eggplant dish. Thanks, Mum. Sure, no problem."

She walked down the corridor to her daughter's room. The door was open. Chloe sat on the rug with photos strewn across the floor as she selected some for her scrapbook album.

"I'll see you later darling. Alex will heat up some dinner when you're hungry. I'll talk to you later."

"Bye Mum."

Having had a pleasant time at the Quails as always, she came home to find Wolfie sitting up in bed reading, which was unusual, as normally he never waited up for her.

"How was your evening?" he asked.

"Good. Josephine and Ezra said to say hello. So, hello. Are you feeling better?" she asked as she undressed.

"A little."

"That's good. Maybe you just needed to relax. Did you eat something?"

"Yeah, I just made myself some toast and had some yoghurt. I didn't feel like lasagne." When alone he usually just gorged himself on sweets and soft drinks.

"How were the kids?" She stepped into their en-suite bathroom.

"The kids did their own thing and so did I."

"Okay. Cool. I'm just going to have a quick shower before coming to bed," she said, closing the door.

She was on the toilet when she heard him exclaim. "Do I have to hear that? Can you do that a little more quietly?"

"Can you leave me alone and mind your own business! Stop listening!"

"You sound like a high-pressure gurney!"

"Can you shut up! You're just jealous that I can still pee in a steady stream, unlike you who stands there for hours with a trickle, trickle." He laughed.

"How am I supposed to make love to you? Next time, I'll be thinking of you on the toilet and nothing will happen."

"Well, don't think about it! It's a normal, human bodily function."

She turned on the water which drowned out any further protests or remarks from him. She exited the bathroom in her pyjamas ready for bed and was plunged into darkness. Wolfie was lying with his back turned to her.

Take a hint! Guess there won't be any action tonight!

"Good night sweetheart," he mumbled.

"Good night Wolfie."

The following Sunday, Mia invited the Becker's for lunch. Entertaining always seemed to lift his mood. Orlando was of German descent so Wolfie tended to listen to his opinion. Aria was, in contrast, very spiritual. They were an older couple that she thought were a good influence on him.

Wolfie could hear Mia in the kitchen rattling containers of glass and shuffling iron pans as he sat at the computer in his study. A culinary orchestra tuning up and clattering toward the finale. The smells of her delicious meal were wafting through the house. She had cooked veal that she had wrapped with ham and cheese held together by toothpicks, baked in a cheesy Béchamel sauce with a selection of roasted vegetables and had made a Caesar salad. Now they were sitting down, hoeing into her chocolate mousse cake.

Orlando said, "I was pulled over the other day for speeding."

"Those bastards are always revenue raising!" protested Wolfie.

"Well, I was actually speeding. I was trying out my new Audi, seeing what she could do. Anyway, it was a lady cop, and I apologised. She complimented me on the colour of my car, and we started talking. I asked her how her day had been. She sent me off with a warning."

"You were lucky! They're such cocksuckers! Such pricks!"

"No, Wolfie, they're just doing their job like you and me. If you're polite and show them respect, it goes a long way."

The coffee steamed as Mia poured Aria another cup, its aroma wafting through the house; she then carefully added milk from the creamer that she held a few inches above the cup. Aria was talking to Mia, "I wish I'd had more children, at least another, but when Dahlia was five, I thought it was too late. Looking back on it now, I realise that it would have been okay. It didn't help that we didn't have any family support. It made things difficult."

"I know what you mean about the lack of support. We didn't have much either and found it tough. I had a boss once, called Vivienne, a lovely lady, who had four kids. All of them were exactly five years apart. Every five years she would pop out another one. It worked for her."

Wolfie interrupted, "Kids are overrated! They're more trouble than their worth. I wish I'd never had any."

"Wolfie, how can you say that?" asked Orlando.

"I mean it. Is it worth it? Besides mine might not actually be mine." Aria and Orlando chortled.

"Whose would they be then? The postman's? He is blonde, blue-eyed and has buck teeth. I never would have gone there," replied Mia.

"I was just reading online that it's more common than you think," replied Wolfie.

"Oh, Wolfie," giggled Aria.

"What are we going to do with you, Wolfie?" softly chuckled Orlando.

"You can have a DNA test anytime you want. They're definitely yours! The only way they would not be yours is if they had accidentally been switched at birth by the hospital, in which case, they would not be mine either." Everyone laughed.

Once their guests had left and Mia had cleaned up, Wolfie sat with her drinking a cup of coffee. When he had finished, he announced, "I'm going to go spend some time on the computer." He stood up as he bellowed, "Alex! Come down and clean the kitchen!"

"Wolfie, I've just cleaned the kitchen. It's only one mug. It can wait until dinner."

He disappeared. Alex didn't come downstairs, and Mia sat there finishing her coffee. Wolfie picked on him incessantly. He often put him down in front of their friends by ridiculing him, and she always came to his rescue. Wolfie would constantly swear at him and indulge in name-calling like a child. Again, she would intervene.

There was a time when Mia went grocery shopping and as she pulled up in the driveway, she could hear Wolfie roaring inside. She walked into the house and went upstairs to find him standing in the doorway to Alex's bedroom as he berated him.

"What the hell is going on? Everyone can hear you from the street."

"I don't fucking care! I'm tired of this fucking little shit and his attitude!"

"Can you calm down and tell me what happened?" Alex looked terrified and was quietly sitting on his bed with downcast eyes and hands fumbling nervously in his lap.

"Take his fucking side again, just like you always do. You bloody bitch!"

She felt that familiar jab of pain. It bothered her that he was always quick to call her names and it was always he who started with the expletives and never her.

"Okay! That's enough! Go downstairs! Get back on your computer because that's all you're good at."

He now hurled insults at her. His anger had shifted but at least he had moved away from Alex and was making his way downstairs.

When he was out of ear shot, she asked Alex, "Are you okay? What happened?"

"I walked into the house and he started yelling at me accusing me of having slammed the door when I hadn't. He wanted me to go outside, come back in and quietly close the door behind me. I told him, 'I didn't slam the door and I'm going to my room.' He chased me up the stairs and punched me in the back."

"What!? Are you alright?"

"I thought he was going to kill me. I hate him, Mum." She felt pangs of pain for her son's suffering, but mostly sadness at their disintegrating relationship, which was all Wolfie's doing. She had stayed in the marriage to protect her children but now wondered if this was not damaging Alex.

"I'll try and talk to him when he's calmed down and make him see sense. Don't worry about it. You haven't done anything wrong," she said, trying to comfort and reassure him.

Mia tried to discuss this incident later with Wolfie but he had continued insulting her and accused her of taking Alex's side.

"I will take his side when you're doing the wrong thing. What do you hope to achieve treating him in that manner?"

"I want respect."

"I think all you're doing is damaging the relationship you have with him."

"I don't care!"

He was jealous of their bond. What he failed to see was that Mia had cultivated this connection with Alex since he was a baby, always involving him in her life and being interested in him. Wolfie had never bothered with either of their children, yet she often heard him say, "I'm an excellent father."

In what dimension or which parallel universe are you referring to?

This was not the first time, and nor would it be the last, that he would brutalise their son. The physical abuse would only stop when Alex was taller and stronger than him. When Wolfie could no longer discipline him with physical punishment, he resorted to threatening to kick him out of the house.

Wolfie said to Mia, "I want Alex to move out."

"Why …? What's happened now?"

"He's a little shit and he's old enough to move out," he replied with malevolence.

"He's just finished his HSC and done well, considering you uprooted all of us in his final year of exams! He'll be starting Uni, and he doesn't give us any problems. He doesn't drink or smoke. He doesn't do drugs. He isn't a wild party animal. He's NEVER given us any grief. I don't understand why you're forever picking on him."

"I've had enough of him and the way he talks to me."

"Maybe if you were nicer to him."

"Take his side why don't you! I never have your support, you're always on his side." He sniffed loudly with disdain.

"That's SO NOT TRUE, but when you pick on him unnecessarily, when he's done nothing wrong and you're unreasonable, then yes, I will take his side; someone has to. He's in his room most of the time avoiding you, because all you do is yell and pick on him."

"Good! That's where he belongs! You can just never support me, can you? Even when I'm asking you for it?"

She walked away. Sometimes there was just no point trying to discuss things with him. She behaved differently with the children and never swore at them and tried never to swear in front of them. The worst thing she had ever called Alex was a "ding-dong", to which he had exclaimed, "Oh, so now I'm the sound of a doorbell?" At that moment, she could have throttled Alex but she did not, and he lived to tell the tale.

Band-Aid
Chapter 23

Mia had had a terrible year. Nonna had died in her sleep at the age of 98, earlier in the year, without suffering. Mia thought she would like to pass this way when her time came. On the other hand, three months later her girlfriend Michelle had died, two months after being diagnosed with a cancerous brain tumour, a secondary cancer caused by her first illness, breast cancer. She had only been 46. These deaths preyed on Wolfie's mind. He started often making comments like, "You never know how long you've got," "I might only be here for another year or two," and, "I could just drop dead so who cares about eating healthy. I'm going to eat what I want when I want."

"Do you know something I don't? Do you have cancer? Are you going into renal failure? Has the doctor only given you months to live? Are you dying?" She asked as she sat in the sun in the living room on their sofa.

"No, not yet" he answered sardonically, looking up from his newspaper while he reclined on the other leather couch.

"Well, if you're going to die, make sure it's instantaneous and not that you end up needing 24-hour care. I can tell you I've had enough of all the extra effort in looking after Chloe, and I'm not interested in doing that again. Every night, while you'll be sitting helplessly in your wheelchair at the dinner table, we'll be asking, 'Who fed Dad last night? Whose turn is it?' Just like the kids currently do with Delilah." Mia said with a chuckle.

Wolfie laughed, "Thank you very much."

"Isn't it great being part of a loving caring family?" she replied sarcastically.

Wolfie nodded, still laughing.

Unbeknownst to her, he was struggling again, due to those deaths. His way of coping was limited to getting up, going to work, and providing for his family. That's where it began and ended. It was as if he had reverted to survival mode and was not really living. He would come home and go straight to his computer to unwind. Like him, Mia worked on the computer all day, and could not think of anything worse than spending the evening on one as well.

He said, "I just need half an hour to myself to relax," but the pattern developed of reading the news and playing online games. Again, after she had called him numerous times, he would join the family for dinner, and once finished, return to his self-appointed exile. Mia spent her evenings in the lounge room with the children watching television, playing board games, listening to music and spending time with them, but she craved attention from her husband, any attention. She was slowly becoming weary of the same routine.

Now and then, she would go and see how Wolfie was doing, coming up behind him and giving him a bear hug and a kiss on the cheek. It was always well-received. She brought him bottomless cups of coffee and tea and an endless supply of snacks and would keep him company, sitting and talking to him. She came over to him later that evening.

"I've made you a rosehip tea. Where would you like it?" He had quickly minimised the screen as she entered the study.

"Thanks darling. Here, just place it here." He shuffled some papers on his antique desk clearing a space for her and laying down a coaster.

"What were you watching?"

He spoke to her with exhilaration, "I looked online for the story about that guy they beheaded and look what's popped up; it's amazing. There are all these videos of people getting murdered, and it's all real. I can't believe how easy it is to find this stuff on the internet. Here, watch this."

He played a video of a man driving his Jeep being pursued by men in a small truck armed with semi-automatic machine guns. The driver jumped out of his vehicle and was being chased by these armed men firing at him. He looked terrified.

"Oh, my goodness! I don't want to watch anymore. That's dreadful."

"It's unbelievable!"

"I don't think you should watch that sort of thing. I don't think it's good for your mind."

"You should see some of the other stuff I've found. There was a guy having sex with a sheep."

"That's disturbing. You'd better be careful watching that sort of thing."

He played her a video of a girl on her knees giving fellatio to two enormous penises. She was gagging and watching her made Mia's eyes water.

"I've seen enough. She looks like she's about to puke. How old is she? She looks underage to me. I'm sure that watching snuff videos, bestiality and child pornography sets off alarm bells somewhere. The last thing you want to do is end up on a sex offender's register."

"Don't be dramatic. She doesn't look like a kid to me."

"Do me a favour and make sure our children don't walk in on you watching this inappropriate stuff."

"Yeah, I know. I know. I'm being careful."

She tried luring him over to watch a movie with her, especially when the kids had gone to bed but he refused. "I've just started playing a new game and I'm happy here."

She tried talking to him about it, "Listen darling," she began, "it would be nice if we saw you sometimes and you maybe came over and watched a movie with us."

"There's nothing suitable that I want to watch."

"I don't like the way you're always by yourself in the study, watching dubious videos. It's like you're not even home. I'm always alone with the children in the other room, and we don't see you. I do everything with them. At times, I feel like a widow. When I call you over for dinner, you put your feet under the table for five minutes, eat and disappear. You don't spend any time with me or them. I'm like a single mum. I'd like to spend some time with you too. I'm not happy with the way things are going."

"Well, if you're not happy, that's your problem, because I am."

Really, is that so?

Eventually, the hugs and cups of tea became less prevalent. She was withdrawing. He didn't notice. She would try to broach the subject with him again, but he would stubbornly refuse to discuss it. The matter according to him, was closed. At about this time, some of her single girlfriends were going out dancing at night clubs on weekends. She felt envious listening to their tales and decided to join them when they invited her.

Why not? He doesn't care if I'm here or not and I love to dance. I haven't gone out dancing in ages and I need to blow off some steam.

She ensured the children had full bellies and were content in their rooms. Her girlfriends would pick her up on Saturday night at 9.30pm, and she made certain that she was home before midnight. For the first couple of times, he was not interested, but after a while he began disapproving of this arrangement. He was, of course, thinking the worst, that Mia was hooking up with other men, but this was not the case, and had never been.

"You know, I'm not happy with you going out dancing every week."

She quickly responded, picking up her bag and coat, "Well if you're not happy, then I guess that's your problem because I am." And left with her girlfriends. He got the message.

Things had reached crisis point between them again. He seemed to drag her down whenever there was an issue that he was unable to deal with. This time he decided to see their family doctor about his anti-depressant medication. He had not had a check-up in a while even though she had begged him on numerous occasions to seek professional help. Whilst there, he updated him on the stress he had been feeling, and the tension at home.

Dr Knight asked, "She isn't having an affair, is she?" Wolfie came home to share this with Mia.

"What!? What did you say?" She was outraged.

"I told him I don't know. I don't think so."

"Good one, Wolfie! Thanks for sticking up for me! Where on earth would I find the time to have an affair?! I'm so busy! Plus, I have the kids with me all the time! Would I sit them on the sofa and be like, "Hey Kids, watch this," she continued. "What a bastard! He knows me. We've been seeing him as our family physician for years and that's what he thinks of me? That I'm a hoe! Some sort of scarlet woman!? What an arsehole! Thanks for defending me!" She was furious.

Having an affair was the furthest thing from her mind. The way she saw it, she already had one major headache in her life, her husband. He was like a constant migraine. Why would she want to complicate things by having an affair? Have two headaches? No thanks! She thought it was time to look around for another doctor.

Later, Wolfie would find out that Dr Knight's wife had been having an affair with his best friend and had left him. It made sense to her now why he had thought the worst of her, but she was not about to forgive him. Wolfie organised for them to see Michael again. In his office, Mia sat rigid with her hands tightly clenched in her lap and wore a pout. Turning to Michael she said, "I can't believe we're here again! I'm wondering what the point of coming here every five or six years, actually is? You make recommendations that are put in place and then shortly after Wolfie goes back to his old ways or doesn't really improve. When he calls me to tell me he's running late, he calls at 6.30pm, when dinner is done or well under way, and he still never greets me with a kiss when he walks through the door! What's the point of marriage counselling?!" She continued giving Michael many examples of Wolfie's selfishness and disrespect, "I don't say anything when I get up to pee at night and I find on the toilet seat covered in his urine because he's completely missed the bowl! He never cleans the drops of pee he leaves behind on the seat or on the floor. Nor does he clean the skid marks, he leaves down the sides of the bowl, because he knows maid Mia will take care of it!"

She also never said anything to him about the toilet roll being on backwards if he bothered to change it. It irritated her that the paper hung toward the wall rather than forwards. Mia was certain that there were many married couples who cohabited in peace and harmony and did not need to run to a marriage counsellor every few years. Her parents were a living example of that. Why did he always need this drama in his life? If it had been up to her, their relationship would have been effortless, warm and always loving. She was not the one always making sarcastic comments, poking fun, and putting people down. He needed to continually belittle everyone to bolster himself.

Eventually, after a few more sessions, Mia and Wolfie worked things out, and they settled back down into their married life. He seemed to be calm again and was listening to her.

One evening they were in the study chatting. Mia said, "I'm starting to think that running to Michael is just a band-aid. You need to hear me and listen to me when I talk to you. We need to be able to stand on our own two feet and work things out. I don't want to run to marriage counsellors anymore. What's the purpose of me speaking if you're not listening?"

He replied, "Why don't you come to me when I'm in a good mood, and when you're calm, and not screeching at me? Then maybe I'll hear you."

Wolfie was on his computer and Mia in a chair next to him. She had just brought him a hot chocolate and a slice of warm cake she had baked.

Frosting dripped from Wolfie's lips as each layer of chocolate sponge seemed to melt on his tongue.

"But how do I do that? So many times, I've tried that approach. I often come to you calmly to discuss something, but you immediately disassociate yourself, get on your high horse and stonewall me."

"What rubbish! You can never discuss anything! You always attack!", his demeanour becoming unpleasant.

"Hello! Look at what's happening now. I've come to you with my hat in hand. I have not raised my voice. I'm not yelling at you or insulting you and you're already on the defensive."

"That's because you're attacking me!"

"How am I doing that? I'm trying to have a discussion with you, a conversation."

"There you go again, you silly cow, always starting a fight. Talking to me in that tone." Wolfie was a shouter. It needed very little to get him to raise his voice. It was something that had irritated the entire family for years.

"I give up!" She left the room. Inside she was fuming.

You can be such an arsehole! What a lost cause! With the next upheaval that you cause, I'll be ripping that band-aid off, once and for all!

The next morning, after her shower, Mia was surprised as she caught her refection in the mirror. It was not half bad, but after two pregnancies and breast feeding her children, her breasts had changed shape. Wolfie watching her was dissatisfied, "If I'd known what breast feeding would've done to your breasts, I never would've allowed it!"

As if the decision was yours to make!

He continued, "Why don't you get a boob job?"

He showed her photos of women on the internet who had had breast enlargements, and which ones he thought were the best. He seemed to like what Mia would describe as "large floatation devices"; these women would never need to wear a life jacket again. He emphasized how beautiful and feminine they looked, his face full of appreciation, telling Mia that she could easily look like that too.

At first surprised by his suggestion, she eventually agreed to make some enquiries and get more information. Initially, they consulted with two cosmetic surgeons. Both suggested a breast lift before getting implants. The first surgeon they met, had a bulbous bald head and gave the impression that he was arrogant and conceited. She decided to go with the second surgeon, Dr Rupert, who reminded her of a sweet grandfather.

Dr Rupert said that Mia had breast atrophy and could therefore recover some money from Medicare as this was a correction, rather than just a cosmetic procedure. Wolfie was pleased that this would lower the cost, but if not, he still believed that this expense was justifiable and encouraged her to get it done. He was just excited at the prospect of new toys to play with. Mia agreed to the lift, believing that this was a repair, rather than an improvement for vanity's sake. A date was set.

On the eve of Mia's surgery, a girlfriend invited her over for dinner. She lived alone in a rented granny flat and had just come out of a relationship. She felt vulnerable as her close friends and family resided in Melbourne. Mia explained the situation to Wolfie, and that she wanted to be there for her friend. He agreed.

Naomi had made a salad and a lasagne. They sat around chatting while it baked in the oven. It was 8.30pm when Naomi said, "*Sex in the City*" is on tonight. Let's watch it."

"Cool. I love that show, I'll watch it and then I'd better make tracks."

At 8.35pm, Mia's mobile rang.

"Hello?"

"When are you coming home?" asked Wolfie, seething.

"Well, we've just sat down to watch Sex in the City and I'll be home after that."

"I want you home now!"

"What …?" Mia laughed. "I've just had a glass of wine. I'm feeling lightheaded so I'll have to wait a while before I can drive. I'll leave at 9.30pm. I'll see you later." She hung up and wondered what that had been about.

By the time she got home, Wolfie had worked himself up into an irrational frenzy. He yelled at her and she yelled back. The animosity was almost tangible between them. As usual, he swore at her and called her names. Again, they both went to bed angry.

In the morning, Wolfie drove Mia to the hospital which took nearly an hour. The whole trip he continued berating her, annoyed that she had gone out. She had come home at a reasonable hour and he had given her his blessing. What was his problem? At the hospital, they went through her paperwork, took her into a cubicle, and she slipped into a gown. Wolfie accompanied her and continued his angry barrage. She was crying.

The staff could see the tension between them. A nurse, Shelley, with a trim figure and a cherubic face, asked, "Would you like to reschedule your surgery?"

Mia declined, "No. I'm here now, let's just get it over and done with." Mia wanted to get away from Wolfie, and she would rather undergo the knife then be in the same room as him for one minute longer.

In the recovery room, she slowly opened her eyes feeling ghastly; a thick bandage was wrapped around her chest and her mouth felt dry. The first person she saw was Wolfie, leaning over her, peering into her face. She was filled with terror and fear.

Oh goodness! Not again! Not him!

He was smiling, his face warm and friendly. There was love in his eyes. In the gentlest, softest voice, he asked, "Mia, are you okay? Look at you with all your tubes and bandages. Are you okay?"

She was stunned. He was again acting like a real-life Dr Jekyll and Mr Hyde. She had not done anything to provoke his wrath, nor had she done anything for him to calm down, but now he seemed placated.

When she was discharged, Wolfie drove her home. He was kind and caring as she spent most of the car ride throwing up into an emesis bag given to her by the hospital. After returning home, she slowly slipped back into her routine. She sat in the lounge room. Two lorikeets flew past the window in quick succession. As they squawked, a car engine started, and the postman passed by the house on his motorcycle. No bills today. She sat resting in the lounge room and noticed a broken nail. She bit the broken end off but this left it feeling jagged and rough, so she chewed at this to make it smooth and before she knew it, she had bitten it down to the quick.

She still had a meal ready on the table when he walked in the door. She still helped the children but did not clean the house, knowing it would wait for her. Her birthday came and went while she recuperated. He had penned a card, something that was now infrequent in their marriage. The card had a picture of a Gothic looking girl on the front standing over a table covered in candles. It read, "Someone's hoarding a lot of birthday candles this year, and I hate to point fingers but …"

Inside the card, Wolfie had written, "Happy Birthday Mia!"

"I hope you have a lovely day. We wish you a very happy birthday, even though you may not wish to celebrate it." She wasn't enthused with the idea of getting older.

He continued, "Love your new breasts, can't wait to test them out. Wolfie xxxx"

That was her Wolfie, crazy one minute, tranquil the next. When he was in a good mood, they got along well, and were the best of friends. Conversation flowed well between them. He would take her out to gourmet restaurants, and on special occasions, he would shower her with jewellery. Sometimes he would whisk her away for the weekend, just the two of them. He would talk to her about politics, world events, and religion. It would be an intelligent discussion, and he would frequently tell her, "I love you, Mia." She always enjoyed this time together. When everything was fine, it was better than fine. It was phenomenal.

As soon as he felt down, or something had not quite gone his way, his mood darkened, and she was the one he took it out on. When she eventually retaliated and started swearing at him, the way he did at her, he would take offense. When she pointed out, that it was always him who yelled and swore first, he fervently denied it. She did, at times, find him impossible, but still loved him. She was his wife. She had a home with him, and she had his children to think of, not to mention one with a disability who was as much work as twins. She enjoyed his company when he was rational and showed her respect.

Sometimes I feel trapped because I'm not free. I'm a servant. I serve my boss at work and my family at home. I'm like a robot. He never helps me, though he always promises to. He doesn't lose his cool as frequently as he used to. I think with age, he seems to have mellowed, but his requests to try sexually perverted things and his need for debauchery has increased. Sometimes he can't hear me when I say NO! But I must stay, I've lasted this long. It's best for the children, for him, and even me. How would I manage financially on my own? I still love him, and we have made a lovely life together, with our home and adorable family. One thing's for sure, I'm not doing any more marriage counselling. I think that's just a band-aid. He needs to be able to hear, listen and understand me on his own.

Mia would do her best to keep Wolfie busy, because when he was distracted, he would be less moody and not misbehave. Perhaps this was another band-aid measure, but it also gave them the chance to spend quality time together and to connect.

One Summer, when the children were 14 and 17, they had been invited to one of Wolfie's stepsister's wedding. Carolyn had finally decided to marry Bob who was ten years younger than her. They had chosen a venue at Terrigal and had booked The Plaza Hotel for their guests. Wolfie and Mia arrived at the hotel and were directed to their room. It was a small space with a double bed. This immediately worried Mia as she would have no escape from Wolfie's excessively loud snoring.

She had not had a good night's sleep in months and would go to extreme lengths to try and get some rest. When at home, she would try sleeping on the sofa downstairs and had resorted to lying upside down next to him in bed. This was dangerous, because she would quite often be woken by a swift kick in the back. His neurologist diagnosed "restless leg syndrome", and there was no cure.

That's great news! NOT!

Approximately 100 guests attended the bare foot beach wedding, mostly family members from both sides. Due to the spiralling list of invitees, Alex and Chloe had not been invited, and were relieved; the thought of attending had filled them with dread.

After a sumptuous dinner, those who were staying retired to their rooms. Wolfie was spent from the drive up, even though it had only taken a couple of hours. Unfortunately for Mia, Wolfie fell asleep before she did and she had no chance of getting to sleep with his reverberating snoring. There was no sofa to retreat to. There was no escape in their small hotel room. She tried her trick of sleeping upside down but tonight it did not help. She yearned for the ear plugs she had left at home, even though she knew they did very little except aggravate her, as they made their own little rustling sounds and were uncomfortable to wear.

She was so tired that she saw herself reaching for her pillow and smothering him with it, until the terrible sonorous racket subsided. In the end, she took out her mobile phone and decided to record him. She would play it back to him, so he could hear for himself what she had to put up with. She eventually fell asleep.

In the morning, they both got up, showered, dressed, and went downstairs for breakfast. Sam and Tammy were at a table talking with some of the guests. As they approached, Sam made introductions. "This is my son, Wolfie, and his wife, Mia." There was the customary hand shaking, smiling and greetings.

Wolfie turning to Sam, "So how did you sleep last night?"

"I actually got a good night's sleep. The bed was very comfy. What about you?"

"I had a terrible night, thanks to Mia. She kept waking me up! All night, she kept shushing and shushing me, and I hardly slept a wink!" He turned to look at Mia, "All night long, shhhhhh, shhhhhhh, that's all I got from you."

Sam was laughing, his large cackling chortle.

"I mean seriously, Mia, did you have a flat tyre or something? All night. Shhh, shhhh."

"You were snoring," said Mia defensively.

"Were you making snake impersonations or something?" Wolfie was entertaining everyone at the table. They were all laughing.

Everyone was looking at Mia, judging her for what seemed like a ridiculous level of sheer selfishness. She reached for her mobile phone and pressed play as she placed it in the centre of the table. Suddenly, the air was filled with the loud offensive sounds of Wolfie's snores.

Sam stopped, as he looked at Mia and asked, "What's that?"

"That would be the sound of your son snoring last night," replied a calm Mia.

"That's terrible," said Sam as he listened and looked disbelievingly at Wolfie.

Tammy was laughing as they listened to the sound of his droning snores reaching a crescendo, crashing down and starting all over again. "Oh, Mia," she laughed, "oh, Mia."

"He sounds like he is grinding gravel, all that grumbling and grating. It doesn't stop. If he's on his side, or on his back, it makes no difference. It just doesn't stop! I couldn't sleep so that's why I shushed him, which by the way didn't help." She threw Wolfie a glance.

Sam turned to Wolfie, "That's bad. You need to do something about that."

Sam asked her to put her phone away. Tammy was still chuckling. Wolfie had become uncharacteristically quiet. He no longer wanted to be the centre of attention and sat quietly eating his breakfast. He had stopped clowning around and trying to blame Mia, who felt slightly victorious.

Kinky
Chapter 24

When he was in an amorous mood, he would lean closer and whisper seductively, "Do you want to go up and have your shower?" That was his come-on line. Or sometimes he would ask, "Do you want to go up and get ready?" This was her cue to have a shower, slip into something comfortable that he had bought, and wait for him in bed. Yet, all she really wanted was for him to look at her the way he used to, with a teasing smile and love in his eyes.

For her birthday, the following year, he gave her sexy underwear. She felt like these were more of a gift for him but never expressed her disappointment. She had more underwear than outer wear, and always had to dress up, to get sex from him. He made lovemaking feel like a chore. Sometimes, she would walk into the bedroom and find, already laid out on the bed, what he had chosen for her to wear for their upcoming sex session. Today, a black lacy bra with matching panties and suspender belt, and of course, a new packet of stockings. It was his fetish. Wolfie had bought her every type of suspender belt on the market and each had a matching bra and panties, of every shade of every colour and every combination of patterns with a vast array of stockings: lace tops, vintage nylons, black seams, full lace, spotted, striped, as well as stay ups, and fishnets.

There was never any spontaneity, and she found his bedroom antics dull, but again, she never voiced her boredom. She understood that it was difficult with children around, but even if they went away or were alone together, it was always the same, "Do you want to go and have your shower?" Set in his ways, he never deviated from the same routine. She wished that he would be more romantic, maybe sometimes offer a massage which could lead to something more, but he had never been fond of her giving these, although she frequently massaged his back when it was sore.

Every so often, he would follow her to the bathroom and whisper, "I want to shave your pussy," and she would oblige. On this occasion, he asked her to stand naked while he changed the blade in his razor to a new one. He knelt in front of her and applied shaving cream before gently shaving her in downward strokes in the direction of the hair's growth. He was pedantic and used small strokes and held the skin taut with the fingers of his other hand to protect against nicks and cuts, as he methodically removed every bit of hair that bothered him, regularly rinsing his blade as the water continued running in the sink. His breathing became shallower as he concentrated on the task at hand. Since he was also naked, as he trimmed and shaped her pubic hair, his penis grew and became firmer. It gave her a fresh sense of pleasure to witness his growing erection and she felt her breath and heartbeat quicken. He tenderly took her by the hips and moved her gingerly to the edge of the bathtub, where he sat her with her legs spread, and continued shaving her until there was no more hair, except for the floating landing strip above her pubic bone. He then instructed her to stand up and lean forward and pull her derriere cheeks apart, so he could shave her there.

This is weird!

Though she was compliant, she wondered where all these kinky ideas came from. It never occurred to him that she did not share his peculiarities. When finished, he rinsed her in the shower with the retractable shower head, trying different speeds and strengths of water to arouse her. It did nothing. He would play with her with his fingers. He purred his version of dirty talk in her ear, "I love licking and sucking pussy" and, "I love your cunt! You've got such a nice cunt! I just love it."

When he'd had enough, he would bend her forward, so she was in a downward dog position, and take her from behind. He easily slipped inside her, his penis hard and her body yielding, sucking him in. She gripped her ankles, and sometimes lent on the wall for support, as he pounded away, the water running down her back and over her shoulders. She enjoyed this position because he was his deepest inside her and she could feel the length of him as he hit her inner walls. She felt her muscles tightening and her body quivering with every thrust. If he did not climax, they would continue in the bedroom, but he was usually quick to finish and when he was done, so was everybody else. Though she had enjoyed most of what had transpired, he never managed to make her climax. He would sometimes say, "Tell me what to do and I'll do it to make you cum," but he would inevitably get tired and give up. She would always have to finish herself off later.

He got off watching her masturbate and frequently asked her to pleasure herself in front of him. He said, "I want to watch and learn. See how you do it." Mia did feel self-conscious lying naked in front of him even though she more often than not still had stockings and suspenders on, while he lay at her feet intently watching. With her legs spread and the middle finger of her right hand vigorously circling her clitoris and her left hand firmly on her lower stomach, she began pleasuring herself. She closed her eyes to avert his intense gaze. He would sometimes partake in her exploits when she was about to climax by inserting a finger or two. She did find this annoying and was quite happy bringing herself to orgasm solo. He was always amazed at how quickly she came, her body tensing and her head rocking as she moaned in pleasure.

He had bought her sex toys online and also some from an adult shop which he had taken her to one weekend afternoon. One of his favourites was "the black smiley man". It was a dildo about six inches long with a wide girth and a vibrator, which had the image of a smiley face. He loved to have her lie on the bed with her legs spread and he would gently insert the dildo as he placed the vibrator on high speed on her clitoris, moving it around for the best reaction from her. In no time, she could feel her stomach knot in pent-up desire, the muscles tightening throughout her body as she squeezed handfuls of bedding, pinned down to the bed in sheer ecstasy, as her back arched, and she reached the brink, and then the scream that passed her lips as she felt the sweet release, the flood of liquid fire that rippled through every nerve ending in her body. And then a blissful calm. He always looked pleased with himself when he made her cum, and this was the only way he could ever achieve this. Afterwards, they lay on the bed, damp bodies spooned together, naked except for her stockings and suspenders in soft lamplight.

He liked to order her around in the bedroom. "Come up here and sit on my face." Other times, he would suggest things she had never heard of. Late one night, when the children were in bed, and they were alone in their bedroom, he stood naked in front of her, as she gave him fellatio, he gently asked, "Can you tea bag me?"

She was also naked and sat back on her heels, as she looked up at him and asked innocently, "What's that?" Compared to him, she was naïve about sex.

"You take my balls in your mouth."

Mia thought this sounded tamer than some of his previous requests, such as, "Can I cum on your face?" and "Can you open your mouth and stick out your tongue, so that I can cum on it?". Being open minded and willing to try new things, she thought she would please him by giving it a go. It dawned on her why it was called "tea bagging", when her mouth formed the shape of a teacup.

With her mouth full, she asked, "Now what?"

"Glide your tongue over them."

She complied and gagged, spitting out his testicles, "Urgh! That's so gross! It's hairy and vile! Yuck!"

He stood stroking his erection, his other hand cupping his balls, as he replied defensively, "But I've shaved."

"No. I'm sorry. That's just revolting. I can taste hair and the texture is like tough, raw chicken skin. It's disgusting. I'm not doing that!"

She found if she made suggestions about what she might like them to try, such as having sex at night in the pool when they were alone, or new positions instead of the standard doggy and missionary, he would always decline. She had the idea of going on a picnic, somewhere remote and having a quickie and an experience out in the open. He was appalled and flatly refused. When he decided against something, then his decision was final.

One weekend, they were driving to the movies. The route was familiar: the straight hill up, through the roundabout, past the school and then the dog park. He started pestering her again saying, "Before I die, I'd like to have sex with someone else, just for the experience."

"But Hubby, everybody fucks the same."

"I'd like to try a threesome. It's every guy's fantasy," he replied, "and most women's too."

"We've had this discussion before. It's not mine and never has been!"

When he could see that she was becoming upset, he would stop asking but every now and then it would start again. It was as if they were stuck in that same revolving door. This was their strange sex life, which swung between the borderline kinky and the lacklustre.

Glitches
Chapter 25

Wolfie screamed, "I'm sick of hearing about your work dramas!", as he stormed off to the study.

"My work dramas?" Mia called out loudly after him. "That's absurd!" She paused. "What about your years of work dramas?! You do have a short-term memory, don't you?" He slammed the door.

Mia was in the kitchen cleaning the oven and continued scrubbing as she thought about where she had worked. A lot of her experience was with medium-sized companies and her bosses, though outstanding in their chosen fields, had minimal people skills. They were usually arrogant and refused to take directives from others, as they believed them to be incompetent. Consequently, though they were brilliant, they were invariably difficult to deal with. They lacked rapport with everyone, and never considered the way they treated their staff and how unimportant this made them feel. Unlike him, she tried to resolve things and waited to see if they improved; perhaps that was why she had plenty of stories to share with Wolfie. That was the difference between them. At the first sign of trouble, he would up and leave. She had never been a quitter. If she thought about it, she could see the opportunities afforded to him, as a man in his field, had been far better than hers. Her roles had been more stressful than his and there also seemed to be a glass ceiling which he would never encounter.

Every day he would ask, "Hey, Mia, how was your day?" and she would answer, "I was flat out doing payroll", or "It was pretty good." Often, she came home wishing to leave work issues at the door, and would reply, "Fine", not wanting to discuss the drama she had been part of.

He would try to coax her, "Just fine? Nothing out of the ordinary happen?" or, "What about Nicky? Did she stuff anything up today?"

"You won't believe it! She signed some fake yellow pages advertising campaign, locking the business into paying thousands of dollars! Dickhead was so pissed! He asked her to come up with a budget of areas she could cut back on to recoup these lost funds. Of course, she couldn't do it and came to me for help, so I did it for her …"

Eventually, he would interrupt, "Look, I'll give you another 15 minutes and then I don't want to hear any more about it!"

Why ask me if you don't want to hear the answers? Am I only supposed to tell you positive stories? Do you ask only to reinforce your delusion that nobody else except you has problems? Did you think I should just storm out like you do?

Mia became aware that the differences in their attitudes to work were profound. She had always tried to keep it professional and refrained from losing her temper in front of her superiors. His constant instability was wearing her down. Mia had always changed jobs to further her career and chase more money for the benefit of her family. She sometimes lamented the fact that she felt she could have achieved so much more professionally but had always put her family first. She looked at the careers some of her single girlfriends had with a pinch of envy, because she had always wanted to have that big, important career.

What she failed to see was that she had managed to become a financial controller earning a salary of well over $100,000 whilst raising a family including a child with a disability mainly on her own. She knew that her girlfriends pined for the life she had. She seemed to have it all in perfect balance: the career, the family, and the loving husband. Little did they know!

She understood that if she had been a high-flyer, she would have earned more money and worked longer hours, but she would not have necessarily been happier. She was elated spending time with her family. Mia often said that being in business meant that she "worked with bastards all day, every day". She was glad to come home, kick off her shoes, talk to her children, walk the dog, go to the gym and unwind. She often doubted what she had achieved. She was proud of Chloe and the bright girl she had become and of her brilliant son, Alex, but what about the endless hamster wheel she seemed caught up in?

All I'm accomplishing is making someone else richer, but what good am I doing? I haven't found a cure for cancer or some other terminal disease. Who am I helping? What have I achieved with my life?

She mentioned this inner turmoil to her friend Zara as they chatted over the phone.

"What are you talking about, Mia?! Look at Chloe! She's only as good as she is thanks to you, and no one else, and what about Wolfie? You're the reason he's still alive!"

Mia eventually snapped out of her negativity, sure that it was a stage that everyone with a conscience went through at some point in their life. She had watched and listened to others struggle with the concept of "Why are we here? What is the point of it all?" Having Chloe, had defined her life's purpose. She had just craved and yearned for more as she had so much unused potential.

The traumatising experience she had had with Norman, made her sensitive to any inappropriate and unwanted male attention. Some of the experiences she had to endure as a woman, Wolfie would never ever face. When the children were younger, she had once worked for a business consultancy practice, where she and Mandy, the receptionist, were the only female members of an otherwise male dominated practice. When the business was facing a downturn, the bosses let Mandy go, a complete shock to them both. The business moved into the boss's house which was a suburb away.

Her boss, Jake, was going through a divorce, his wife having left him for a younger man. One morning Mia arrived at work with her hair still a little damp. Jake was sitting next to one of the other consultants as they studied something on the computer.

Mia greeted them, "Morning Jake! Morning Stuart!"

"Oh no! Oh no! Now that you've walked in here with wet hair, I'm having visions of you in the shower naked!" cried out Jake.

Never loquacious, Mia was now lost for words. She looked at him blankly. Stuart was laughing. From that day on Stuart would make lewd comments to her each time he saw her.

Though business was conducted from his suburban home, she still came to work in professional attire, suit, high heels, lipstick on and nails gleaming, carrying her business satchel. On arrival, George, the general manager, greeted her as he snickered, "You should've heard what Jake just said as you were putting on your lipstick in the car."

"I don't want to know," responded an exasperated Mia.

"He said she looks like a call girl coming in to service her client." He roared with laughter. Walking into the office she saw Jake sitting at his desk with a big sheepish grin on his face.

"You forget one thing, Jake, I know how much you earn, and if that were the case, you wouldn't be able to afford me." Again, she used the only weapon available to her. Jake and George roared with laughter.

In the end, she resigned as the level of harassment had become intolerable and she filed a claim for sexual harassment. She won a $10,000 payout. Wolfie had listened to his wife's stories of frustration at the hands of these abusive men for months and was pleased that she had taken positive action and won. This sent a clear message to her boss and colleagues. Mia learned that her replacement would be another female and was glad that the office would now be a safe place free of sexual harassment.

Wolfie decided that with this money, the family should take a week's holiday in Surfers Paradise, the balance to be used by him to have a bespoke cabinet, made with a secret door to hide his safe. He'd taken to collecting gold coins and had an album full of them. Mia had bought him an antique safe for his birthday, which he loved, to store his precious coins in.

It's my fucking money! Why are YOU deciding how it gets spent?!

She gave in to him, because for her it had been about being vindicated and those responsible getting a rap over the knuckles. She was proud of herself for not having acted like a victim. Years later, Wolfie would reproach her, "I still think there was something suspicious about that whole Jake incident. You must have done something to set him off."

Again, Mia did not understand what he was talking about. Jake was 13 years older than her, middle aged, balding, out of shape and flat broke from his divorce. What could Mia have ever seen in him? Why did Wolfie have to let his imagination run away with him like that? The gender biases and behaviours she had faced had possibly shaped both their attitudes in a way that was detrimental for Mia.

He liked that Mia was stunning, but at times it made him feel insecure. When his colleagues or anyone he knew met her for the first time, they would often comment, "You have a very attractive wife." This made him beat his chest like Tarzan. When Mia would complain about unwanted male attention, he often intimated that it was her fault, something she had done, and he would sulk.

Men adored her. It was a combination of her attractive characteristics, a care-free, playful and fun-loving attitude, along with her hourglass figure and fabulous dress sense. As a result, this always caught their eye, and there could have been plenty of opportunities for her to have had affairs, if she had so desired. Many times, she had begged and pleaded with him to come to a wedding with her, a birthday party, a work Christmas function, anything, but he would decline, saying, "You can go. I'm happy to stay at home." It was hard work for her to get him to accept a social invitation, even from friends.

It was Saturday morning, and outside the bushman's alarm rang loudly. A family of kookaburras sat in the eucalypts, performing their morning laughs that sounded like a variety of trills, chortles, belly laughs and hoots. Ezra and Josephine had invited them to their place for dinner that evening.

"Again! Do we have to go?" asked Wolfie.

"You already didn't come the last time they invited you. Do you want to keep them as friends? You can't always turn them down and then expect them to remain friends. You have to nurture relationships. All relationships."

Reluctantly, he agreed.

Josephine had made a salad and a roast with vegetables. Mia brought a New York baked cheesecake for dessert. There was always a good drop of red at their place. Mia liked catching up with the Quails. Conversation always flowed freely. Josephine always had interesting stories about the people she knew.

"One of Ezra's friends, Larry, is a successful dentist. Married with three kids, house paid off, investment properties, the lot. Anyway, this new 17-year-old dental assistant starts working for him. One thing led to another, and before you know it, he's in love and wants to leave his wife of 30 years."

"You're kidding," replied Mia.

"Nah, nah, so what happens is, she then falls pregnant, and he divorces Amy. He's in love and wants to marry his dental assistant. The wife got everything in the divorce. He lost his house and investments. His kids don't talk to him. He got married and now, in his fifties, he's a dad again and miserable."

"Trophy wife," said Mia.

"You see them at the early morning soccer games at the park. Some pretty little young thing walking with some old bastard trailing behind her. When I see that, I just think to myself, 'You idiot.' I couldn't think of anything worse than going through the baby stage again in my fifties," replied Ezra.

"Sounds like he deserves it. He made his bed and now he can lie in it, right?" said Mia with a chuckle at her own pun.

"He made his bed alright," laughed Ezra. "He's got nothing in common with his young wife and misses the conversations he used to have with Amy.

They liked the same art, wine, foreign films and had lots in common. He doesn't have any of that with his new wife. He wishes he was still married to Amy. He's so depressed."

"What a dickhead," Wolfie said, sniggering.

"He regrets ever leaving her and his family. He says he's too old to be going through the baby stage again. His new wife is now 18 but he can't have a decent conversation with her. He's lost everything except his practice. I've never seen him so crestfallen," added Josephine. Wolfie was laughing.

"Serves him right," said Wolfie.

"Why do men do that? Sounds like a midlife crisis. Men seem to have these more than women. It never ends well. Why do they do it?" Mia continued, "You seem to know so many people getting divorced. Why do you know so many? Is it because they're older?"

"I don't know, but yeah, we do know quite a lot of divorced couples. They're usually older so maybe after a certain point they've just had enough of each other," laughed Josephine.

Mia looked at Wolfie, "We don't know anyone who's divorced, not in our immediate circle anyway; maybe Stephanie but that's it. Of all our friends, I can't think of anyone who would get divorced. Can you?"

"No. There's no one." He was shaking his head.

"I know they say one in three marriages ends in divorce, but all of our friends seem to still be going strong. I can't imagine any of them ever going their separate ways."

After dinner, they sat on the back porch. There was pink behind the trees. It tinged the bottom of the clouds that streaked across the darkening sky. They were drinking coffee, eating cheesecake and lamenting about getting older.

Ezra said, "You know, you've got great skin, Mia. Look at you, your skin is clear, healthy, you don't have any wrinkles. You don't look your age."

Wolfie interrupted, "I don't know about that. She's got those big lines on her face." As he said this, he pointed to the laughter lines from his nose to his mouth.

Josephine let out a small chuckle. She did this because of the theatrical effort Wolfie was making in drawing invisible lines on his face.

"Oh, come on. Look at her. She's hardly got any wrinkles, and she has no blemishes," continued Ezra, turning to Wolfie as he said this.

"No way! Look at those deep lines." He was still outlining the laughter lines on his face.

"Everyone has those," piped in Mia, "as soon as you move your face and laugh, you get those lines."

"I don't know; they're pretty deep," replied Wolfie.

"She looks pretty good," replied Ezra.

"What about that big one she's got up here?" asked Wolfie as he pointed to his brow.

Ezra looked momentarily dumbfounded as he glanced from Mia to Wolfie. Finally, he turned to Wolfie and asked, "Did you want to walk home tonight, mate?"

Wolfie sniggered and in a mocking tone said, "No. Why? Do you? Do you want to walk home tonight?"

Mia was not upset by Wolfie's jeering comments. Ezra was the one offended for her. It was as if she was standing under a giant invisible umbrella, his comments bouncing and rolling off, like water droplets do on a rainy day. Had she become immune or brainwashed to switch off?

The Climax
Chapter 26

With New Year's Eve fast approaching, Wolfie thought he would surprise his wife of 25 years with a weekend away. He booked two night's accommodation at the Hilton in Sydney, using frequent flyer points from his Diamond membership. The fact that he organised this at no cost on New Year's Eve impressed her. A full buffet breakfast was also included which sounded very enticing. Mia was looking forward to their romantic getaway since they had not done anything for New Year's Eve in a while. Despite all the challenges they had overcome and all the difficulties they had faced, she was looking forward to lots of travel with her husband in the imminent future. They had also done all the hard work with their children who were now grown up. Alex was nearly 21 and Chloe was now 17. She looked ahead with hope and positivity to a bright future with Wolfie.

As their Saturday afternoon began, he was very attentive to her, always giving her his arm, and asking if he could buy her anything. Mia enjoyed the attention. Who wouldn't? He took her shopping at the exclusive Queen Victoria Building and to an upmarket designer boutique called Seduce. Despite loving this label, Mia had never dared to shop there, because even on sale, it was expensive.

"If you buy two dresses, you get the second one at half price," said Wolfie.

"That's still pricey."

"Go on. Get two. You deserve it."

He was in a good mood. Usually, he would have teased her with what he called "female logic". Whenever she came home proudly announcing,

"Look at the bargain I got today. This dress was normally $299.99 but I got it for $29.40. It was the last one and it fits perfectly."
"So, you had to spend money to save some, is that right?"

"Look at the saving!"

"Did you need it?" She understood his point. She already had a vast array of clothing for every occasion.

"Yes, I don't have anything like it. Besides, you want me to look pretty, don't you? Now I'll have something nice to wear the next time you take me out somewhere special. You know I only ever buy things when they're heavily reduced. I need clothes, I mean it's not like I can walk around naked, can I?" she teased.

Wolfie laughed.

The dress that she chose was a halter-neck with tulle in the skirt. It was a deep eye-catching navy-blue, with bright red polka dots. It was a fun dress. It was her! It showed off her very shapely figure, even now at 45 and after two children. He chose the second one, a sophisticated and elegant black dress with a scoop neck and lace bodice covered in colourful embroidered flowers. He also took her to a lingerie store called La Coquette and bought her two pairs of sexy seamed stockings.

They returned to their hotel room and had what he called "afternoon delight". She felt very much in love at this point and was looking forward to entering the next phase of their life together, growing old, becoming grandparents and travel.

Later, they went out for a simple and inexpensive dinner. It was wonderful to forget about work and life's responsibilities and just focus on each other. As they walked back to their hotel, he asked her again, "So do you think you might be interested in trying a threesome one day?" He had started asking this question again.

She calmly responded, "I know you keep asking me that, in the hope that I will change my mind, but it's just not me and I'll never be interested."

"There's no harm in asking and one day you might change your mind."

"I know you're hopeful, but I know myself and I will never want to try it. I've already explained that it's just not me," she continued firmly.

"One day, you'll change your mind."

Is this your delusion talking or are you just plain deaf?

"What about if I try it, and I like it better than having sex with you, and I leave you to be with my girlfriend? Like that doctor personality did? That Dr Pippa Black." Recently, a well-known TV personality had been outed. Her husband had suggested they try a threesome "to spice things up". They had, and she realised that she preferred women to men and had left him and her children to be with her girlfriend.

"That's a risk I'm willing to take," he replied.

You big, fat, filthy pig!

They walked in silence back to their hotel room.

On Sunday, after a hearty breakfast they went for a walk around their old inner-city haunts. This was where they had bought their first little one-bedroom apartment all those years ago. The traffic stopped, and they crossed with a small crowd of people. Ahead of them was a young girl, with a svelte figure walking her tiny, fluffy dog on his bejewelled lead. Her rounded derriere was accentuated by active wear that clung to her body like a second skin.

Wolfie whispered in low tones to Mia, "Whoa, look at that. What a nice butt that girl has. What I'd like to do to her." He paused. "I'd like to grab it and give it a good squeeze."

Mia, taken aback, replied, "And what would happen after that?"

"I don't know."

"I know," and she made some rather exaggerated snoring noises. She had always been quick-witted with a fast comeback, and he enjoyed having someone who could take him on and challenge him.
Wolfie chuckled, "You're probably right. You're probably right."

Though vexed by her husband's comments, she had become used to ignoring them and did not want to spend the weekend fighting. She had noticed his roving eye when it came to younger girls and had even started calling him "DOM" when he was doing it, which stood for "dirty old man". He had laughed. She thought it was just a phase. After all, he still had her, and she was stunning. When Mia pointed out that some girls he was ogling were younger than his own daughter, he had tried to save face, saying that he had been looking at their "assets" and suitable "talent" for their son. Mia knew otherwise.

I'm getting that uncomfortable feeling again. I wonder if another episode is imminent.

New Year's Eve was Sunday night, and Mia was looking forward to saying goodbye to the challenging year she had experienced and welcoming the wonderful year she hoped would soon arrive. Wolfie had decided that they would have dinner at the casino, gamble a little, and then go back to their hotel room to relax, have some room service and celebrate the arrival of the New Year together. He made it clear that he did not want sex again, his potency waning now that he was getting older.

Wolfie loved to gamble and at the Casino his eyes showed how alive he felt. He was joyous and his euphoria was palpable, until he started to lose. He would then stand up abruptly muttering and try his luck at another table, often with the same result. Sometimes, his gambling would get out of hand. Mia would try to talk reasonably to him, saying things like, "The odds are in the casino's favour, which is why you'll never win the jackpot playing Blackjack," or "How many people have you heard of who have won it big at a casino?" Of course, he knew none.

"The next time I tell you I want to go to the Casino, say no, we're not going." He would then say, "I know that's what I told you to say but let's just go for an hour," but it was never just an hour. When nothing seemed to deter him, she would simply say, "Just remember, whatever you lose

tonight, I'll spend the same amount on clothes, shoes or jewellery when I go shopping next, and I'll even double what you've lost." This seemed to be the only thing that curbed the amount that he would lose.
She always had to outsmart him, which she found easy to do. He believed himself to be the more intelligent one because he was well-informed on current affairs. Though Mia was far too busy to read as much as he did, she was much more astute on so many levels. He may have had smarts when it came to political events and important happenings in the world, but he lacked emotional intelligence.

As it was New Year's Eve, activity was brisk at the casino. Punters sat at slot machines watching the endless spinning symbols, the occasional flashing light and ringing bell, to announce a winner and enticing them to part with more money. All around, there was the jittering sound of coins falling and joyous and energetic voices. There were more young girls than usual, wearing short skirts and having trouble balancing in their six-inch heels. As they were approaching the ATM, Wolfie remarked, "Ohhhhh, look at her."

A young twenty-something brunette was approaching them, wearing a black mini skirt, a gold sequined top and high heels. She had bare legs that seemed to go on forever and was a golden-brown all over. He continued breathlessly, "Look! She isn't wearing a bra, and she's got big ones. Ohhh, I'd love to suck those titties."

Mia was appalled.

"Ohhh, she's also got big ones," indicating another girl to their left, who had just exited the lift.

"When I see big ones, I want to do this."

With that, he heatedly did some squeezing actions with both hands, as if he was kneading stress balls.

"I'd like to squeeze hers." Mia was too poleaxed to react, but his comments stung.

That can't be right. Did I hear him correctly? What despicable things to say! Here I am dressed to kill, and you haven't even noticed! Yet you're drooling over girls younger than your own daughter! What's wrong with you? Where's my compliment? The evening continued without further drama, as tediously as usual. They caught a taxi back to their hotel room to avoid the throngs of people starting to amass at key vantage points to watch the New Year's Eve fireworks. Back in their hotel room, Mia had changed into her cotton pyjamas and turned on the television. As he was about to jump into bed, he paused and asked, "I just want to ask a question, I know you've said 'no' before, but I just want to make sure … so you're definitely not interested in having a threesome?"

Unfucking believable!

"For goodness' sake, how many times do I have to tell you? I don't want to have a threesome! I will never want to have a threesome! Ever! I've told you that I'm not interested!"

He had begun complaining again, that as Mia was his first and only sexual experience, he would like to have sex with someone else before he died.

"I've already told you, if you want to have sex with someone else so badly, just go do it and get it out of your system. Be discreet, use a condom and DON'T TELL ME ABOUT IT!"

He replied eagerly, "So, I can go try?"

Mia screamed, "I DON'T WANT TO KNOW! DON'T TELL ME ABOUT IT!"

"Do you mind if I look now?" He jumped into bed with his iPad. He looked like a child on Christmas morning about to open his first present.

Go ahead you stupid bastard! I haven't got the energy to deal with your shit! I'm so sick of your kinky obsessions!

She threw up her hands, "DO WHAT YOU WANT! I DON'T CARE!" She felt the rage starting to escalate.

Slavering at the mouth, he chose a website and then proceeded to salivate at the pictures of girls in their lingerie. He was looking at young high-class hookers, oblivious to the anguish he was causing her.
How can you do this to me? What's wrong with you?

"Here, come over and help me pick one," he offered.

"I don't want to help you pick one," barely able to control herself.

She continued breathing deeply, "So, if you're having an experience? Does that mean I can have one too?"

He paused as a little smile curled the corners of his mouth, "I don't see why not. If I'm having one, then I think it's only fair that you have one too."

She tried to remain calm, as she asked, "Are we having an open marriage now?"

"No, no, that's not what I'm saying, but I think it's only fair that if I have an experience, then you should have one too."

"Will this be a one off?" Mia asked, trying to sound like they were having a friendly chat over a hot cup of tea.

You fucking arsehole!

"I don't know," came his reply, again with that same little smile curling up the corners of his mouth, greedily going through the photos. He had not looked up at her once. Mia felt crushed.

What am I doing here? How can he treat me like this? Where is the love and respect? That's it!

Standing up and changing into her clothes, she started packing and stuffing everything into her large overnight bag. She zipped it up and was heading for the door when he finally looked up.

"Where are you going?" he asked, surprised. "What's wrong?"

Mia yelled, “I’m going home. I don’t want to be here! How dare you ask me to help you pick another woman that you can go fuck?!”
“But you said it was okay. You said it was okay to look. I thought you were okay with it.” The look on his face was that of a child whose hand had been slapped as he tried to sneak a cookie out of the cookie jar.

“Do I look okay with it?” Mia screamed as she pointed to the tears freely flowing down her cheeks.

“I don’t understand where this is coming from. Why are you so upset? You said I could. You have to understand that I’m curious. You’re the only woman I’ve ever been with; even you’ve had another experience.”

There was that familiar stab of pain and guilt again.

“The non-consensual experience, the assault, the rape?”

He sneered, “Not when it happens twice.” He had never acknowledged the truth of what had happened to her.

“Why do you keep bringing that up?” she yelled. “That was 25 years ago! Why bring it up again now?”
“Well, I’m just saying that you had another experience so why can’t you understand that I’d like to have one too?”

“That was hardly an experience worth remembering or talking about! Maybe you need to get gang banged and see if you like it! You promised that you wouldn’t bring it up again! You said you forgave me. Remember?”

“But you still had an experience with someone else, didn’t you?” He was stabbing her with the memory of Norman.

“So, what is this? Tit for tat? Are we comparing notches now?”

“Of course not.”

"I also told you to go and have a 'sexual experience', and NOT tell me about it but you want to keep rubbing my nose in it."

"No, I just want to be honest with you."
"I've told you before, I DON'T WANT TO KNOW ABOUT IT! But you want to give me a detailed account of who you've been with and what you've been up to. I can't handle that!"

"It wouldn't be a blow-by-blow account, but I want to be honest with you."

"You can't do that. It would kill me!"

Eventually, he persuaded her to stay, reminding her that it was New Year's Eve and that there were drunken hooligans outside. He thought it was best to wait until morning when he would drive them home. Again, she acquiesced, and begrudgingly stayed. Wolfie would not let the matter rest, on and on he continued, "I don't know why you're so upset. You said I could."

"YOU HURT ME!" she shrieked, tears still streaming down her face.

At that moment, she saw a softening in his eyes. He hurriedly said, "I'm sorry. That was insensitive of me. I handled that badly. I'm sorry."
When Wolfie usually displeased her, their normal pattern would be that she would completely ignore him for days, before he would say, "I apologise." Mia would only forgive him when he used what she felt were genuine words.

Before 7am the next day, Mia had showered, dressed, packed and was ready to go. He asked her to have breakfast with him, and then they would leave together. Mia was feeling devastated.

"If I had the money, I would leave you right now and that would be the last thing you ever said to me." But she agreed to have breakfast with him.

He said, "I know you're hurt but I've already apologised. The way I behaved was inappropriate and it was badly handled … I know you're upset, but I want you to know that I'm going to give you a month to calm down, but if that's the way you truly feel, don't let money stop you from leaving."

"What?! You'll give ME a month to calm down? Are you FUCKING SERIOUS?" asked a seething Mia.
"I know you're upset and angry, but I think once you've calmed down, you'll see things differently."

"Was the whole weekend one big fucking set up, to get me to pander to your sexual perversion? What were you thinking, Wolfie? Did you buy me dresses and were you nice to me, in the hope of buttering me up so that I would agree to your disgusting demands? Have you just been manipulating me this whole time?"

"No. I'm not that smart," but he still had that same little wicked smile curling the corners of his mouth.

A couple of days later, once back at home, Mia received delivery of two bunches of flowers from Wolfie. One bunch had Tiger Lilies with an assortment of giant green leaves, the other, pink roses. This was something he seldom did. The note read, "To My Best Friend and Wife, Love Wolfie xx."

MIA WASN'T FALLING FOR IT THIS TIME.

The two of them had not spoken to each other since the incident. They were both back at work. Daily life stops for no one.

On Friday morning, as he was making himself a coffee before heading to work, Mia asked him venomously, "Was there any other behaviour on the weekend, apart from the obvious, where you might have acted inappropriately; said something you shouldn't have; behaved in a way that showed a total lack of respect or love for me? What do you think? Anything come to mind?"

"Look, I'm tired," he replied brushing her off. "I really can't think now. Let's talk about it tomorrow."

The next day, when Mia broached the subject again, he said dejectedly, "Yes. Yes. Okay. What I said about those other women was inappropriate. My behaviour that weekend was appalling. I don't know what came over me."

"How could you even say those things to me, your beloved wife and partner for over 25 years. Why would you even say that? I would never and have never disrespected you like that."

"I don't know. I've already apologised. I don't know what more I can do."

She still was not hearing any real remorse. In fact, he seemed to be getting worse. He would not let up and continued, "I don't want to be on my death bed and think, "I was such a good man, I only ever slept with one woman." He was still obsessing about his need for "sexual experiences".

When he saw that she was not calming down and forgiving him as she usually did, he began asking, "Give me until the end of the year. By then, you will have calmed down and you'll see things differently."

Now he doesn't just want me to give him a month, he wants a whole fucking year! What the fuck is wrong with him?!

He then admitted, "This past year has been difficult for me. I've found it tough to get up in the morning when all I've wanted to do was stay in bed. I finally told myself that going to work and doing my job well was the one thing that I had to focus on. It was important because I had to support my family. I funnelled all my energy into the job. I had to."

"It's not normal to feel that way! Not for a whole year! Nobody feels like that!" exclaimed Mia, "Why don't you talk to someone like a doctor or a health care professional? I think you need help that I can't give you."

He scoffed, "What good would that do? What can they do?"

"They can look at your medication for starters. Maybe the dose is wrong. They can evaluate you and they can help. Why don't you see what they can do, find out? You could also talk to someone like that guy you used to see? The one who retired that you liked. That psychologist or psychiatrist dude?"

"I wouldn't know where to start," came his despondent reply. Their conversation continued like a game of cricket, Wolfie whacking all her suggestions out of the field for a six.
The following Friday she gave him a sheet of paper, with a line down the middle and two lists.

Option 1	**Option 2**
• Beautiful wife	• Prostitutes
• A family life	• Threesomes
• A wonderful home	• Orgies
• A comfortable life	
• Financial freedom	
• No visiting prostitutes	
• No anal sex	
• No porn	

Later that evening he wanted to discuss the lists with her. He was lying on the bed, and she sat on a chair with her feet up on the bed.

"Come and lie on the bed with me," he said.

"No thanks." She never wanted to be in a bed with him again.

After much deliberation, he finally said, "Of course, I choose option one." He excitedly folded his pillow in half and stuffed it under his head, as he rolled onto his left to face her, "So does that mean you're going to be more adventurous in the bedroom?"

"What …?" a disbelieving Mia asked.

Didn't you just choose option 1, you stupid prick with ears?!

He asked again, "Does that mean you're going to be more adventurous in the bedroom?"

"What does that mean?" she asked, exasperated.

"Are you going to be more adventurous in bed?"

"What do you want?" she retorted almost in a growl.
"I'd like longer blow jobs. I want you to swallow it, like it and enjoy it."

What's wrong with you? Do you think you're speaking to a porn star? Are you stuck in fantasy land? Are you visiting Numbskull Island again? Gaga Land perhaps? Have you lost touch with reality? Of all the porn movies you've made me watch, the actresses never swallow. They do this weird spitting thing. Now you're treating me even worse than a porn star. What planet are you on?

"No, that's never going to happen," Mia replied. "We've had this discussion before, when you've ejaculated, you're done. It makes no difference where it goes. It's all about you having power and control over me. There is no need for me to swallow it!"

"It's nice."

"Why?"

"It just is nice."

"It's never going to happen," she replied curtly.

"It would be nice if you could deep throat me too."

Mia almost laughed out loud.

You poor deluded fool! Are you stuck in some second-rate porn flick?

"I won't do that! I don't have a flip-top head and I have a very strong gag reflex. I'll vomit."

"Would you be willing to learn?" came his earnest reply.

You're so vile and repulsive! You're despicable! Can you hear yourself? That's ludicrous! What was the point of all that marriage counselling?

"No," came Mia's succinct and definite answer. "Where do you get all of these ideas from anyway? Wanting to come all over my face, tea bagging, queening, pig on a spit, DP, pearl necklace, tag team, golden showers, fisting, pegging, wanting to be deep-throated. I know you watch porn."

"Sometimes." He had that same culpable smile.

"I know it's more than sometimes. When do you watch it? When I've gone to bed and you stay up for hours on end on your own?"

"Yes, but it doesn't matter."

"If it doesn't matter, why do you look so guilty?" she quizzed.

"Look, I just need you to be more adventurous in bed," he said in an almost whiny voice. "It's boring, doing the same thing over and over again for more than 25 years."

"I beg your pardon! I'm the one who's been having cum all over her face for the last 18 months because you thought it was 'nice'. Even though I told you that I hated it, that it made me feel degraded, like you were pissing or shitting on me. You still wanted it, ignored my pleas and persisted in wearing me down to get what you wanted! Never mind me! So, don't tell me that I haven't been adventurous. I always do what you want to try to please you."

Whatever was I thinking?

"Well, you are my wife, if I can't come to you to ask for what I want, then who should I go to?"

"Because I'm your wife, you should be respecting and listening to me when I say I don't want to do something."

"Can't you understand that I'm bored?"

"Why is it boring to make love? I mean every night is 'movie night' at 8.30pm. It doesn't matter if you've seen that movie two or three times, you'll still watch it again. That's dull and mundane!"
"I know I'm boring, and you're right. I go to work. I come home. I have dinner. I watch TV, I go to bed, and then I do it all over again the next day. I know I'm boring."

"Well then why don't YOU do something about it? Take up a hobby? An interest? Read a book. Do some exercise. Instead of asking me to act like a slut or a whore."

"Just because you do the things that I like, doesn't make you a slut or a whore, but you're my wife. You should be willing to do these things because I'm asking you as your husband."

"You can ask for whatever you want from a prostitute. She'll happily do the kinky things you want. She'll also be happy to have cum on her face and will have anal sex with you, because you will be paying her and probably paying extra for those services. Do you see any money here?" Mia asked as she tapped on her bedside table, "There's no money here because I'm your wife and not a whore!"

"I pay."

"What …?" asked a perplexed Mia. Their conversation was going from bad to worse.

"I pay."

"What do you mean you pay?"

"I take you on holidays. I buy you things, like clothes. I pay."

"Excuse me, but I work too, and when I come home, I continue working, unlike you who gets to relax and put his feet up. Are you calling me a whore?"

"No, but I'm saying that I pay."

"I thought you were choosing option one, because I don't think anything has changed for you. You still want to stick your dick in prostitutes, and you want me to act like a whore which will never happen!"

They continued to argue, but something was different. Normally, he could be reasoned with, and she could bring him back to her, but not this time. She stared out the window but was unsure what more she could say in her defence.

Awakened
Chapter 27

Mia was done. She finally realised her marriage was over. The breaking point had come with her husband's persistent need to have his lustful desires fulfilled at any cost! Maybe she had been living in her own fantasy land with her ideal of happily ever after. She felt she was clearly seeing everything around her for the first time in a long while.

Mia now reviewed her relationship and thought back to their courtship days, wondering if she had made a mistake. Perhaps she should have listened to that soft little voice in the back of her head. Should she have left him after those first three weeks? Why had she given him another chance? Although she had picked up bad vibrations, their physical attraction had been so strong. Mia realised when something about a person or situation did not feel right, she should have trusted her intuition. Knowing this, she knew she would never disregard her gut instincts again.

With hindsight, she wondered if dragging her to a sex therapist should have set off alarm bells? Was this a precursor to the man he would eventually become? Why did she accept this? Had she missed another red flag? Now she realised she had been too kind and forgiving, and wondered why, on the night of his ruined dinner she had not stood up to him, "If you don't like what I've cooked, then cook for yourself!."

In retrospect, she wondered how she'd missed these warning signs. The woman she was today would not have allowed herself to associate with a man who mocked and ridiculed her, especially if he supposedly loved her. Sadly, she had missed the fact that she had been donning an over-sized pair of diamanté encrusted rose-coloured glasses. A red flag would not have stood out, her insight blinded by the sparkle

Reflecting upon these early days, she understood the oafishness that appeared to be ingrained in him. Mia never spoke ill of strangers they passed on the street. He was relentless with his deprecatory remarks. He denounced everything and everyone. Not her. Him. If she laughed at his comments, it only encouraged him. She had also tried to ignore his callous remarks to no avail. Even with her repertoire of dirty jokes, she had never been as deliberately crude and inappropriate as he had. His bullying and erratic behaviour had been incorrigible.

Though Mia admired her integrity and commitment, she felt duped and taken advantage of. Looking back, she had never seen his colossal anger or mood swings until they were wed. True, during the three months they lived together, she saw snippets, but she wished they had spent more time together before they married. Whilst dating, he always appeared to be happy and in control.

Mia would not stay with a man who clearly did not love and respect her. She realised that being strong had not helped her in her marriage. It meant that she had been able to stay and tolerate his abuse, but had it been worth it? She had suffered much abuse at the hands of her so called, beloved husband. It had made him feel better about himself, to yell and rant at her when he was in a lousy mood, and she had largely ignored this mistreatment.

He had continually castigated her taste in clothing, music and anything she liked. She had laughed most of it off, but he had also regularly, publicly humiliated her, so much so that she had stopped realising he was doing it. It was only when others pointed it out and stood up for her, that she became aware. The blatant exaggeration of Mia's flaws just to entertain himself reminded her of "the boy who cried wolf" to entice the villagers from their homes and brighten up his day. He did not realise that the consequences were piling up. Immature pranksters of any age never do. Now, she realised, she had not reacted because she had become numb from being used to it! However, on a deeper level, it had chipped away at her love for him. Something he did not understand.

He had criticised some of her friends so much so that she had stopped seeing them. She could see he had always been this way. It had been well hidden and lain dormant for years. The little creature would occasionally

pop its head up to peer around from its burrow like a whack-a-mole. She had used humour as her weapon of choice to abate his remarks.
While he would spend as much time with her as he wanted, he insisted on being free to do whatever he wanted when he wanted. Admittedly, Mia was thankful for the respite, as it had enabled her to breathe and have some freedom.

He had financially abused her by controlling her spending. Screaming and berating her for buying clothes or shoes, yet he would be willing to spend ten times more on a dress of his choosing. When she eagerly modelled an item she had purchased, he would also condemn her choice, but he would inevitably compliment her, "That's a lovely dress. It really suits you."

She would reply astounded, "What are you on about? You told me it was a revolting colour and style."

"No, no. It's really nice."

Mia had learned to switch off to these types of criticism. Her skin was thick from years of his abusive words, and though at times they had pierced her skin and made their way to her heart, her soul had remained intact. She was confident and knew exactly what colours suited her and what styles flattered her beautiful figure. Even though it would have been nice to have his approval, she had not needed it.

Even in the bedroom, she could only wear what he wanted, what he had bought her. He had spent thousands buying unwanted gifts of sexy underwear. Every time they had sex, she had to slip into a matching bra, panties, garter belt and stockings. If she tried initiating play, first thing in the morning, after a shower, her skin moisturised and smelling sweet, she would climb back into bed, and cuddle him, trying to unwrap him from the sheets that bound him. She would slide her hand into his track pants as she kissed his neck, stroking his manhood, feeling it grow in the palm of her hand, eventually he would roll over and say, "Alright! Alright, but at least put on a garter belt and stockings." She wished that he would make love to her naked sometimes, but he never did. She had tried to surprise him by buying lingerie that she liked, and something different, like crotchless knickers or a body stocking. He always said her choices looked "cheap and nasty", and what he bought was "classy" in comparison. Since she could never please him, she stopped trying. During their love making, she felt like his life-sized Barbie doll.

Mia had conquered the pain, learned a lesson, grown stronger and moved forward. Her scars were medals of triumph and she decided not to become a hostage to them. She did not want her anger to consume her and become bitter and twisted.

He had moaned about wanting to kill himself for years and had never forgiven Mia for calling his bluff. She could not understand why he did not go about his daily life as she did. To her, he seemed happiest when he was languishing in the misery he made up in his head. Always positive, she said, "Stop worrying about it. Everything's fine. Come on. Snap out of it." He seemed fixated on the negative, whilst she was a born optimist. He used to ask her how she kept being so positive and persistent all the time. Her reply was simple, "What other choice is there? You either get up, dust yourself off and keep going or you lie down and die. I choose to get up and keep going."

She had understood his weakness and had felt sorry for him and tried to help him get over himself but in the end, her efforts had been futile. He would answer, "But don't you get tired?" to which she would respond, "Sometimes, but then I figure I can rest when I'm dead. Until then, there is still so much to see and do." He could not relate or understand. To her it seemed simple. She was stronger than him, and she would not let him break her. He had always reproached her for her strength.

Throughout their marriage, she had lamented that they had nothing in common except for the children. He had been most upset by this, but she had always been able to face the inconvenient truths.

Maybe that's why we were together, after all, don't opposites attract?

He could not have survived on his own. She had rescued him. Because of his weaknesses, he believed that she had not supported him through his mental illness, but she had, having always taken her vows seriously and

believed in doing anything to save their marriage. However, he could never do the same for her.
Her view had always been that their children would be better off with a father figure in their lives and their biological father would be the best. She had wanted them to grow up in a stable, safe and loving environment. In addition, she felt a solid family structure was best for Wolfie, and she had worked hard to build one. However, he had dragged his 13-year-old son by the scruff of the neck through the dining room and the foyer before he had slammed him up against the wall with his hands around his throat. Alex never forgave him for this. She had loved him, trusted him. She had made children with him, and this had meant very little to him.

When she had voiced her concerns, he had ignored her pleas and persisted in the behaviour he enjoyed. He did not care about the suffering he had caused her and the children. She was beginning to see past events for what they truly were - ABUSE!!!

She was confused as to why she had endured so much for so long and felt used. Looking back, she wondered if it would have been better to have let him go earlier. Perhaps it would have been better if she had never met him and wished she could go back in time. Now, at 45, she was living this nightmare, being separated and getting divorced, which was the worst thing that had ever happened to her. This should have been a time for grandchildren, travel and stress-free living.

Mia realised she had stayed because she had patiently waited for the return of the sweet boy who had courted her all those years ago, who had remained fondly in her memory, hoping to see him again soon. However, she finally accepted that she never would.

Lastly, a part of her had always felt guilty about what had happened with Norman. She knew that she was a good person, but feeling she had betrayed Wolfie, she suffered his punishment. Therefore, she felt beholden and always tried to make amends. Now Mia decided to see two separate counsellors and explain the Norman incident in detail. One said, "That's assault," and the other confirmed, "That's rape." It unburdened her for a third party to acknowledge that she was not the sneaky, adulterous woman that Wolfie painted. Even when she had explained every painful detail to him as he had demanded, he had still shamed her and never conceded that it was rape! Having already been wounded by this experience, his words only added to her pain. It bothered her that she had acted like a victim and had thus become one, but she had learned from the experience. Though it was a tough lesson, she knew that today she would handle the situation differently.

She pondered this for some time. Had this influenced his ill-treatment of her? Looking back, she could see that he had begun to change as soon as they had become man and wife, well before her rape. When he had placed that wedding band on her finger, it had become their destiny. She had become his chattel to do with as he pleased.

Mia had developed coping mechanisms during her marriage. Much of what Wolfgang said and did could be ignored by switching off. However, this was not healthy for her, and not positive for either one of them. This meant that he had continued with his self-indulgent behaviour as there had been no repercussions. Thus, Mia had continually been maltreated, subliminally unaware of it. It had become her normal.

What was the point of my marriage?

She met with her girlfriends over the next few weeks to discuss her situation with them. Her girlfriend, Petra said, "It's the universe testing your resolve. I know it feels like nothing is going your way, but that's because there are gifts around the corner for you. Many gifts. Just wait and see."

"I love the sentiment, Petra, but I wish the universe would kindly fuck off! Leave me alone! And go pick on someone else."

Aria gave her an answer that sat better with her. "The spiritual journey in life has nothing to do with being nice and kind to others. It's about being real and authentic, having boundaries and honouring your space first, and others second. In this space of self-care, being nice will just happen. It will flow naturally, not motivated by fear but by love. You gave yourself entirely to another and didn't keep anything for yourself. This is what a lot of people misunderstand. You are your own temple."

Recently, Mia read something inspiring, "When you're in a dark place, you sometimes tend to think that you've been buried alive. Perhaps you've been planted. Bloom." As a result, she made the decision to bloom.

Her friend, Zara offered, "I read something the other day and it made me think of you. It said we often choose a life partner, not necessarily for the journey but for the lesson, forcing you to go through experiences with them so that you become your empowered self. Enabling you to find your soul's purpose, and break generational patterns and traumas, and ultimately heal yourself, propelled in the direction of what you really want in a partner and out of life. This journey partner is often referred to as a narcissist, sociopath, or lost soul because of the darkness they depict. Know that it's not about the person but the lesson they teach."

"That's a pretty tough way to become enlightened but okay, point taken."

Zara added, "Knowing when to walk away is wisdom. Being able to is courage."

Mia felt victorious like a warrior on the battlefield. It was as if she were wearing the silver armour of a knight, shimmering in the sunlight. While she seemed to have a few chinks in her sheathing, chinks that she could have done without, she had come out of her 30-year battle relatively unscathed. Her integrity was intact, and she felt stronger and more independent than ever. It felt good to be free.

As she stood there wondering what was next, she heard a friendly voice in her head that she had not heard in a while. It was loud and it was clear, *"YOU'VE GOT THIS! YOU CAN DO IT!"*

Book Club Questions

1. Describe Wolfie in up to five words.
2. Describe Mia in up to five words.
3. Why was Mia so committed to her marriage and family?
4. Why did Mia put up with so much for so long?
5. What do you think of Wolfie's choices?
6. If you were Mia, what would you do differently?
7. How many more Mia's do you think are out there?
8. How many Wolfie's do you think are out there?
9. If you become aware of a Mia in your life, what could you do to help her?
10. What do you think of this abuse statement, "Don't say it would never happen to you, we didn't think it would ever happen to us either."?
11. Are you a Mia?

CPSIA information can be obtained
at www.ICGtesting.com
Printed in the USA
LVHW051049110522
718474LV00012B/1676